John Gibson Lockhart

Memoirs of the Life of Sir Walter Scott

Vol. 2

John Gibson Lockhart

Memoirs of the Life of Sir Walter Scott
Vol. 2

ISBN/EAN: 9783741183409

Manufactured in Europe, USA, Canada, Australia, Japa

Cover: Foto ©Raphael Reischuk / pixelio.de

Manufactured and distributed by brebook publishing software
(www.brebook.com)

John Gibson Lockhart

Memoirs of the Life of Sir Walter Scott

LIFE

OF

SIR WALTER SCOTT, BART

VOL. II.

MEMOIRS

OF THE

LIFE OF SIR WALTER SCOTT, BART.

BY

J. G. LOCKHART, ESQ.

VOL. II.

EDINBURGH:

ADAM AND CHARLES BLACK

1862.

CONTENTS

OF VOLUME SECOND.

MEMOIRS

LIFE OF SIR WALTER SCOTT.

CHAPTER IX.

*Early Married Life — Lasswade Cottage — Monk
Lewis — Translation of Goetz von Berlichingen,
published — Visit to London — House of Aspen
— Death of Scott's Father — First Original
Ballads — Glenfinlas, &c. — Metrical Fragments — Appointment to the Sheriffship of Selkirkshire.*

1798–1799.

SCOTT carried his bride to a lodging in George
Street, Edinburgh; a house which he had taken in
South Castle Street not being quite prepared for her
reception. The first fortnight, to which she had

looked with such anxiety, was, I believe, more than
sufficient to convince her husband's family that, however rashly he had formed the connexion, she had the
sterling qualities of a good wife. Notwithstanding
the little leaning to the pomps and vanities of the
world, which her letters have not concealed, she had
made up her mind to find her happiness in better
things; and so long as their circumstances continued
narrow, no woman could have conformed herself to
them with more of good feeling and good sense.
Some habits, new in the quiet domestic circles of
Edinburgh citizens, did not escape criticism; and in
particular, I have heard herself, in her most pros-
perous days, laugh heartily at the remonstrances of
her George Street landlady, when it was discovered
that the *southron* lodger chose to sit usually, and
not on high occasions merely, in her drawing-room,
— on which subject the mother-in-law was disposed
to take the thrifty old-fashioned dame's side.

I cannot fancy that Lady Scott's manners or ideas
could ever have amalgamated very well with those of
her husband's parents; but the feeble state of the old
gentleman's health prevented her from seeing them
constantly; and without any affectation of strict intimacy, they soon were, and always continued to be,
very good friends. Anne Scott, the delicate sister
to whom the Ashestiel Memoir alludes so tenderly,
speedily formed a warm and sincere attachment for

the stranger; but death, in a short time, carried off
that interesting creature, who seems to have had
much of her brother's imaginative and romantic temperament, without his power of controlling it.

Mrs Scott's arrival was welcomed with unmingled
delight by the brothers of *the Mountain.* The two
ladies, who had formerly given life and grace to their
society, were both recently married. We have seen
Miss Erskine's letter of farewell; and I have before
me another not less affectionate, written when Miss
Cranstoun gave her hand (a few months later) to
Godfrey Wenceslaus, Count of Purgstall, a nobleman
of large possessions in Styria, who had been spend-
ing some time in Edinburgh. Scott's house in South
Castle Street — (soon after exchanged for one of the
same sort in North Castle Street, which he purchased,
and inhabited down to 1826) — became now to *the
Mountain* what Cranstoun's and Erskine's had been
while their accomplished sisters remained with them.
The officers of the Light Horse, too, established a
club among themselves, supping once a-week at each
other's houses in rotation. The young lady thus
found two somewhat different, but both highly agreeable circles ready to receive her with cordial kindness; and the evening hours passed in a round of
innocent gaiety, all the arrangements being conducted
in a simple and inexpensive fashion, suitable to young
people whose days were mostly laborious, and very

few of their purses heavy.   Scott and Erskine had
always been fond of the theatre; the pretty bride was
passionately so — and I doubt if they ever spent a
week in Edinburgh without indulging themselves in
this amusement.   But regular dinners and crowded
assemblies were in those years quite unthought of.
Perhaps nowhere could have been found a society
on so small a scale including more of vigorous intellect, varied information, elegant tastes, and real
virtue, affection, and mutual confidence.   How often have I heard its members, in the midst of the
wealth and honours which most of them in due
season attained, sigh over the recollection of those
humbler days, when love and ambition were young
and buoyant — and no difference of opinion was able
to bring even a momentary chill over the warmth of
friendship.

" You will imagine," writes the Countess Purgstall
to Scott, from one of her Styrian castles, " how my
heart burnt within me, my dear, dear friend, while I
read your thrice welcome letter.   Had all the gods
and goddesses, from Saturn to La Liberté, laid their
heads together, they could not have presented me with
any thing that so accorded with my fondest wishes.
To have a conviction that those I love are happy,
and don't forget me — I have no way to express my
feelings—they come in a flood and destroy me.   Could
my George but light on another Charlotte, there

would be but one crook left in my lot *— to wit, that
Reggersburg does not serve as a vista for the Parliament Square.† Would some earthquake engulf the
vile tract between, or the spirit of our rock introduce
me to Jack the Giant-Queller's shoemaker; Lord,
Lord, how delightful! Could I choose, I should
just for the present patronise the shoemaker, and
then the moment I got you all snug in this old hall,
steal the shoes, and lock them away till the indignation of the Lord passes by poor Old England! Earl
Walter would play the devil with me, but his Charlotte's smiles would speak thanks ineffable, and the
angry clouds pass as before the sun in his strength.
How divinely your spectre scenes would come in
here! Surely there is no vanity in saying that earth
has no mountains like ours. O, how delightful to
see the lady that is blessed with Earl Walter's love,
and that had mind enough to discover the blessing.
Some kind post, I hope, will soon tell me that your

* A long-popular manual of Presbyterian Theology is entitled,
" The Crook in the Lot:"—the author's name Thomas Boston,
Minister of Ettrick.

† The ancient castle of Reggersburg (if engravings may be
trusted, one of the most magnificent in Germany) was the chief
seat of the Purgstalls. In situation and extent it seems to re-
semble the castle of Stirling. The Countess writes thus, about
the same time, to another of *the Mountain* :—" As for Scott
and his sweet little wife, I consider them as a sort of papa and
mamma to you all, and am happy the gods have ordered it so."

happiness is enlarged, in the only way it can be enlarged, for you have no chance now I think of taking
Buonaparte prisoner. What sort of a genius will he
be, is a very anxious speculation indeed; whether the
philosopher, the lawyer, the antiquary, the poet, or
the hero will prevail — the spirit whispers unto me
a happy *melange* of the two last — he will lisp in
numbers, and kick at *la Nourrice*. On his arrival,
present my fondest wishes to his honour, and don't,
pray, give him a name out of your list of round-table
knights, but some simple Christian appellation from
the House of Harden. And is it then true, my
God, that Earl Walter is a Benedick, and that I am
in Styria?   Well, bless us all, prays the separated
from her brethren,   J. A. P."

        " Hainfeld, July 20, 1798."

Another extract from the *Family Bible* may close
this letter — " *M. C. Scott puerum edidit* 14*to die
Octobris* 1798, *qui postero die obiit apud Edin-
burgum*."

In the summer of this year Scott had hired a
pretty cottage at Lasswade, on the Esk, about six
miles from Edinburgh, and there, as the back of
Madame de P.'s letter shows, he received it from the
hands of Professor Stewart. It is a small house, but
with one room of good dimensions, which Mrs Scott's

taste set off to advantage at very humble cost — a paddock or two — and a garden (commanding a most beautiful view) in which Scott delighted to train his flowers and creepers. Never, I have heard him say, was he prouder of his handiwork than when he had completed the fashioning of a rustic archway, now overgrown with hoary ivy, by way of ornament to the entrance from the Edinburgh road. In this retreat they spent some happy summers, receiving the visits of their few chosen friends from the neighbouring city, and wandering at will amidst some of the most romantic scenery that Scotland can boast — Scott's dearest haunt in the days of his boyish ramblings. They had neighbours, too, who were not slow to cultivate their acquaintance. With the Clerks of Pennycuick, with Mackenzie the Man of Feeling, who then occupied the charming villa of Auchendinny, and with Lord Woodhouselee, Scott had from an earlier date been familiar; and it was while at Lasswade that he formed intimacies, even more important in their results, with the noble families of Melville and Buccleuch, both of whom have castles in the same valley

> " Sweet are the paths, O passing sweet,
>   By Esk's fair streams that run,
>   O'er airy steep, thro' copsewood deep
>   Impervious to the sun;

> " From that fair dome where suit is paid
>   By blast of bugle free, *
>   To Auchendinny's hazel shade,
>   And haunted Woodhouselee.

> " Who knows not Melville's beechy grove,
>   And Roslin's rocky glen;
>   Dalkeith, which all the virtues love,
>   And classic Hawthornden?"

Another verse reminds us that

> " There the rapt poet's step may rove;"—

and it was amidst these delicious solitudes that he
did produce the pieces which laid the imperishable
foundations of all his fame. It was here, that when
his warm heart was beating with young and happy
love, and his whole mind and spirit were nerved by
new motives for exertion; it was here, that in the
ripened glow of manhood he seems to have first felt
something of his real strength, and poured himself
out in those splendid original ballads which were at
once to fix his name.

I must, however, approach these more leisurely.
When William Erskine was in London in the spring
of this year, he happened to meet in society with
Matthew Gregory Lewis, M. P. for Hindon, whose
romance of The Monk, with the ballads which it
included, had made for him, in those barren days, a

* Pennycuick.

brilliant reputation. This good-natured fopling, the
pet and plaything of certain fashionable circles, was
then busy with that miscellany which at length came
out in 1801, under the name of Tales of Wonder,
and was beating up in all quarters for contributions.
Erskine showed Lewis, Scott's versions of Lenore
and the Wild Huntsman; and when he mentioned
that his friend had other specimens of the German
diablerie in his portfolio, the collector anxiously
requested that Scott might be enlisted in his cause.
The brushwood splendour of " The Monk's" fame,

> " The false and foolish fire that's whisk't about
> By popular air, and glares, and then goes out,

had a dazzling influence among the unknown aspi-
rants of Edinburgh; and Scott, who was perhaps
at all times rather disposed to hold popular favour
as the surest test of literary merit, and who certainly
continued through life to over-estimate all talents
except his own, considered this invitation as a very
flattering compliment. He immediately wrote to
Lewis, placing whatever pieces he had translated
and imitated from the German *Volkslieder* at his
disposal. The following is the first of Lewis's letters
to him that has been preserved — it 'is without date,
but marked by Scott " 1798."

* Oldham.

" *To Walter Scott, Esq. Advocate, Edinburgh.*

" Sir,

" I cannot delay expressing to you how much I feel obliged to you, both for the permission to publish the ballads I requested, and for the handsome manner in which that permission was granted. The plan I have proposed to myself, is to collect all the *marvellous* ballads which I can lay hands upon. Ancient as well as modern will be comprised in my design ; and I shall even allow a place to Sir Gawaine's Foul Ladye, and the Ghost that came to Margaret's door and tirled at the pin. But as a ghost or a witch is a *sine-qua-non* ingredient in all the dishes of which I mean to compose my hobgoblin repast, I am afraid the ' Lied von Treue' does not come within the plan. With regard to the romance in Claudina von Villa Bella, if I am not mistaken, it is only a fragment in the original ; but, should you have finished it, you will oblige me much by letting me have a copy of it, as well as of the other *marvellous* traditionary ballads you were so good as to offer me.

" Should you be in Edinburgh when I arrive there, I shall request Erskine to contrive an opportunity for my returning my personal thanks. Meanwhile, I beg you to believe me your most obedient and obliged

M. G. Lewis."

When Lewis reached Edinburgh, he met Scott accordingly, and the latter told Allan Cunningham, thirty years afterwards, that he thought he had never felt such elation as when the " Monk" invited him to dine with him for the first time at his hotel. Since he gazed on Burns in his seventeenth year, he had seen no one enjoying, by general consent, the fame of a poet; and Lewis, whatever Scott might, on maturer consideration, think of his title to such fame, had certainly done him no small service; for the ballads of " Alonzo the Brave and the Fair Imogine," and " Durandarte," had rekindled effectually in his breast the spark of poetical ambition. Lady Charlotte Campbell (now Bury), always distinguished by her passion for elegant letters, was ready, " in pride of rank, in beauty's bloom," to do the honours of Scotland to the " Lion of Mayfair;" and I believe Scott's first introduction to Lewis took place at one of her Ladyship's parties. But they met frequently, and, among other places, at Dalkeith —as witness one of Scott's marginal notes, written in 1825, on Lord Byron's Diary : — " Poor fellow," says Byron, " he died a martyr to his new riches — of a second visit to Jamaica.

> ' I'd give the lands of Deloraine
> Dark Musgrave were alive again ; '

that is,

> ' I would give many a sugar-cane
> Monk Lewis were alive again.' "

To which Scott adds: — " I would pay my share ! how few friends one has whose faults are only ridiculous. His visit was one of humanity to ameliorate the condition of his slaves. He did much good by stealth, and was a most generous creature . . . . Lewis was fonder of great people than he ought to have been, either as a man of talent or as a man of fashion. He had always dukes and duchesses in his mouth, and was pathetically fond of any one that had a title. You would have sworn he had been a *parvenu* of yesterday, yet he had lived all his life in good society . . . . Mat had queerish eyes — they projected like those of some insects, and were flattish on the orbit. His person was extremely small and boyish — he was indeed the least man I ever saw, to be strictly well and neatly made. I remember a picture of him by Saunders being handed round at Dalkeith House. The artist had ingeniously flung a dark folding-mantle around the form, under which was half-hid a dagger, a dark lantern, or some such cut-throat appurtenance; with all this the features were preserved and ennobled. It passed from hand to hand into that of Henry, Duke of Buccleuch, who, hearing the general voice affirm that it was very like, said aloud, ' Like Mat Lewis ! Why that picture's like a MAN !' He looked, and lo, Mat Lewis's head was at his elbow. This boyishness went through life with him. He was a child, and a

spoiled child, but a child of high imagination; and
so he wasted himself on ghost-stories and German
romances. He had the finest ear for rhythm I ever
met with — finer than Byron's."

During Lewis's stay in Scotland this year, he
spent a day or two with Scott at Musselburgh, where
the yeomanry corps were in quarters. Scott received
him in his lodgings, under the roof of an ancient
dame, who afforded him much amusement by her
daily colloquies with the fishwomen — the *Muckle-
backets* of the place. His delight in studying the
dialect of these people is well remembered by the
survivors of the cavalry, and must have astonished
the stranger dandy. While walking about before
dinner on one of these days, Mr Skene's recitation of
the German *Kriegslied*, " Der Abschied's Tag ist
da" (the day of departure is come), delighted both
Lewis and the Quarter-Master; and the latter produced next morning that spirited little piece in the
same measure, which, embodying the volunteer ardour of the time, was forthwith adopted as the troop-
song of the Edinburgh Light-Horse.*

In January 1799, Mr Lewis appears negotiating
with a bookseller, named Bell, for the publication of
Scott's version of Goethe's Tragedy, " Goetz von
Berlichingen of the Iron Hand." Bell seems finally

* See Poetical Works (Edition 1833), Vol. IV. p. 230.

to have purchased the copy-right for twenty-five
guineas, and twenty-five more to be paid in case of a
second edition — which was never called for until
long after the copy-right had expired.   Lewis writes,
" I have made him distinctly understand, that, if you
accept so small a sum, it will be only because this
is your first publication."   The edition of " Lenore"
and the " Yäger," in 1796, had been completely forgotten ; and Lewis thought of those ballads exactly
as if they had been MS. contributions to his own
Tales of Wonder, still lingering on the threshold
of the press.   The *Goetz* appeared accordingly,
with Scott's name on the title-page, in the following
February.

In March 1799, he carried his wife to London,
this being the first time that he had seen the metropolis since the days of his infancy.   The acquaintance
of Lewis served to introduce him to some literary
and fashionable society, with which he was much
amused ; but his great anxiety was to examine the
antiquities of the Tower and Westminster Abbey,
and to make some researches among the MSS. of
the British Museum.   He found his Goetz spoken
of favourably, on the whole, by the critics of the
time ; but it does not appear to have attracted general attention.   The truth is, that, to have given
Goethe any thing like a fair chance with the English
public, his first drama ought to have been translated

at least ten years before. The imitators had been
more fortunate than the master, and this work, which
constitutes one of the most important landmarks in
the history of German literature, had not come even
into Scott's hands, until he had familiarized himself
with the ideas which it first opened, in the feeble and
puny mimicries of writers already forgotten.   He
readily discovered the vast gulf which separated
Goethe from the German dramatists on whom he
had heretofore been employing himself; but the public in general drew no such distinctions, and the
English Goetz was soon afterwards condemned to
oblivion, through the unspairing ridicule showered on
whatever bore the name of *German play*, by the
inimitable caricature of The Rovers.

The tragedy of Goethe, however, has in truth
nothing in common with the wild absurdities against
which Canning and Ellis levelled the arrows of their
wit.   It is a broad, bold, free, and most picturesque
delineation of real characters, manners, and events;
the first fruits, in a word, of that passionate admiration for Shakspeare, to which all that is excellent
in the recent imaginative literature of Germany must
be traced. With what delight must Scott have found
the scope and manner of our Elizabethan drama re-
vived on a foreign stage at the call of a real master!
with what double delight must he have seen Goethe
seizing for the noblest purposes of art, men and modes

of life, scenes, incidents, and transactions, all claiming
near kindred with those that had from boyhood formed
the chosen theme of his own sympathy and reflection!
In the baronial robbers of the Rhine, stern, bloody,
and rapacious, but frank, generous, and, after their
fashion, courteous—in their forays upon each other's
domains, the besieged castles, the plundered herds,
the captive knights, the browbeaten bishop, and the
baffled liege-lord, who vainly strove to quell all these
turbulences—Scott had before him a vivid image of
the life of his own and the rival Border clans, familiarized to him by a hundred nameless minstrels. If
it be doubtful whether, but for Percy's Reliques, he
would ever have thought of editing their Ballads, I
think it not less so, whether, but for the Ironhanded
Goetz, it would ever have flashed upon his mind,
that in the wild traditions which these recorded, he
had been unconsciously assembling materials for more
works of high art than the longest life could serve
him to elaborate.

As the version of the Goetz has at length been
included in Scott's poetical works, I need not make
it the subject of more detailed observation here. The
reader who turns to it for the first time will be no
less struck than I was under similar circumstances
a dozen years ago, with the many points of resemblance between the tone and spirit of Goethe's delineation, and that afterwards adopted by the translutor

in some of the most remarkable of his original works. One example, however, may be forgiven :—

" *A loud alarm, with shouts and firing—* Selbiss *is borne in wounded, by two Troopers.*

Selbiss. Leave me here, and hasten to Goetz.

1st Trooper. Let us stay—you need our aid.

Sel. Get one of you on the watch-tower, and tell me how it goes.

1st Troop. How shall I get up?

2d Troop. Get upon my shoulder; you can then reach the ruined part.

1st Troop. (On the tower.) Alas! Alas!

Sel. What seest thou?

Troop. Your cavaliers fly to the hill.

Sel. Hellish cowards! I would that they stood, and that I had a ball through my head! Ride one of you at full speed—Curse and thunder them back to the field! See'st thou Goetz?

Troop. I see the three black feathers in the midst of the tumult.

Sel. Swim, brave swimmer—I lie here.

Troop. A white plume! Whose is that?

Sel. The Captain.

Troop. Goetz gallops upon him—Crash—down he goes.

Sel. The Captain?

Troop. Yes.

Sel. Bravo!—bravo!

Troop. Alas! alas! I see Goetz no more.

Sel. Then die, Selbiss!

Troop. A dreadful tumult where he stood. George's blue plume vanishes too.

Sel. Climb higher—See'st thou Lerse?

Troop. No—every thing is in confusion.

Sel. No further — come down — tell me no more.
Troop. I cannot — Bravo! I see Goetz.
Sel. On horseback?
Troop. Ay, ay — high on horseback — victory! —they fly!
Sel. The Imperialists?
Troop. Standard and all — Goetz behind them — he has it — he has it!"

The first hint of this (as of what not in poetry?) may be found in the Iliad—where Helen points out the persons of the Greek heroes, to old Priam seated on the walls of Troy; and Shakspeare makes some use of the same idea in his Julius Cæsar. But who does not recognise in Goethe's drama the true original of the death-scene of Marmion, and the storm in Ivanhoe?

Scott executed about the same time his " House of Aspen," rather a *rifacimento* than a translation from one of the minor dramatists that had crowded to partake the popularity of Goetz of the Ironhand. It also was sent to Lewis in London, where having first been read and much recommended by the celebrated actress, Mrs Esten, it was taken up by Kemble, and I believe actually put in rehearsal for the stage. If so, the trial did not encourage further preparation, and the notion was abandoned. Discovering the play thirty years after among his papers, Scott sent it to one of the literary almanacks (the Keepsake of 1829.) In the advertisement he says, " he had lately chanced to look over these scenes with feelings very different

from those of the adventurous period of his literary
life during which they were written, and yet with
such, perhaps, as a reformed libertine might regard
the illegitimate production of an early amour." He
adds, " there is something to be ashamed of, certainly ;
but after all, paternal vanity whispers that the child
has some resemblance to the father." This piece
being also now included in the general edition of his
works, I shall not dwell upon it here. It owes its
most effective scenes to the *Secret Tribunal,* which
fountain of terror had first been disclosed by Goethe,
and had by this time lost much of its effect through
the " clumsy alacrity " of a hundred followers. Scott's
scenes are interspersed with some lyrics, the numbers of which, at least, are worthy of attention. One
has the metre—and not a little of the spirit, of the
boat-song of Roderick Dhu and Clan Alpin :—

> " Joy to the victors, the sons of old Aspen,
> Joy to the race of the battle and scar!
> Glory's proud garland triumphantly grasping,
> Generous in peace, and victorious in war.
>> Honour acquiring,
>> Valour inspiring,
> Bursting resistless through foemen they go,
>> War axes wielding,
>> Broken ranks yielding,
> Till from the battle proud Roderick retiring,
> Yields in wild rout the fair palm to his foe."

Another is the first draft of " the Maid of Toro;

and perhaps he had forgotten the more perfect copy
of that song, when he sent the original to the Keepsake.

I incline to believe that the House of Aspen
was written after Scott's return from London; but
it has been mentioned in the same page with the
Goetz, to avoid any recurrence to either the German or the Germanized dramas. His return was
accelerated by the domestic calamity which forms the
subject of the following letter : —

" *To Mrs Scott, George's Square, Edinburgh.*

"London, 19th April 1799.

" My Dear Mother,

" I cannot express the feelings with which I sit
down to the discharge of my present melancholy
duty, nor how much I regret the accident which has
removed me from Edinburgh, at a time, of all others,
when I should have wished to administer to your
distress all the consolation which sympathy and affection could have afforded. Your own principles of
virtue and religion will, however, I well know, be
your best support in this heaviest of human afflictions. The removal of my regretted parent from
this earthly scene, is to him, doubtless, the happiest
change, if the firmest integrity and the best spent

life can entitle us to judge of the state of our de-
parted friends.   When we reflect upon this we ought
. almost to suppress the selfish feelings of regret that
he was not spared to us a little longer, especially
when we consider that it was not the will of Heaven
that he should share the most inestimable of its
earthly blessings, such a portion of health as might
have enabled him to enjoy his family.   To my dear
father, then, the putting off this mortal mask was
happiness, and to us who remain, a lesson so to live
that we also may have hope in our latter end; and
with you, my dearest Mother, remain many blessings
and some duties, a grateful recollection of which will,
I am sure, contribute to calm the current of your
affliction.   The affection and attention which you
have a right to expect from your children, and which
I consider as the best tribute we can pay to the
memory of the parent we have lost, will also, I am
sure, contribute its full share to the alleviation of
your distress.   The situation of Charlotte's health,
in its present delicate state, prevented me from setting off directly for Scotland, when I heard that immediate danger was apprehended.   I am now glad
I did not do so, as I could not with the utmost expedition have reached Edinburgh before the lamented
event had taken place.   The situation of my affairs
must detain me here for a few days more; the instant I can I will set off for Scotland.   I need not

tell you not even to attempt to answer this letter —
such an exertion would be both unnecessary and
improper.   John or Tom will let me know how my
sister and you do.   I am, ever, dear Mother, your
dutiful and affectionate son,   W. S."

" P.S.—Permit me, my dear Madam, to add a line
to Scott's letter, to express to you how sincerely I
feel for your loss, and how much I regret that I am
not near you to try by the most tender care to soften
the pain that so great a misfortune must inflict on
you and on all those who had the happiness of being
connected with him.   I hope soon to have the pleasure
of returning to you, and to convince you of the
sincere affection of your daughter,   M. C. S."

The death of this worthy man, in his 70th year,
after a long series of feeble health and suffering, was
an event which could only be regarded as a great
deliverance to himself.   He had had a succession of
paralytic attacks, under which, mind as well as body
had by degrees been laid quite prostrate.   When the
first Chronicles of the Canongate appeared, a near
relation of the family said to me — " I had been out
of Scotland for some time, and did not know of my
good friend's illness, until I reached Edinburgh, a
few months before his death.   Walter carried me to
visit him, and warned me that I should see a great

change. I saw the very scene that is here painted
of the elder Croftangry's sickroom — not a feature
different — poor Anne Scott, the gentlest of creatures, was treated by the fretful patient precisely like
this niece." [a]

I have lived to see the curtain rise and fall once
more on a like scene.

Mr Thomas Scott continued to manage his father's
business. He married early; he was in his circle of
society extremely popular; and his prospects seemed
fair in all things. The property left by the old gentleman was less than had been expected, but sufficient
to make ample provision for his widow, and a not
inconsiderable addition to the resources of those
among whom the remainder was divided.

Scott's mother and sister, both much exhausted
with their attendance on a protracted sickbed, and
the latter already in the first stage of the malady
which in two years more carried her also to her
grave, spent the greater part of the following summer and autumn in his cottage at Lasswade.

There he was now again labouring assiduously in
the service of Lewis's " hobgoblin repast," and the
specimens of his friend's letters on his contributions, as they were successively forwarded to London, which were printed by way of appendix to the

* See Chronicles — Waverley Novels, vol. xli. p. 13.

Essay on Imitations of the Ancient Ballad, in 1830,* may perhaps be sufficient for the reader's curiosity. The versions from Bürger were, in consequence of Lewis's remarks, somewhat corrected; and, indeed, although Scott speaks of himself as having paid no attention " *at the time*," to the lectures of his " martinet in rhymes and numbers"—" lectures which were," he adds, " severe enough, but useful eventually, as forcing on a young and careless versifier criticisms absolutely necessary to his future success") — it is certain that his memory had in some degree deceived him when he used this language, for, of all the false rhymes and Scotticisms which Lewis had pointed out in these " lectures," hardly one appears in the printed copies of the ballads contributed by Scott to the Tales of Wonder.

As to his imperfect *rhymes* of this period, I have no doubt he owed them to his recent zeal about collecting the ballads of the Border. He had, in his familiarity with compositions so remarkable for merits of a higher order, ceased to be offended, as in the days of his devotion to Langhorne and Meikle he would probably have been, with their loose and vague assonances, which are often, in fact, not rhymes at all; a license pardonable enough in real minstrelsy, meant to be chanted to moss-troopers

---

* See Minstrelsy, vol. iv. p. 79.

with the accompanying tones of the war-pipe, but
certainly not worthy of imitation in verses written
for the eye of a polished age.   Of this carelessness
as to rhyme, we see little or nothing in our few
specimens of his boyish verse, and it does not occur,
to any extent that has ever been thought worth
notice, in his great works.

But Lewis's collection did not engross the leisure
of this summer.   It produced also what Scott justly
calls his " first serious attempts in verse ;" and of
these the earliest appears to have been the Glenfinlas.
Here the scene is laid in the most favourite district
of his favourite Perthshire Highlands ; and the Gaelic
tradition on which it is founded was far more likely
to draw out the secret strength of his genius, as well
as to arrest the feelings of his countrymen, than any
subject with which the stores of German *diablerie*
could have supplied him.   It has been alleged, however, that the poet makes a German use of his
Scottish materials ; that the legend, as briefly told
in the simple prose of his preface, is more *affecting*
than the lofty and sonorous stanzas themselves ; that
the vague terror of the original dream loses, instead
of gaining, by the expanded elaboration of the detail.
There may be something in these objections : but no
man can pretend to be an impartial critic of the piece
which first awoke his own childish ear to the power
of poetry and the melody of verse.

The next of these compositions was, I believe, the
Eve of St John, in which Scott repeoples the tower
of Smailholm, the awe-inspiring haunt of his infancy;
and here he touches, for the first time, the one superstition which can still be appealed to with full and
perfect effect; the only one which lingers in minds
long since weaned from all sympathy with the machinery of witches and goblins. And surely this
mystery was never touched with more thrilling skill
than in that noble ballad. It is the first of his original pieces, too, in which he uses the measure of his
own favourite Minstrels; a measure which the mo-
notony of mediocrity had long and successfully been
labouring to degrade, but in itself adequate to the
expression of the highest thoughts, as well as the
gentlest emotions; and capable, in fit hands, of as
rich a variety of music as any other of modern times.
This was written at Mertoun-house in the autumn
of 1799. Some dilapidations had taken place in the
tower of Smailholm, and Harden, being informed
of the fact, and entreated with needless earnestness
by his kinsman to arrest the hand of the spoiler,
requested playfully a ballad, of which Smailholm
should be the scene, as the price of his assent. The
stanza in which the groves of Mertoun are alluded
to, has been quoted in a preceding page.

Then came The Grey Brother, founded on another superstition, which seems to have been almost

as ancient as the belief in ghosts ; namely, that the
holiest service of the altar cannot go on in the presence of an unclean person — a heinous sinner un-
confessed and unabsolved. The fragmentary form of
this poem greatly heightens the awfulness of its impression; and in construction and metre, the verses
which really belong to the story appear to me the
happiest that have ever been produced expressly in
imitation of the ballad of the middle age. In the
stanzas, previously quoted, on the scenery of the
Esk, however beautiful in themselves, and however
interesting now as marking the locality of the composition, he must be allowed to have lapsed into
another strain, and produced a *pannus purpureus*
which interferes with and mars the general texture.

He wrote at the same period the fine chivalrous
ballad entitled The Fire-King, in which there is
more than enough to make us forgive the machinery.

It was in the course of this autumn that he first
visited Bothwell Castle, the seat of Archibald Lord
Douglas, who had married the Lady Frances Scott,
sister to Henry, Duke of Buccleuch ; a woman
whose many amiable virtues were combined with
extraordinary strength of mind, and who had, from
the first introduction of the young poet at Dalkeith,
formed high anticipations of his future career. Lady
Douglas was one of his dearest friends through life ;
and now, under her roof, he improved an acquaint-

ance (begun also at Dalkeith) with one whose abilities and accomplishments not less qualified her to .
estimate him, and who still survives to lament the
only event that could have interrupted their cordial
confidence — the Lady Louisa Stuart, daughter of
the celebrated John Earl of Bute. These ladies,
who were sisters in mind, feeling, and affection, he
visited among scenes the noblest and most interesting that all Scotland can show — alike famous in
history and romance; and he was not unwilling to
make Bothwell and Blantyre the subject of another
ballad. His purpose was never completed. I think,
however, the reader will not complain of my introducing the fragment which I have found among his
papers.

====

" When fruitful Clydesdale's apple-bowers
        Are mellowing in the noon;
    When sighs round Pembroke's ruin'd towers
        The sultry breath of June;

" When Clyde, despite his sheltering wood,
        Must leave his channel dry;
    And vainly o'er the limpid flood
        The angler guides his fly;

" If chance by Bothwell's lovely braes
        A wanderer thou hast been,
    Or hid thee from the summer's blaze
        In Blantyre's bowers of green,

" Full where the copsewood opens wild
    Thy pilgrim step hath staid,
  Where Bothwell's towers in ruin piled
    O'erlook the verdant glade ;

" And many a tale of love and fear
    Hath mingled with the scene —
 'Of Bothwell's banks that bloom'd so dear
    And Bothwell's bonny Jean.

" O, if with rugged minstrel lays
    Unsated be thy ear,
  And thou of deeds of other days
    Another tale wilt hear,

" Then all beneath the spreading beech
    Flung careless on the lea,
  The Gothic muse the tale shall teach
    Of Bothwell's sisters three.

" Wight Wallace stood on Deckmont head,
    He blew his bugle round,
  Till the wild bull in Cadyow wood
    Has started at the sound.

" St George's cross, o'er Bothwell hung,
    Was waving far and wide,
  And from the lofty turret flung
    Its crimson blaze on Clyde;

" And rising at the bugle blast
    That marked the Scottish foe,
  Old England's yeomen muster'd fast,
    And bent the Norman bow.

> " Tall in the midst Sir Aylmer rose,
>   Proud Pembroke's Earl was he—
> While"——   . . . . . .

One morning, during his visit to Bothwell, was spent on an excursion to the ruins of Craignethan Castle, the seat, in former days, of the great Evandale branch of the house of Hamilton, but now the property of Lord Douglas; and the poet expressed such rapture with the scenery, that his hosts urged him to accept, for his lifetime, the use of a small habitable house, enclosed within the circuit of the ancient walls. This offer was not at once declined; but circumstances occurred before the end of the year, which rendered it impossible for him to establish his summer residence in Lanarkshire. The castle of Craignethan is the original of his " Tillietudlem." *

Another imperfect ballad, in which he had meant to blend together two legends familiar to every reader of Scottish history and romance, has been found in the same portfolio, and the handwriting proves it to be of the same early date. Though long and very

---

* The name *Tillietudlem* was no doubt taken from that of the ravine under the old castle of Lanark—which town is near Craignethan. This ravine is called Gillytudlem.

unfinished, it contains so many touches of his best manner that I cannot withhold

· THE SHEPHERD'S TALE.

. . . .

" And ne'er but once, my son," he says,
  " Was yon sad cavern trod,
In persecution's iron days,
  When the land was left by God.

From Bewlie bog, with slaughter red,
  A wanderer hither drew,
And oft he stopt and turned his head,
  As by fits the night wind blew;

For trampling round by Cheviot edge
  Were heard the troopers keen,
And frequent from the Whitelaw ridge
  The death-shot flashed between.

The moonbeams through the misty shower
  On yon dark cavern fell;
Through the cloudy night the snow gleamed white,
  Which sunbeam ne'er could quell.

" Yon cavern dark is rough and rude,
  And cold its jaws of snow;
But more rough and rude are the men of blood,
  That hunt my life below;

" Yon spell-bound den, as the aged tell,
 Was hewn by demon's hands;
But I had lourd* melle with the fiends of hull,
 Than with Clavers and his band."

He heard the deep-mouthed bloodhound bark,
 He heard the horses neigh,
He plunged him in the cavern dark,
 And downward sped his way.

Now faintly down the winding path
 Came the cry of the faulting hound,
And the muttered oath of baulked wrath
 Was lost in hollow sound.

He threw him on the flinted floor,
 And held his breath for fear;
He rose and bitter cursed his foes,
 As the sounds died on his ear.

" O bare thine arm, thou battling Lord,
 For Scotland's wandering band;
Dash from the oppressor's grasp the sword,
 And sweep him from the land!

" Forget not thou thy people's groans
 From dark Dunnotter's tower,.
Mix'd with the seafowl's shrilly moans,
 And ocean's bursting roar!

" O in fell Clavers' hour of pride,
 Even in his mightiest day,
As bold he strides through conquest's tide,
 O stretch him on the clay!

    * *Lourd; i. e.* liefer—rather.

" His widow and his little ones,
    O may their tower of trust
Remove its strong foundation stones,
    And crush them in the dust!"—

" Sweet prayers to me," a voice replied,
    " Thrice welcome, guest of mine!"—
And glimmering on the cavern side,
    A light was seen to shine.

An aged man, in amice brown,
    Stood by the wanderer's side,
By powerful charm, a dead man's arm
    The torch's light supplied.

From each stiff finger stretched upright,
    Arose a ghastly flame,
That waved not in the blast of night
    Which through the cavern came.

O deadly blue was that taper's hue,
    That flamed the cavern o'er,
But more deadly blue was the ghastly hue
    Of his eyes who the taper bore.

He laid on his head a band like lead,
    As heavy, pale, and cold :—
" Vengeance be thine, thou guest of mine,
    If thy heart be firm and bold.

" But if faint thy heart, and caitiff fear
    Thy recreant sinews know,
The mountain erne thy heart shall tear,
    Thy nerves the hooded crow."

The wanderer raised him undismay'd :
  " My soul, by dangers steeled,
Is stubborn as my border blade,
  Which never knew to yield.

" And if thy power can speed the hour
  Of vengeance on my foes,
Theirs be the fate, from bridge and gate
  To feed the hooded crows."

The Brownie looked him in the face,
  And his colour fled with speed —
" I fear me," quoth he, " uneath it will be
  To match thy word and deed.

" In ancient days when English bands
  Sore ravaged Scotland fair,
The sword and shield of Scottish land
  Was valiant Halbert Kerr.

" A warlock loved the warrior well,
  Sir Michael Scott by name,
And he sought for his sake a spell to make,
  Should the Southern foemen tame :

" Look thou," he said, " from Cessford head,
  As the July sun sinks low,
And when glimmering white on Cheviot's height
  Thou shalt spy a wreath of snow.
The spell is complete which shall bring to thy feet
  The haughty Saxon foe.

" For many a year wrought the wizard here,
  In Cheviot's bosom low,

Till the spell was complete, and in July's heat
  Appeared December's snow ;
But Cessford's Halbert never came
  The wondrous cause to know.

" For years before in Bowden aisle
  The warrior's bones had lain,
And after short while, by female guile,
  Sir Michael Scott was slain.

" But me and my brethren in this cell
  His mighty charms retain, —
And he that can quell the powerful spell
  Shall o'er broad Scotland reign."   .

He led him through an iron door
  And up a winding stair,
And in wild amaze did the wanderer gaze
  On the sight which opened there.

Through the gloomy night flashed ruddy light, —
  A thousand torches' glow ;
The cave rose high, like the vaulted sky,
  O'er stalls in double row.

In every stall of that endless hall
  Stood a steed in barbing bright ;
At the foot of each steed, all armed save the head,
  Lay stretched a stalwart knight.

In each mailed hand was a naked brand ;
  As they lay on the black bull's hide,
Each visage stern did upwards turn,
  With eyeballs fixed and wide.

A launcegay strong, full twelve ells long,
  By every warrior hung ;
At each pommel there, for battle yare,
  A Jedwood axe was slung.

The casque hung near each cavalier ;
  The plumes waved mournfully
At every tread which the wanderer made
  Through the hall of Gramarye ;

The ruddy beam of the torches' gleam
  That glared the warriors on,
Reflected light from armour bright,
  In noontide splendour shone.

And onward seen in lustre sheen,
  Still lengthening on the sight,
Through the boundless hall, stood steeds in stall,
  And by each lay a sable knight.

Still as the dead lay each horseman dread,
  And moved nor limb nor tongue ;
Each steed stood stiff as an earthfast cliff,
  Nor hoof nor bridle rung.

No sounds through all the spacious hall
  The deadly still divide,
Save where echoes aloof from the vaulted roof
  To the wanderer's step replied.

At length before his wondering eyes,
  On an iron column borne,
Of antique shape, and giant size,
  Appear'd a sword and horn.

" Now choose thee here," quoth his leader,
  " Thy venturous fortune try;
Thy wo and weal, thy boot and bale,
  In yon brand and bugle lie."

To the fatal brand he mounted his hand,
  But his soul did quiver and quail;
The life-blood did start to his shuddering heart,
  And left him wan and pale.

The brand he forsook, and the horn he took
  To 'say a gentle sound;
But so wild a blast from the bugle brast,
  That the Cheviot rock'd around.

From Forth to Tees, from seas to seas,
  The awful bugle rung;
On Carlisle wall, and Berwick withal,
  To arms the warders sprung.

With clank and clang the cavern rang,
  The steeds did stamp and neigh;
And loud was the yell as each warrior fell
  Sterte up with hoop and cry.

" Wo, wo," they cried, " thou caitiff coward
  That ever thou wert born!
Why drew ye not the knightly sword
  Before ye blew the horn?'

The morning on the mountain shone,
  And on the bloody ground
Hurled from the cave with shiver'd bone,
  The mangled wretch was found.

And still beneath the cavern dread,
  Among the glidders gray,
A shapeless stone with lichens spread
  Marks where the wanderer lay."

      *   *   *   *   *   *

The reader may be interested by comparing with this ballad the author's prose version of part of its legend, as given in one of the last works of his pen. He says, in the Letters on Demonology and Witchcraft, 1830 : — " Thomas of Ercildowne, during his retirement, has been supposed, from time to time, to be levying forces to take the field in some crisis of his country's fate. The story has often been told, of a daring horse-jockey having sold a black horse to a man of venerable and antique appearance, who appointed the remarkable hillock upon Eildon hills, called the Lucken-hare, as the place where, at twelve o'clock at night, he should receive the price. He came, his money was paid in ancient coin, and he was invited by his customer to view his residence. The trader in horses followed his guide in the deepest astonishment through several long ranges of stalls, in each of which a horse stood motionless, while an armed warrior lay equally still at the charger's feet. ' All these men,' said the wizard in a whisper, ' will awaken at the battle of Sheriffmuir.' At the extremity of this extraordinary depôt hung a sword and, a horn, which the prophet pointed out to the horse-

dealer as containing the means of dissolving the spell.
The man in confusion took the horn and attempted
to wind it. The horses instantly started in their
stalls, stamped, and shook their bridles, the men
arose and clashed their armour, and the mortal, ter-
rified at the tumult he had excited, dropped the horn
from his hand. A voice like that of a giant, louder
even than the tumult around, pronounced these
words : —

> ' Wo to the coward that ever he was born,
> That did not draw the sword before he blew the horn.'

A whirlwind expelled the horse-dealer from the
cavern, the entrance to which he could never again
find. A moral might be perhaps extracted from the
legend, namely, that it is best to be armed against
danger before bidding it defiance."

One more fragment, in another style, and I shall
have exhausted this budget. I am well aware that
the introduction of such things will be considered by
many as of questionable propriety ; but on the whole,
it appears to me the better course to omit nothing
by which it is in my power to throw light on this
experimental period.

* * * * *

> " Go sit old Cheviot's crest below,
> And pensive mark the lingering snow
> In all his scaurs abide,

And slow dissolving from the hill
In many a sightless, soundless rill,
   Feed sparkling Bowmont's tide.

" Fair shines the stream by bank and lea,
As wimpling to the eastern sea
   She seeks Till's sullen bed,
Indenting deep the fatal plain,
Where Scotland's noblest, brave in vain,
   Around their monarch bled.

" And westward hills on hills you see,
Even as old Ocean's mightiest sea
   Heaves high her waves of foam,
Dark and snow-ridged from Cutsfeld's wold
To the proud foot of Cheviot roll'd,
   Earth's mountain billows come."

*   *   *   *   *

Notwithstanding all these varied essays, and the charms of the distinguished society into which his reputation had already introduced him, Scott's friends do not appear to have as yet entertained the slightest notion that literature was to be the main business of his life. A letter of Kerr of Abbotrule congratulates him on his having had more to do at the autumnal assizes of Jedburgh this year than on any former occasion, which intelligence he seems himself to have communicated with no feeble expressions of satisfaction. " I greatly enjoy this," says Kerr; " go on; and with your strong sense and hourly ripening

knowledge, that you must rise to the top of the tree
in the Parliament House in due season, I hold as
certain as that Murray died Lord Mansfield.   But
don't let many an Ovid,* or rather many a Burns
(which is better), be lost in you.   I rather think men
of business have produced as good poetry in their
by-hours as the professed regulars; and I don't see
any sufficient reason why a Lord President Scott
should not be a famous poet (in the vacation time),
when we have seen a President Montesquieu step so
nobly beyond the trammels in the *Esprit des Loix*.
I suspect Dryden would have been a happier man
had he had your profession.   The reasoning talents
visible in his verses, assure me that he would have
ruled in Westminster Hall as easily as he did at
Button's, and he might have found time enough
besides for every thing that one really honours his
memory for."   This friend appears to have entertained, in October 1799, the very opinion as to the
profession of literature on which Scott acted through
life.

Having again given a week to Liddesdale, in company with Mr Shortreed, he spent a few days at
Rosebank, and was preparing to return to Edinburgh
for the winter, when James Ballantyne called on him

* How sweet an Ovid, Murray was our boast ;
How many Martials were in Pult'ney lost.
                                        Dunciad, b. iv. v. 170.

one morning, and begged him to supply a few paragraphs on some legal question of the day for his
newspaper. Scott complied; and carrying his article
himself to the printing-office, took with him also
some of his recent pieces, designed to appear in
Lewis's collection. With these, especially, as his
Memorandum says, the " Morlachian fragment after
Goethe," Ballantyne was charmed, and he expressed
his regret that Lewis's book was so long in appear-
ing. Scott talked of Lewis with rapture; and, after reciting some of his stanzas, said — " I ought to
apologize to you for having troubled you with any
thing of my own when I had things like this for your
ear."— " I felt at once," says Ballantyne, " that his
own verses were far above what Lewis could ever
do, and though, when I said this, he dissented, yet
he seemed pleased with the warmth of my approbation."   At parting, Scott threw out a casual observation, that he wondered his old friend did not try
to get some little booksellers' work, " to keep his
types in play during the rest of the week."   Ballantyne answered, that such an idea had not before
occurred to him — that he had no acquaintance with
the Edinburgh " trade;" but, if he had, his types
were good, and he thought he could afford to work
more cheaply than town-printers. Scott, " with his
good-humoured smile," said — " You had better try
what you can do. You have been praising my little

ballads ; suppose you print off a dozen copies or so
of as many as will make a pamphlet, sufficient to let
my Edinburgh acquaintances judge of your skill for
themselves." Ballantyne assented ; and I believe
exactly twelve copies of William and Ellen, The
Fire-King, The Chase, and a few more of those
pieces, were thrown off accordingly, with the title
(alluding to the long delay of Lewis's collection) of
" Apology for Tales of Terror — 1799." This first
specimen of a press, afterwards so celebrated, pleased
Scott ; and he said to Ballantyne — " I have been for
years collecting old Border ballads, and I think I
could, with little trouble, put together such a selection from them as might make a neat little volume,
to sell for four or five shillings. I will talk to some
of the booksellers about it when I get to Edinburgh,
and if the thing goes on, you shall be the printer."
Ballantyne highly relished the proposal ; and the
result of this little experiment changed wholly the
course of his worldly fortunes, as well as of his
friend's.

Shortly after the commencement of the Winter
Session, the office of Sheriff-depute of Selkirkshire
became vacant by the death of an early ally of Scott's,
Andrew Plummer of Middlestead, a scholar and antiquary, who had entered with zeal into his ballad researches, and whose name occurs accordingly more

than once in the notes to the Border Minstrelsy.
Perhaps the community of their tastes may have had
some part in suggesting to the Duke of Buccleuch,
that Scott might fitly succeed Mr Plummer in the
magistrature.   Be that as it might, his Grace's influence was used with the late Lord Melville, who,
in those days, had the general control of the Crown
patronage in Scotland, and his Lordship was prepared to look favourably on Scott's pretensions to
some office of this description.   Though neither the
Duke nor this able Minister were at all addicted to
literature, they had both seen Scott frequently under
their own roofs, and been pleased with his manners
and conversation ; and he had by this time come to
be on terms of affectionate intimacy with some of
the younger members of either family.   The Earl of
Dalkeith (afterwards Duke Charles of Buccleuch),
and his brother Lord Montagu, had been partici-
pating, with kindred ardour, in the military patriot-
ism of the period, and had been thrown into Scott's
society under circumstances well qualified to ripen
acquaintance into confidence.   The Honourable Robert Dundas, eldest son of the statesman whose title
he has inherited, had been one of Scott's companions
in the High School ; and he, too, had been of late
a lively partaker in the business of the yeomanry
cavalry ; and, last not least, Scott always remem-

bered with gratitude the strong intercession on this occasion of Lord Melville's nephews, Robert Dundas of Arniston, then Lord Advocate, and afterwards Chief Baron of the Exchequer in Scotland, and the Right Honourable William Dundas, then Secretary to the Board of Control, and now Lord Clerk Register.

His appointment to the *Sheriffship* bears date 16th December, 1799. It secured him an annual salary of £300; an addition to his resources which at once relieved his mind from whatever degree of anxiety he might have felt in considering the prospect of an increasing family, along with the ever precarious chances of a profession, in the daily drudgery of which it is impossible to suppose that he ever could have found much pleasure.* The duties of the office were far from heavy; the district, small, peaceful, and pastoral, was in great part the property of the Duke of Buccleuch; and he turned with redoubled zeal to his project of editing the ballads, many of the best of which belonged to this very

* " My profession and I came to stand nearly upon the footing which honest Slender consoled himself on having established with Mistress Anne Page: ' There was no great love between us at the beginning, and it pleased heaven to decrease it on farther acquaintance.' " — *Introduction to the Lay of the Last Minstrel*, 1830.

district of his favourite Border — those " tales,"
which, as the Dedication of the Minstrelsy expresses
it, had " in elder times celebrated the prowess and
cheered the halls" of his noble patron's ancestors.

CHAPTER X.

The Border Minstrelsy in Preparation — Richard Heber — John Leyden — William Laidlaw — James Hogg — Correspondence, with George Ellis — Publication of the Two First Volumes of the Border Minstrelsy.

1800 – 1802.

JAMES BALLANTYNE, in his *Memorandum*, after mentioning his ready acceptance of Scott's proposal to print the Minstrelsy, adds — " I do not believe, that even at this time, he seriously contemplated giving himself much to literature." I confess, however, that a letter of his, addressed to Ballantyne in the spring of 1800, inclines me to question the accuracy of this impression. After alluding to an intention which he had entertained, in consequence of the delay of Lewis's collection, to *publish* an edition of the ballads contained in his own little volume, entitled " Apology for Tales of Terror," he goes on to detail plans for the future direction of his printer's career, which were, no doubt, primarily suggested by the friendly interest he took in Ballantyne's fortunes; but there are some hints which, considering what afterwards did take place, lead me to suspect, that even thus early the writer contemplated the possibility at least of being himself very intimately connected with the result of these airdrawn schemes.   The letter is as follows : —

" *To Mr J. Ballantyne, Kelso Mail Office, Kelso.*

"Castle Street, 22d April 1800.

" Dear Sir,

" I have your favour, since the receipt of which some things have occurred which induce me to postpone my intention of publishing my ballads, particularly a letter from a friend, assuring me that ' The Tales of Wonder' are actually in the printer's hand. In this situation I endeavour to strengthen my small stock of patience, which has been nearly exhausted by the delay of this work, to which (though for that reason alone) I almost regret having promised assistance.   I am still resolved to have recourse to your press for the Ballads of the Border, which are in some forwardness.

" I have now to request your forgiveness for mentioning a plan which your friend Gillon and I have talked over together with a view as well to the public advantage as to your individual interest. It is nothing short of a migration from Kelso to this place, which I think might be effected upon a prospect of a very flattering nature.

" Three branches of printing are quite open in Edinburgh, all of which I am well convinced you have both the ability and inclination to unite in your person.   The first is that of an editor of a newspaper, which shall contain something of an uniform historical deduction of events, distinct from the farrago of detached and unconnected plagiarisms from the London paragraphs of ' The Sun.'   Perhaps it might be possible (and Gillon has promised to make enquiry about it) to treat with the proprietors of some established paper — suppose the Caledonian Mercury — and we would all struggle to obtain for it some celebrity.   To this might be added a ' Monthly Magazine,' and ' Caledonian Annual Register,' if you will; for both of which, with the excellent literary assistance which Edinburgh at present affords, there is a fair opening.   The next object would naturally be the execution of Session papers, the best paid work which a printer undertakes, and of which, I dare say, you would soon have a considerable share; for as you make it your business to superintend the proofs yourself, your education and abilities would

insure your employers against the gross and provoking blunders which the poor composers are often
obliged to submit to. The publication of works,
either ancient or modern, opens a third fair field for
ambition. The only gentleman who attempts any
thing in that way is in very bad health; nor can I,
at any rate, compliment either the accuracy or the
execution of his press. I believe it is well understood, that with equal attention an Edinburgh press
would have superior advantages even to those of
the metropolis; and though I would not advise
launching into that line at once, yet it would be
easy to feel your way by occupying your press in this
manner on vacant days only.

" It appears to me that such a plan, judiciously
adopted and diligently pursued, opens a fair road to
an ample fortune. In the meanwhile, the ' Kelso
Mail' might be so arranged as to be still a source of
some advantage to you; and I dare say, if wanted,
pecuniary assistance might be procured to assist you
at the outset, either upon terms of a share or otherwise; but I refer you for particulars to Joseph, in
whose room I am now assuming the pen, for reasons
too distressing to be declared, but at which you will
readily guess. I hope, at all events, you will impute
my interference to anything rather than an imperti-
nent intermeddling with your concerns on the part
of, Dear Sir, your obedient servant,

WALTER SCOTT."

The Joseph Gillon here named was a solicitor of some eminence; a man of strong abilities and genuine wit and humour, for whom Scott, as well as Ballantyne, had a warm regard.* The intemperate habits alluded to at the close of Scott's letter gradually undermined his business, his health, and his character; and he was glad, on leaving Edinburgh, which became quite necessary some years afterwards, to obtain a humble situation about the House of Lords—in which he died.† The answer of Ballantyne has not been preserved.

To return to the "Minstrelsy."— Scott found able assistants in the completion of his design. Richard Heber (long Member of Parliament for the University of Oxford) happened to spend this winter in Edinburgh, and was welcomed, as his talents and accomplishments entitled him to be, by the cultivated society of the place. With Scott his multifarious learning, particularly his profound knowledge of the

---

* Calling on him one day in his writing office, Scott said, "Why, Joseph, this place is as hot as an oven." "Well," quoth Gillon, "and isn't it here that I make my bread?"

† The Poet casually meeting Joseph in the streets, on one of his visits to London, expressed his regret at having lost his society in Edinburgh; Joseph responded by a quotation from the Scotch Metrical Version of the Psalms —

" rather in
The Lord's house would I keep a door,
Than dwell in tents of sin."

literary monuments of the middle ages, soon drew
him into habits of close alliance; the stores of his
library, even then extensive, were freely laid open,
and his own oral commentaries were not less valuable.
But through him Scott made acquaintance with a
person still more qualified to give him effectual aid
in this undertaking; a native of the Border — from
infancy, like himself, an enthusiastic lover of its
legends, and who had already saturated his mind with
every species of lore that could throw light upon
these relics.

Few who read these pages can be unacquainted
with the leading facts in the history of John Leyden.
— Few can need to be reminded that this extraordinary man, born in a shepherd's cottage in one of
the wildest valleys of Roxburghshire, and of course
almost entirely self-educated, had, before he attained
his nineteenth year, confounded the doctors of Edinburgh by the portentous mass of his acquisitions in
almost every department of learning. He had set
the extremest penury at utter defiance, or rather he
had never been conscious that it could operate as a
bar; for bread and water, and access to books and lectures, comprised all within the bound of his wishes;
and thus he toiled and battled at the gates of science
after science, until his unconquerable perseverance
carried everything before it; and yet with this mo-
nastic abstemiousness and iron hardness of will,

perplexing those about him by manners and habits
in which it was hard to say whether the moss-trooper
or the schoolman of former days most prevailed, he
was at heart a poet.

Archibald Constable, in after life one of the most
eminent of British publishers, was at this period the
keeper of a small book-shop, into which few, but the
poor students of Leyden's order, had hitherto found
their way. Heber, in the course of his bibliomaniacal
prowlings, discovered that it contained some of

       " The small old volumes, dark with tarnished gold,"

which were already the Delilahs of his imagination;
and, moreover, that the young bookseller had himself
a strong taste for such charmers. Frequenting the
place accordingly, he observed with some curiosity
the barbarous aspect and gestures of another daily
visitant, who came not to purchase, evidently, but
to pore over the more recondite articles of the collection—often balanced for hours on a ladder with
a folio in his hand, like Dominie Sampson. The
English virtuoso was on the look-out for any books
or MSS. that might be of use to the editor of the
projected " Minstrelsy," and some casual colloquy
led to the discovery that this unshorn stranger was
amidst the endless labyrinth of his lore, a master of
legend and tradition — an enthusiastic collector and

most skilful expounder of these very Border ballads
in particular. Scott heard with much interest Heber's
account of his odd acquaintance, and found, when
introduced, the person whose initials, affixed to a
series of pieces in verse, chiefly translations from
Greek, Latin, and the northern languages, scattered,
during the last three or four years, over the pages
of the " Edinburgh Magazine," had often much excited his curiosity, as various indications pointed out
the Scotch Border to be the native district of this
unknown " J. L."

These new friendships led to a great change in
Leyden's position, purposes, and prospects. He was
presently received into the best society of Edinburgh,
where his strange, wild uncouthness of demeanour
does not seem to have at all interfered with the
general appreciation of his genius, his gigantic endowments, and really amiable virtues. Fixing his
ambition on the East, where he hoped to rival the
achievements of Sir William Jones, he at length,
about the beginning of 1802, obtained the promise
of some literary appointment in the East-India
Company's service; but when the time drew near, it
was discovered that the patronage of the season had
been exhausted, with the exception of one *surgeon-
assistant's* commission—which had been with difficulty secured for him by Mr William Dundas; who,
moreover, was obliged to inform him, that if he

accepted it, he must be qualified to pass his medical
trials within six months. This news, which would
have crushed any other man's hopes to the dust, was
only a welcome fillip to the ardour of Leyden. He
that same hour grappled with a new science, in full
confidence that whatever ordinary men could do in
three or four years, his energy could accomplish
in as many months; took his degree accordingly
in the beginning of 1803, having just before published his beautiful poem, the Scenes of Infancy;
sailed to India; raised for himself, within seven short
years, the reputation of the most marvellous of
Orientalists; and died, in the midst of the proud-
est hopes, at the same age with Burns and Byron,
in 1811.

But to return:—Leyden was enlisted by Scott in
the service of Lewis, and immediately contributed a
ballad, called The Elf-King, to the Tales of Terror.
Those highly-spirited pieces, The Cout of Keildar,
Lord Soulis, and The Mermaid, were furnished for
the original department of Scott's own collection:
and the Dissertation on Fairies, prefixed to its second volume, " although arranged and digested by
the editor, abounds with instances of such curious
reading as Leyden only had read, and was originally
compiled by him ;" but not the least of his labours
was in the collection of the old ballads themselves.
When he first conversed with Ballantyne on the

subject of the proposed work, and the printer signified his belief that a single volume of moderate size
would be sufficient for the materials, Leyden exclaimed — " Dash it, does Mr Scott mean another
thin thing like Goetz of Berlichingen? I have more
than that in my head myself: we shall turn out
three or four such volumes at least." He went to
work stoutly in the realization of these wider views.
" In this labour," says Scott, " he was equally interested by friendship for the editor, and by his own
patriotic zeal for the honour of the Scottish borders; and both may be judged of from the following
circumstance. An interesting fragment had been
obtained of an ancient historical ballad ; but the remainder, to the great disturbance of the editor and
his coadjutor, was not to be recovered. Two days
afterwards, while the editor was sitting with some
company after dinner, a sound was heard at a distance like that of the whistling of a tempest through
the torn rigging of the vessel which scuds before it.
The sounds increased as they approached more near ;
and Leyden (to the great astonishment of such of
the guests as did not know him) burst into the
room, chanting the desiderated ballad with the most
enthusiastic gesture, and all the energy of what he
used to call the *saw-tones* of his voice. It turned
out that he had walked between forty and fifty miles
and back again, for the sole purpose of visiting an

old person who possessed this precious remnant of antiquity."[*]

Various allusions to the progress of Leyden's fortunes will occur in letters to be quoted hereafter. I may refer the reader, for further particulars, to the biographical sketch by Scott from which the preceding anecdote is taken. Many tributes to his memory are scattered over his friend's other works, both prose and verse; and, above all, Scott did not forget him when exploring, three years after his death, the scenery of his " Mermaid :"—

> " Scarba's isle, whose tortured shore
> Still rings to Corrievrekan's roar,
>   And lonely Colonsay;—
> Scenes sung by him who sings no more:
> His bright and brief career is o'er,
>   And mute his tuneful strains;
> Quench'd is his lamp of varied lore,
> That loved the light of song to pour;
> A distant and a deadly shore
>   Has Leyden's cold remains !"[†]

During the years 1800 and 1801, the Minstrelsy formed its editor's chief occupation — a labour of love truly, if ever such there was; but neither this nor his sheriffship interfered with his regular attend-

[*] Essay on the Life of Leyden — Scott's Miscellaneous Prose Works, vol. iv., p. 165.

[†] Lord of the Isles, Canto iv. st. 11.

ance at the bar, the abandonment of which was all
this while as far as it ever had been from his imagination, or that of any of his friends. He continued
to have his summer headquarters at Lasswade; and
Mr (now Sir John) Stoddart, who visited him there
in the course of his Scottish tour,* dwells on " the
simple unostentatious elegance of the cottage, and
the domestic picture which he there contemplated—
a man of native kindness and cultivated talent, passing the intervals of a learned profession amidst scenes
highly favourable to his poetic inspirations, not in
churlish and rustic solitude, but in the daily exercise
of the most precious sympathies as a husband, a
father, and a friend." His means of hospitality were
now much enlarged, and the cottage, on a Saturday
and Sunday at least, was seldom without visitors.

Among other indications of greater ease in his
circumstances, which I find in his letter-book, he
writes to Heber, after his return to London in May
1800, to request his good offices on behalf of Mrs
Scott, who had " set her heart on a phaeton, at once
strong, and low, and handsome, and not to cost more
than thirty guineas;" which combination of advantages Heber seems to have found by no means easy
of attainment. The phaeton was, however, discovered; and its springs must soon have been put

* The account of this Tour was published in 1801.

to a sufficient trial, for this was " the first wheeled
carriage that ever penetrated into Liddesdale" —
namely, in August 1800. The friendship of the
Buccleuch family now placed better means of research at his disposal, and Lord Dalkeith had taken
special care that there should be a band of pioneers
in waiting for his orders when he reached Hermitage.

Though he had not given up Lasswade, his sheriffship now made it necessary for him that he should
be frequently in Ettrick Forest. On such occasions
he took up his lodgings in the little inn at Clovenford, a favourite fishing station on the road from
Edinburgh to Selkirk. From this place he could
ride to the county town whenever business required
his presence, and he was also within a few miles of
the vales of Yarrow and Ettrick, where he obtained
large accessions to his store of ballads. It was in
one of these excursions that, penetrating beyond St
Mary's lake, he found a hospitable reception at the
farm of *Blackhouse,* situated on the Douglas-burn,
then tenanted by a remarkable family, to which I
have already made allusion—that of William Laidlaw. He was then a very young man, but the
extent of his acquirements was already as noticeable
as the vigour and originality of his mind; and their
correspondence, where " Sir" passes, at a few bounds,
through " Dear Sir," and " Dear Mr Laidlaw," to

" Dear Willie," shews how speedily this new acquaintance had warmed into a very tender affection.
Laidlaw's zeal about the ballads was repaid by Scott's
anxious endeavours to get him removed from a
sphere for which, he writes, " it is no flattery to say
that you are much too good." It was then, and
always continued to be, his opinion, that his friend
was particularly qualified for entering with advantage on the study of the medical profession ; but
such designs, if Laidlaw himself ever took them up
seriously, were not ultimately persevered in ; and I
question whether any worldly success could, after all,
have overbalanced the retrospect of an honourable
life spent happily in the open air of nature, amidst
scenes the most captivating to the eye of genius, and
in the intimate confidence of, perhaps, the greatest
of contemporary minds.

James Hogg spent ten years of his life in the
service of Mr Laidlaw's father, but he had passed
into that of another sheep farmer in a neighbouring valley before Scott first visited Blackhouse.
William Laidlaw and Hogg were, however, the
most intimate of friends, and the former took care
that Scott should see, without delay, one whose
enthusiasm about the minstrelsy of the Forest was
equal to his own, and whose mother, then an aged
woman, though she lived many years afterwards, was
celebrated for having by heart several ballads in a

more perfect form than any other inhabitant of the
vale of Ettrick. The personal history of James Hogg
must have interested Scott even more than any
acquisition of that sort which he owed to this acquaintance with, perhaps, the most remarkable man
that ever wore the *maud* of a shepherd. But I need
not here repeat a tale which his own language will
convey to the latest posterity. Under the garb
aspect, and bearing of a rude peasant — and rude
enough he was in most of these things. even after no
inconsiderable experience of society — Scott found
a brother poet, a true son of nature and genius, hardly
conscious of his powers. He had taught himself to
write by copying the letters of a printed book as he
lay watching his flock on the hill-side, and had probably reached the utmost pitch of his ambition when
he first found that his artless rhymes could touch the
heart of the ewe-milker who partook the shelter of
his mantle during the passing storm. As yet his
naturally kind and simple character had not been exposed to any of the dangerous flatteries of the world;
his heart was pure — his enthusiasm buoyant as that
of a happy child; and well as Scott knew that reflection, sagacity, wit, and wisdom, were scattered abundantly among the humblest rangers of these pastoral
solitudes, there was here a depth and a brightness
that filled him with wonder, combined with a quaint-
ness of humour, and a thousand little touches of ab-

surdity, which afforded him more entertainment, as I
have often heard him say, than the best comedy that
ever set the pit in a roar.

Scott opened in the same year a correspondence
with the venerable Bishop of Dromore, who seems,
however, to have done little more than express a
warm interest in an undertaking so nearly resembling
that which will ever keep his own name in remembrance.   He had more success in his applications to
a more unpromising quarter — namely, with Joseph
Ritson, the ancient and virulent assailant of Bishop
Percy's editorial character.   This narrow-minded,
sour, and dogmatical little word-catcher had hated
the very name of a Scotsman, and was utterly incap-
able of sympathizing with any of the higher views of
his new correspondent.   Yet the bland courtesy of
Scott disarmed even this half-crazy pedant ; and he
communicated the stores of his really valuable learning in a manner that seems to have greatly surprised
all who had hitherto held any intercourse with him
on antiquarian topics.   It astonished, above all, the
late amiable and elegant George Ellis, whose acquaintance was about the same time opened to Scott
through their common friend Heber.   Mr Ellis was
now busily engaged in collecting the materials for
his charming works, entitled Specimens of Ancient
English Poetry, and Specimens of Ancient English
Romance.   The correspondence between him and

Scott soon came to be constant.   They met personally, not long after the correspondence had commenced, conceived for each other a cordial respect
and affection, and continued on a footing of almost
brotherly intimacy ever after.   To this valuable alliance Scott owed, among other advantages, his early
and ready admission to the acquaintance and familiarity of Ellis's bosom friend, his coadjutor in the Anti-
jacobin, and the confidant of all his literary schemes,
the late illustrious statesman, Mr Canning.

   The first letter of Scott to Ellis is dated March
27, 1801, and begins thus: — " Sir, as I feel myself
highly flattered by your enquiries, I lose no time in
answering them to the best of my ability.   Your eminence in the literary world, and the warm praises
of our mutual friend Heber, had made me long wish
for an opportunity of being known to you.   I enclose
the first sheet of Sir Tristrem, that you may not so
much rely upon my opinion as upon that which a
specimen of the style and versification may enable
your better judgment to form for itself. . . . These
pages are transcribed by Leyden, an excellent young
man, of uncommon talents, patronised by Heber, and
who is of the utmost assistance to my literary under-
takings."

   As Scott's edition of Sir Tristrem did not appear
until May 1804, and he and Leyden were busy with
the Border Minstrelsy when his correspondence with

Ellis commenced, this early indication of his labours
on the former work may require explanation.   The
truth is, that both Scott and Leyden, having eagerly
arrived at the belief, from which neither of them ever
permitted himself to falter, that the " Sir Tristrem "
of the Auchinleck MS. was virtually, if not literally,
the production of Thomas the Rhymer, laird of Ercildoune in Berwickshire, who flourished at the close
of the thirteenth century—the original intention
had been to give it, not only a place, but a very
prominent one, in the Minstrelsy of the Scottish
Border.   The doubts and difficulties which Ellis
suggested, however, though they did not shake Scott
in his opinion as to the parentage of the romance,
induced researches which occupied so much time,
and gave birth to notes so bulky, that he eventually
found it expedient first to pass it over in the two
volumes of the Minstrelsy which appeared in 1802,
and then even in the third, which followed a year
later; thus reserving Tristrem for a separate publication, which did not take place until after Leyden
had sailed for India.

I must not swell these pages by transcribing the
entire correspondence of Scott and Ellis, the greater
part of which consists of minute antiquarian discussion which could hardly interest the general reader;
but I shall give such extracts as seem to throw light
on Scott's personal history during this period.

" To George Ellis, Esq.

" Lasswade Cottage, 20th April 1801.

" My Dear Sir,

" I should long ago have acknowledged your instructive letter, but I have been wandering about in the wilds of Liddesdale and Ettrick Forest, in search of additional materials for the Border Minstrelsy. I cannot, however, boast much of my success. One of our best reciters has turned religious in his later days, and finds out that old songs are unlawful. If so, then, as Falstaff says, is many an acquaintance of mine damned. I now send you an accurate analysis of Sir Tristrem. Philo-Tomas, whoever he was, must surely have been an Englishman ; when his hero joins battle with Moraunt, he exclaims—

' God help Tristrem the Knight,
He fought for Ingland.'

This strain of national attachment would hardly have proceeded from a Scottish author, even though he had laid his scene in the sister country. In other respects the language appears to be Scottish, and certainly contains the essence of Tomas's work. . . . . . . You shall have Sir Otuel in a week or two, and I shall be happy to compare your Romance of Merlin with our *Arthur and Merlin*, which is a

very good poem, and may supply you with some
valuable additions. .. .. I would very fain
lend your elephant* *a lift*, but I fear I can be of little
use to you. I have been rather an observer of de-

---

* This phrase will be best explained by an extract from a
letter, addressed by Sir Walter Scott, on the 12th February
1830, to William Brockedon, Esq. acknowledging that gentleman's
courtesy in sending him a copy of the beautiful work entitled
"Passes of the Alps :"—

"My friend the late George Ellis, one of the most accomplished
scholars, and delightful companions whom I have ever known,
himself a great geographer on the most extended and liberal plan,
used to tell me an anecdote of the eminent antiquary General
Melville, who was crossing the Alps, with Livy and other historical accounts in his post chaise, determined to follow the route of
Hannibal. He met Ellis, I forget where at this moment, on the
western side of that tremendous ridge, and pushed onwards on his
journey after a day spent with his brother antiquary. After journeying more slowly than his friend, Ellis was astonished to meet
General Melville coming back. ' What is the matter, my dear
friend? how come you back on the journey you had so much at
heart ?'—' Alas l' said Melville, very dejectedly, ' I would have
got on myself well enough, but I could not get my *elephants*
over the pass." He had, in idea, Hannibal with his train of
elephants in his party. It became a sort of bye-word between
Ellis and me ; and in assisting each other during a close correspondence of some years, we talked of a lift to the elephants.

"You, Sir, have put this theoretical difficulty at an end, and
show how, without bodily labour, the antiquary may traverse
the Alps with his elephants, without the necessity of a retrograde
movement. In giving a distinct picture of so interesting a country as Switzerland, so peculiar in its habits, and its history, you

tached facts respecting antiquities, than a regular
student.   At the same time, I may mention one or
two circumstances, were it but to place your elephant
upon a tortoise.   From Selkirkshire to Cumberland,
we have a ditch and bulwark of great strength, called
the Catrail, running north and south, and obviously
calculated to defend the western side of the island
against the inhabitants of the eastern half.   Within
this bulwark, at Drummelzier, near Peebles, we find
the grave of Merlin, the account of whose madness
and death you will find in Fordun.   The same author says he was seized with his madness during a
dreadful battle on the Liddle, which divides Cumberland from Scotland.   All this seems to favour
your ingenious hypothesis, that the sway of the
British Champion [Arthur] extended over Cumberland and Strathcluyd, as well as Wales.   Ercildoune
is hardly five miles from the Catrail. . . . . .

    " Leyden has taken up a most absurd resolution
to go to Africa on a journey of discovery. Will you
have the goodness to beg Heber to write to him
seriously on so ridiculous a plan, which can promise
nothing either pleasant or profitable. I am certain
he would get a church in Scotland with a little

have added a valuable chapter to the history of Europe, in which
the Alpine regions make so distinguished a figure. Accept my
best congratulations on achieving so interesting a task."

patience and prudence, and it gives me great pain to
see a valuable young man of uncommon genius and
acquirements fairly throw himself away. Yours truly,

W. Scott."

" *To the Same.*

"Musselburgh, 11th May 1801.

. . . . . " I congratulate you upon the health of
your elephants—as an additional mouthful of pro-
vender for them, pray observe that the tale of Sir
Gawain's Foul Ladie, in Percy's Reliques, is originally Scaldic, as you will see in the history of Hrolfe
Kraka, edited by Torfæus from the ancient Sagas
regarding that prince. I think I could give you
some more crumbs of information were I at home;
but I am at present discharging the duties of quartermaster to a regiment of volunteer cavalry—an
office altogether inconsistent with romance; for where
do you read that Sir Tristrem weighed out hay and
corn; that Sir Lancelot du Lac distributed billets;
or that any Knight of the Round Table condescended
to higgle about a truss of straw ?   Such things were
left for our degenerate days, when no warder sounds
his horn from the barbican as the *preux chevalier*
approaches to claim hospitality.   Bugles indeed we
have; but it is only to scream us out of bed at five
in the morning—hospitality such as the seneschals

of Don Quixote's castles were wont to offer him—
and all. to troopers, to whom, for valour eke and
courtesy, Major Sturgeon* himself might yield the
palm.   In the midst of this scene of motley confusion, I long, like the hart for water-brooks, for the
arrival of your *grande opus.* 'The nature of your
researches animates me to proceed in mine (though
of a much more limited and local nature), even as
iron sharpeneth iron.   I am in utter despair about
some of the hunting terms in ' Sir Tristrem.'   There
is no copy of Lady Juliana Berners' work† in Scotland, and I would move heaven and earth to get a
sight of it.   But as I fear this is utterly impossible,
I must have recourse to your friendly assistance, and
communicate a set of doubts and queries, which, if
any man in England can satisfy, I am well assured
it must be you.   You may therefore expect, in a few
days, another epistle.   Mean time I must invoke the
spirit of Nimrod."

                    " Edinburgh, 10th June 1801.

" My Dear Sir,

        " A heavy family misfortune, the loss of an
only sister in the prime of life, has prevented, for
some time, my proposed communication regarding

* See Foote's farce of The Mayor of Garrat.

† " The Boke of St Albans"— first printed in 1486 — re-
printed by Mr Haslewood in 1810.

the hunting terms of 'Sir Tristrem.' I now enclose
the passage, accurately copied, with such explana-
tions as occur to myself, subject always to your
correction and better judgment. . . . . . . I have as
yet had only a glance of *The Specimens.* Thomson,
to whom Heber intrusted them, had left them to
follow him from London in a certain trunk, which
has never yet arrived. I should have quarrelled
with him excessively for making so little allowance
for my impatience, had it not been that a violent
epidemic fever, to which I owe the loss already
mentioned, has threatened also to deprive me, in
his person, of one of my dearest friends, and the
Scottish literary world of one of its most promising
members.

"Some prospect seems to open for getting Leyden out to India, under the patronage of Mackintosh,
who goes as chief of the intended academical establishment at Calcutta. That he is highly qualified
for acting a distinguished part in any literary undertaking, will be readily granted; nor do I think Mr
Mackintosh will meet with many half so likely to be
useful in the proposed institution. The extent and
versatility of his talents would soon raise him to his
level, even although he were at first to go out in a
subordinate department. If it be in your power to
second his application, I rely upon Heber's interest
with you to induce you to do so."

. . . . " I am infinitely obliged to you, indeed, for
your interference in behalf of our Leyden, who, I am
sure, will do credit to your patronage, and may be
of essential service to the proposed mission.   What
a difference from broiling himself, or getting himself
literally broiled, in Africa.   ' Que diable vouloit-il
faire dans cette galère ?' . . . His brother is a fine
lad, and is likely to enjoy some advantages which he
wanted—I mean by being more early introduced
into society.   I have intermitted his transcript of
' Merlin,' and set him to work on ' Otuel,' of which
I send a specimen." . . . .

.   . " My literary amusements have of late
been much retarded and interrupted, partly by professional avocations, and partly by removing to a
house newly furnished, where it will be some time
before I can get my few books put into order, or
clear the premises of painters and workmen ; not to
mention that these worthies do not nowadays proceed upon the plan of Solomon's architects, whose
saws and hammers were not heard, but rather upon
the more ancient system of the builders of Babel.
To augment this confusion, my wife has fixed upon
this time as proper to present me with a fine chopping
boy, whose pipe, being of the shrillest, is heard amid

the storm, like a boatswain's whistle in a gale of
wind.   These various causes of confusion have also
interrupted the labours of young Leyden on your
behalf; but he has again resumed the task of transcribing ' Arthour,' of which I once again transmit
a part.   I have to acknowledge, with the deepest
sense of gratitude, the beautiful analysis of Mr
Douce's Fragments, which throws great light upon
the romance of Sir Tristrem.   In arranging that, I
have anticipated your judicious hint, by dividing it
into three parts, where the story seems naturally to
pause, and prefixing an accurate argument, referring
to the stanzas as numbered.

" I am glad that Mrs Ellis and you have derived
any amusement from the House of Aspen.   It is a
very hurried dramatic sketch; and the fifth act, as
you remark, would require a total revisal previous
to representation or publication.   At one time I
certainly thought, with my friends, that it might
have ranked well enough by the side of the Castle
Spectre, Bluebeard, and the other drum and trumpet
exhibitions of the day; but the ' Plays of the Passions'* have put me entirely out of conceit with my
Germanized brat; and should I ever again attempt
dramatic composition, I would endeavour after the
genuine old English model. . . . . . . The publica-

* The first volume of Joanna Baillie's " Plays of the Passions"
appeared in 1798.   Vol. II. followed in 1802.

tion of ' The Complaynt'* is delayed. It is a work
of multifarious lore. I am truly anxious about Leyden's Indian journey, which seems to hang fire. Mr
William Dundas was so good as to promise me his
interest to get him appointed Secretary to the Institution;† but whether he has succeeded or not, I
have not yet learned. The various kinds of distress
under which literary men, I mean such as have no
other profession than letters, must labour, in a commercial country, is a great disgrace to society. I
own to you I always tremble for the fate of genius
when left to its own exertions, which, however
powerful, are usually, by some bizarre dispensation
of nature, useful to every one but themselves. If
Heber could learn by Mackintosh, whether anything
could be done to fix Leyden's situation, and what
sort of interest would be most likely to succeed, his
friends here might unite every exertion in his favour. . . . . Direct Castle Street, as
usual ; my new house being in the same street with
my old dwelling."

"Edinburgh, 8th January 1802.

. . . . " Your favour arrived just as I was sitting

* " The Complaynt of Scotland, written in 1548; with a Pre-
liminary Dissertation and Glossary. by John Leyden," was published by Constable in January 1802.

† A proposed Institution for purposes of Education at Calcutta.

down to write to you, with a sheet or two of ' King
Arthur.' I fear, from a letter which I have received
from Mr William Dundas, that the Indian Establishment is tottering, and will probably fall. Leyden
has therefore been induced to turn his mind to some
other mode of making his way to the East ; and
proposes taking his degree as a physician and surgeon, with the hope of getting an appointment in
the Company's Service as surgeon. If the Institution goes forward, his having secured this step will
not prevent his being attached to it ; at the same
time that it will afford him a provision independent
of what seems to be a very precarious establishment.
Mr Dundas has promised to exert himself. . . . I
have just returned from the hospitable halls of Hamilton, where I have spent the Christmas." . . . .

                                    "14th February 1802.

    " I have been silent, but not idle. The tran-
script of King Arthur is at length finished, being a
fragment of about 7000 lines. Let me know how I
shall transmit a parcel containing it, with the *Complaynt* and the Border Ballads, of which I expect
every day to receive some copies. I think you will
be disappointed in the Ballads. I have as yet touched
very little on the more remote antiquities of the
Border, which, indeed, my songs, all comparatively
modern, did not lead me to discuss. Some scattered

herbage, however, the elephants may perhaps find.
By the way, you will not forget to notice the mountain called *Arthur's Seat*, which overhangs this city.
When I was at school, the tradition ran that King
Arthur occupied as his throne a huge rock upon its
summit, and that he beheld from thence some naval
engagement upon the Frith of Forth.   I am pleasantly interrupted by the post; he brings me a letter
from William Dundas, fixing Leyden's appointment
as an assistant-surgeon to one of the India settle-
ments — which, is not yet determined ; and another
from my printer, a very ingenious young man, telling
me, that he means to escort the ' Minstrelsy' up
to London in person.   I shall, therefore, direct him
to transmit my parcel to Mr Nicol." . . . .

                              " 2d March 1802.

   " I *hope* that long ere this you have received
the Ballads, and that they have afforded you some
amusement.   I hope, also, that the *threatened* third
volume will be more interesting to Mrs Ellis than
the dry antiquarian detail of the two first could
prove.   I hope, moreover, that I shall have the
pleasure of seeing you soon, as some circumstances
seem not so much to call me to London, as to furnish me with a decent apology for coming up some
time this spring ; and I long particularly to say, that
I know my friend Mr Ellis *by sight* as well as *inti-*

mately. I am glad you have seen the Marquess of
Lorn, whom I have met frequently at the house of
his charming sister, Lady Charlotte Campbell, whom,
I am sure, if you are acquainted with her, you must
admire as much as I do.   Her Grace of Gordon, a
great admirer of yours, spent some days here lately,
and, like. Lord Lorn, was highly entertained with
an account of our friendship *à la distance.* I do not,
nor did I ever, intend to fob you off with twenty
or thirty lines of the second part of Sir Guy. Young
Leyden has been much engaged with his studies,
otherwise you would have long since received what
I now send, namely, the combat between Guy and
Colbronde, which I take to be the cream of the romance. . . . . If I do not come to London this
spring, I will find a safe opportunity of returning
Lady Juliana Berners, with my very best thanks for
the use of her reverence's work."

The preceding extracts are picked out of letters,
mostly very long ones, in which Scott discusses
questions of antiquarian interest, suggested sometimes by Ellis, and sometimes by the course of his
own researches among the MSS. of the Advocates'
Library.   The passages which I have transcribed
appear sufficient to give the reader a distinct notion
of the tenour of Scott's life while his first considerable work was in progress through the press.   In

fact, they place before us in a vivid light the chief
features of a character which, by this time, was
completely formed and settled — which had passed
unmoved through the first blandishments of worldly
applause, and which no subsequent trials of that sort
could ever shake from its early balance : — His calm
delight in his own pursuits — the patriotic enthusiasm which mingled with all the best of his literary
efforts ; his modesty as to his own general merits,
combined with a certain dogged resolution to maintain his own first view of a subject, however assailed ; his readiness to interrupt his own tasks
by any drudgery by which he could assist those
of a friend ; his steady and determined watchful-
ness over the struggling fortunes of young genius
and worth.

The reader has seen that he spent the Christmas
of 1801 at Hamilton Palace, in Lanarkshire.   To
Lady Anne Hamilton he had been introduced by her
friend, Lady Charlotte Campbell, and both the late
and the present Dukes of Hamilton appear to have
partaken of Lady Anne's admiration for Glenfinlas,
and the Eve of St John.   A morning's ramble to
the majestic ruins of the old baronial castle on the
precipitous banks of the Evan, and among the adjoining remains of the primeval Caledonian forest,
suggested to him a ballad, not inferior in execution
to any that he had hitherto produced, and especially

interesting as the first in which he grapples with
the world of picturesque incident unfolded in the
authentic annals of Scotland. With the magnificent localities before him, he skilfully interwove the
daring assassination of the Regent Murray by one of
the clansmen of "the princely Hamilton." Had the
subject been taken up in after years, we might have
had another Marmion or Heart of Mid-Lothian; for
in Cadyow Castle we have the materials and outline
of more than one of the noblest of ballads.

About two years before this piece began to be
handed about in Edinburgh, Thomas Campbell had
made his appearance there, and at once siezed a high
place in the literary world by his " Pleasures of
Hope." Among the most eager to welcome him
had been Scott; and I find the brother-bard thus
expressing himself concerning the MS. of Cadyow:—

" The verses of Cadyow Castle are perpetually
ringing in my imagination—

> ' Where, mightiest of the beasts of chase
>   That roam in woody Caledon,
>   Crashing the forest in his race,
>   The mountain bull comes thundering on—'

and the arrival of Hamilton, when

> ' Reeking from the recent deed,
>   He dashed his carbine on the ground.'

I have repeated these lines so often on the North
Bridge that the whole fraternity of coachmen know
me by tongue as I pass.   To be sure, to a mind in
sober, serious street-walking humour, it must bear
an appearance of lunacy when one stamps with the
hurried pace and fervent shake of the head, which
strong, pithy poetry excites."

Scott finished Cadyow Castle before the last sheets
of the second volume of his Minstrelsy had passed
through the press; but " the two volumes," as Ballantyne says, " were already full to overflowing;"
so it was reserved for the " threatened third."   The
two volumes appeared in the course of January
1802, from the respectable house of Cadell and
Davies, in the Strand; and, owing to the cold
reception of Lewis's Tales of Wonder, which had
come forth a year earlier, these may be said to have
first introduced Scott as an original writer to the
English public.

In his Remarks on the Imitation of Popular
Poetry, he says:—" Owing to the failure of the
vehicle I had chosen, my first efforts to present
myself before the public as an original writer proved
as vain as those by which I had previously endeavoured to distinguish myself as a translator.   Like
Lord Home, however, at the Battle of Flodden, I
did so far well, that I was able to stand and save
myself; and amidst the general depreciation of the

Tales of Wonder, my small share of the obnoxious
publication was dismissed without censure, and in
some cases obtained praise from the critics. The
consequences of my escape made me naturally more
daring, and I attempted in my own name, a collection
of ballads of various kinds, both ancient and modern,
to be connected by the common tie of relation to the
Border districts in which I had collected them. The
edition was curious, as being the first example of
a work printed by my friend and schoolfellow, Mr
James Ballantyne, who at that period was editor of
a provincial paper. When the book came out, the
imprint, Kelso, was read with wonder by amateurs
of typography, who had never heard of such a place,
and were astonished at the example of handsome
printing which so obscure a town had produced. As
for the editorial part of the task, my attempt to imitate the plan and style of Bishop Percy, observing
only more strict fidelity concerning my originals, was
favourably received by the public."

The first edition of volumes I. and II. of the
Minstrelsy consisted of eight hundred copies, fifty
of which were on large paper. One of the embellishments was a view of Hermitage castle, the history
of which is rather curious. Scott executed a rough
sketch of it during the last of his " Liddesdale raids"
with Shortreed, standing for that purpose for an
hour or more up to his middle in the snow. Nothing

can be ruder than the performance, which I have
now before me; but his friend William Clerk made
a better drawing from it; and from his, a third and
further improved copy was done by Hugh Williams,
the elegant artist, afterwards known as "Greek
Williams." *   Scott used to say, the oddest thing of
all was, that the engraving, founded on the labours
of three draughtsman, one of whom could not draw
a straight line, and the two others had never seen
the place meant to be represented, was nevertheless
pronounced by the natives of Liddesdale to give a
very fair notion of the ruins of Hermitage.

The edition was exhausted in the course of the
year, and the terms of publication having been that
Scott should have half the clear profits, his share
was exactly £78 : 10s.—a sum which certainly could
not have repaid him for the actual expenditure
incurred in the collection of his materials. Messrs
Cadell and Davies, however, complained, and probably with good reason, that a premature advertisement of a " second and improved edition" had
rendered some copies of the first unsaleable.

I shall transcribe the letter in which Mr George
Ellis acknowledges the receipt of his copy of the
book : —

---

* Mr Williams's Travels in Italy and Greece were published
in 1820.

" *To Walter Scott, Esq. Advocate, Castle Street,*
Edinburgh.

" Sunning Hill, March 5, 1802.

" My Dear Sir,

" The volumes are arrived, and I have been
devouring them, not as a pig does a parcel of grains
(by which simile you will judge that I must be
brewing, as indeed I am), putting in its snout, shutting its eyes, and swallowing as fast as it can without
consideration — but as a schoolboy does a piece of
gingerbread; nibbling a little bit here, and a little
bit there, smacking his lips, surveying the number
of square inches which still remain for his gratification, endeavouring to look it into larger dimensions,
and making at every mouthful a tacit vow to pro-
tract his enjoyment by restraining his appetite. Now,
therefore—but no! I must first assure you on the
part of Mrs E., that if you cannot, or will not come
to England soon, she must gratify her curiosity and
gratitude, by setting off for Scotland, though at the
risk of being tempted to pull caps with Mrs Scott
when she arrives at the end of her journey. Next,
I must request you to convey to Mr Leyden my very
sincere acknowledgment for his part of the precious
parcel. How truly vexatious that such a man should
embark, not for the ' fines Atticæ,' but for those of

Asia; that the genius of Scotland, instead of a poor *Complaint*, and an address in the style of ' Navis, quæ tibi creditum debes Virgilium — reddas incolumem, precor,' should not interfere to prevent his loss.   I wish to hope that we should, as Sterne says, ' manage these matters better' in England; but now, as regret is unavailing, to the main point of my letter.

" You will not, of course, expect that I should as yet give you anything like an opinion, *as a critic*, of your volumes; first, because you have thrown into my throat a cate of such magnitude that Cerberus, who had three throats, could not have swallowed a third part of it without shutting his eyes; and secondly, because, although I have gone a little farther than George Nicol the bookseller, who cannot cease exclaiming, ' What a beautiful book!' and is distracted with jealousy of your Kelso Bulmer, yet, as I said before, I have not been able yet to *digest* a great deal of your ' Border Minstrelsy.'   I have, however, taken such a survey as satisfies me that your plan is neither too comprehensive nor too contracted; that the parts are properly distinct; and that they are (to preserve the painter's metaphor) *made out* just as they ought to be.   Your introductory chapter is, I think, particularly good; and I was much pleased, although a little surprised, at finding that it was made to serve as a *recueil des pièces justificatives* to your view of the state of manners among your Borderers, which I venture to say will be more thumbed than any part of the volume.

" You will easily believe that I cast many an anxious look for the annunciation of ' Sir Tristrem,' and will not be surprised that I was at first rather disappointed at not finding any thing like a solemn engagement to produce him to the world within some fixed and limited period.   Upon reflection, however, I really think you have judged wisely, and that you have best promoted the interests of literature, by sending, as the *harbinger* of the ' Knight of Leonais,' a collection which must form a parlour-window book in every house in Britain which contains a parlour and a window.   I am happy to find my *old favourites* in their natural situation—indeed in the only situation which can enable a Southern reader to estimate their merits.   You remember what somebody said of the Prince de Condé's army during the wars of the Fronde, viz.—" that it would be a very fine army whenever it came of age."   Of the Murrays and Armstrongs of your Border Ballads, it might be said that they might grow, when the age of good taste should arrive, to a Glenfinlas or an Eve of St John. Leyden's additional poems are also very beautiful. I meant, at setting out, a few simple words of thanks, and behold I have written a letter ; but no matter —

I shall return to the charge after a more attentive perusal.   Ever yours very faithfully,

G. Ellis."

I might fill many pages by transcribing similar letters from persons of acknowledged discernment in this branch of literature; John Duke of Roxburgh is among the number, and he conveys also a complimentary message from the late Earl Spencer; Pinkerton issues his decree of approbation as *ex cathedrâ;* Chalmers overflows with heartier praise; and even Joseph Ritson extols his presentation copy as " the most valuable literary treasure in his possession." There follows enough of female admiration to have been dangerous for another man; a score of fine ladies contend who shall be the most extravagant in encomium—and as many professed blue stockings come after; among, or rather above the rest, Anna Seward, " the Swan of Lichfield," who laments that her " bright luminary," Darwin, does not survive to partake her raptures; — observes, that " in the Border Ballads the first strong rays of the Delphic orb illuminate Jellon Graeme;" and concludes with a fact indisputable, but strangely expressed, viz. that " the Lady Anne Bothwell's Lament, Cowdenknowes, &c. &c., *climatically* preceded the treasures of Burns, and the consummate Glenfinlas and Eve of St John."   Scott felt as acutely as any malevolent

critic the pedantic affectations of Miss Seward's epis-
tolary style, but in her case sound sense as well as
vigorous ability had unfortunately condescended to
an absurd disguise; he looked below it, and was far
from confounding her honest praise with the flat
superlatives either of worldly parrots or weak en-
thusiasts.

CHAPTER XI.

*Preparation of Volume III. of the Minstrelsy—
and of Sir Tristrem — Correspondence with
Miss Seward and Mr Ellis—Ballad of the
Reiver's Wedding—Commencement of the Lay
of the Last Minstrel — Visit to London and
Oxford — Completion of the Minstrelsy of the
Scottish Border.*

1802–1803.

THE approbation with which the first two volumes
of the Minstrelsy were received, stimulated Scott to
fresh diligence in the preparation of a third; while
" Sir Tristrem"—it being now settled that this romance should form a separate volume—was transmitted, without delay, to the printer at Kelso.   As
early as March 30th, 1802, Ballantyne, who had just
returned from London, writes thus:—

" *To Walter Scott, Esq., Castle Street, Edinburgh.*

" Dear Sir,

" By to-morrow's Fly I shall send the remaining materials for Minstrelsy, together with three
sheets of Sir Tristrem. . . . I shall ever think the
printing the Scottish Minstrelsy one of the most
fortunate circumstances of my life. I have gained,
not lost by it, in a pecuniary light; and the prospects it has been the means of opening to me, may
advantageously influence· my future destiny. I can
never be sufficiently grateful for the interest you
unceasingly take in my welfare. Your query respecting *Edinburgh,* I am *yet* at a loss to answer.
To say truth, the expenses I have incurred in my
resolution to acquire a character for elegant printing,
whatever might be the result, cramp considerably my
present exertions. A short time, I trust, will make
me easier, and I shall then contemplate the road
before me with a steady eye. One thing alone is
clear—that Kelso cannot be my abiding place for
aye; sooner or later emigrate I must and will; but,
at all events, I must wait till my plumes are grown.
I am, Dear Sir, your faithful and obliged

                                    J. B."

On learning that a third volume of the Minstrelsy

was in progress. Miss Seward forwarded to the Editor
" Rich Auld Willie's Farewell," a Scotch ballad of
her own manufacture, meaning, no doubt, to place it
at his disposal, for the section of " Imitations." His
answer (dated Edinburgh, June 29, 1802), after
many compliments to the *Auld Willie*, of which he
made the use that had been intended, proceeds as
follows :—

  " I have some thoughts of attempting a Border
ballad in the comic manner ; but I almost despair of
bringing it well out. A certain Sir William Scott,
from whom I am descended, was ill-advised enough
to plunder the estate of Sir Gideon Murray of
Elibank, ancestor to the present Lord Elibank. The
marauder was defeated, seized, and brought in fetters
to the castle of Elibank, upon the Tweed. The
Lady Murray (agreeably to the custom of all ladies
in ancient tales) was seated on the battlements, and
descried the return of her husband with his prisoners.
She immediately enquired what he meant to do with
the young Knight of Harden, which was the *petit
titre* of Sir William Scott. ' Hang the robber, as-
suredly,' was the answer of Sir Gideon.   ' What !'
answered the lady, ' hang the handsome young knight
of Harden, when I have three ill-favoured daughters
unmarried ! No, no, Sir Gideon, we'll force him to
marry our Meg.' Now tradition says, that Meg

Murray was the ugliest woman in the four counties,
and that she was called, in the homely dialect of the
time, *meikle-mouthed Meg* (I will not affront you
by an explanation.)*   Sir Gideon, like a good husband and tender father, entered into his wife's sentiments, and proffered to Sir William the alternative
of becoming his son-in-law, or decorating with his
carcase the *kindly* gallows of Elibank.   The lady
was so very ugly, that Sir William, the handsomest
man of his time, positively refused the honour of her
hand.   Three days were allowed him to make up his
mind; and it was not until he found one end of a
rope made fast to his neck, and the other knitted to
a sturdy oak bough, that his resolution gave way,
and he preferred an ugly wife to the literal noose.
It is said, they were afterwards a very happy couple.
She had a curious hand at pickling the beef which
he stole; and, marauder as he was, he had little
reason to dread being twitted by the pawky gowk.
This, either by its being perpetually told to me when
young, or by a perverted taste for such anecdotes,
has always struck me as a good subject for a comic
ballad, and how happy should I be were Miss Seward
to agree in opinion with me.

" This little tale may serve for an introduction to

* It is commonly said that all Meg's descendants have inherited something of her characteristic feature.   The Poet certainly was no exception to the rule.

some observations I have to offer upon our popular
poetry. It will at least so far disclose your correspondent's weak side, as to induce you to make
allowance for my mode of arguing. Much of its
peculiar charm is indeed, I believe, to be attributed
solely to its *locality*. A very commonplace and ob-
vious epithet, when applied to a scene which we have
been accustomed to view with pleasure, recalls to us
not merely the local scenery, but a thousand little
nameless associations, which we are unable to separate or to define. In some verses of that eccentric
but admirable poet, Coleridge, he talks of

> ' An old rude tale that suited well
> The ruins wild and hoary.'

I think there are few who have not been in some
degree touched with this local sympathy. Tell a
peasant an ordinary tale of robbery and murder, and
perhaps you may fail to interest him; but to excite
his terrors, you assure him it happened on the very
heath he usually crosses, or to a man whose family
he has known, and you rarely meet such a mere
image of Humanity as remains entirely unmoved.
I suspect it is pretty much the same with myself,
and many of my countrymen, who are charmed by
the effect of local description, and sometimes impute
that effect to the poet, which is produced by the recollections and associations which his verses excite.

Why else did Sir Philip Sydney feel that the tale of
Percy and Douglas moved him like the sound of a
trumpet? or why is it that a Swiss sickens at
hearing the famous Ranz des Vaches, to which the
native of any other country would have listened for
a hundred days, without any other sensation than
ennui? I fear our poetical taste is in general much
more linked with our prejudices of birth, of educa-
cation, and of habitual thinking, than our vanity will
allow us to suppose; and that, let the point of the
poet's dart be as sharp as that of Cupid, it is the
wings lent it by the fancy and prepossessions of the
gentle reader which carry it to the mark. It may
appear like great egotism to pretend to illustrate my
position from the reception which the productions
of so mere a ballad-monger as myself have met with
from the public; but I cannot help observing that
all Scotchmen prefer the Eve of St John to Glenfinlas, and most of my English friends entertain precisely an opposite opinion. . . . I have been writing
this letter by a paragraph at a time for about a
month, this being the season when we are most devoted to the

    'Drowsy bench and babbling hall.'

  " I have the honour," &c. &c. . . . . .

Miss Seward, in her next letter, offers an apology

for not having sooner begged Scott to place her name among the *subscribers* to his third volume. His answer is in these words : —

" Lasswade, July, 1802.

" I am very sorry to have left you under a mistake about my third volume.   The truth is, that highly as I should feel myself flattered by the encouragement of Miss Seward's name, I cannot, in the present instance, avail myself of it, as the Ballads are not published by subscription.   Providence having, I suppose, foreseen that my literary qualifications, like those of many more distinguished persons, might not, *par hazard*, support me exactly as I would like, allotted me a small patrimony, which, joined to my professional income, and my appointments in the characteristic office of Sheriff of Ettrick Forest, serves to render my literary pursuits more a matter of amusement than an object of emolument. With this explanation, I hope you will honour me by accepting the third volume as soon as published, which will be in the beginning of next year, and I also hope, that under the circumstances, you will hold me acquitted of the silly vanity of wishing to be thought a *gentleman*-author.

" The ballad of The Reiver's Wedding is not yet written, but I have finished one of a tragic cast, founded upon the death of Regent Murray, who was

shot in Linlithgow, by James Hamilton of Bothwellhaugh.   The following verses contain the catastrophe, as told by Hamilton himself to his chief and
his kinsmen :—

> ' With hackbut bent,' &c. &c.
>
> *   *   *   *   *
> *   *   *   *   *

" This Bothwellhaugh has occupied such an un-
warrantable proportion of my letter, that I have
hardly time to tell you how much I join in your
admiration of Tam o' Shanter, which I verily believe
to be inimitable, both in the serious and ludicrous
parts, as well as the singularly happy combination of
both.   I request Miss Seward to believe," &c.

The " Reiver's Wedding" never was completed,
but I have found two copies of its commencement,
and I shall make no apologies for inserting here
what seems to have been the second one.   It will
be seen that he had meant to mingle with Sir William's capture, Auld Wat's Foray of the Bassened
Bull, and the Feast of Spurs ; and that, I know not
for what reason, Lochwood, the ancient fortress of
the Johnstones in Annandale, has been substituted
for the real locality of his ancestor's drum-head
Wedding Contract :—

" THE REIVER'S WEDDING.

' O will ye hear a mirthful bourd ?
  Or will ye hear of courtesie ?
Or will ye hear how a gallant lord
  Was wedded to a gay ladye ?

' Ca' out the kye,' quo the village herd,
  As he stood on the knowe,
' Ca' this ane's mine and that ane's ten,
  And hauld Lord William's cow.'

' Ah ! by my sooth,' quoth William then,
  ' And stands it that way now,
When knave and churl have nine and ten,
  That the Lord has but his cow ?

' I swear by the light of the Michaelmas moon
  And the might of Mary high,
And by the edge of my braidsword brown,
  They shall soon say Harden's kye.'

He took a bugle frae his side,
  With names carved o'er and o'er —
Full many a chief of meikle pride,
  That Border bugle bore —*

He blew a note baith sharp and hie,
  Till rock and water rang around —

---

* This celebrated horn is still in the possession of Lord Polwarth.

Three score of mosstroopers and three
    Have mounted at that bugle sound.

The Michaelmas moon had entered then,
    And ere she wan the full,
Ye might see by her light in Harden glen
    A bow o' kye and a bassened bull.

And loud and loud in Harden tower
    The quaigh gaed round wi' meikle glee ;
For the English beef was brought in bower,
    And the English ale flowed merrilis.

And mony a guest from Teviotside
    And Yarrow's Braes were there ;
Was never a lord in Scotland wide
    That made more dainty fare.

They ate, they laugh'd, they sang and quaff'd,
    Till nought on board was seen,
When knight and squire were boune to dine,
    But a spur of silver sheen.

Lord William has ta'en his berry brown steed —
    A sore sbent man was he ;
' Wait ye, my guests, a little speed —
    Weel feasted ye shall be.'

He rode him down by Falsehope burn,
    His cousin dear to see,
With him to take a riding turn —
    Wat-draw-the-sword was he.

And when he came to Falsehope glen,
    Beneath the trysting tree,

On the smooth green was carved plain,*
  ' To Lochwood bound are we.'

' O if they be gane to dark Lochwood
  To drive the Warden's gear,
Betwixt our names, I ween, there's feud:
  I'll go and have my share:

' For little reck I for Johnstone's feud,
  The Warden though he be.'
So Lord William is away to dark Lochwood,
  With riders barely three.

The Warden's daughters in Lochwood sate,
  Were all both fair and gay,
All save the Lady Margaret,
  And she was wan and wae.

The sister, Jean, had a full fair skin,
  And Grace was bauld and braw;
But the leal-fast heart her breast within
  It weel was worth them a'.

Her father 's pranked her sisters twa
  With meikle joy and pride;

---

* " At Linton, in Roxburghshire, there is a circle of stones surrounding a smooth plot of turf, called the *Tryst*, or place of appointment, which tradition avers to have been the rendezvous of the neighbouring warriors. The name of the leader was cut in the turf, and the arrangement of the letters announced to his followers the course which he had taken."—*Introduction to the Minstrelsy*, p. 185.

But Margaret maun seek Dundrennan's wa' —
  She ne'er can be a bride.

On spear and casque by gallants gent
  Her sisters' scarfs were borne,
But never at tilt or tournament
  Were Margaret's colours worn.

Her sisters rode to Thirlstane bower,
  But she was left at hame
To wander round the gloomy tower,
  And sigh young Harden's name.

' Of all the knights, the knight most fair,
  From Yarrow to the Tyne,'
Soft sighed the maid, ' is Harden's heir,
  But ne'er can he be mine :

Of all the maids, the foulest maid
  From Teviot to the Dee,
Ah !' sighing sad, that lady said,
  ' Can ne'er young Harden's be' —

She looked up the briery glen,
  And up the mossy brae,
And she saw a score of her father's men
  Yclad in the Johnstone grey.

O fast and fast they downwards sped
  The moss and briers among,
And in the midst the troopers led
  A shackled knight along."

*   *   *   *   *   *   *

As soon as the autumn vacation set Scott at
liberty, he proceeded to the Borders with Leyden.
" We have just concluded," he tells Ellis on his
return to Edinburgh, " an excursion of two or
three weeks through my jurisdiction of Selkirkshire,
where, in defiance of mountains, rivers, and bogs
damp and dry, we have penetrated the very recesses
of Ettrick Forest, to which district if I ever have
the happiness of welcoming you, you will be convinced
that I am truly the sheriff of the ' cairn and the
scaur.' In the course of our grand tour, besides the
risks of swamping and breaking our necks, we encountered the formidable hardships of sleeping upon
peat-stacks, and eating mutton slain by no common
butcher, but deprived of life by the judgment of
God, as a coroner's inquest would express themselves. I have, however, not only escaped safe ' per
varios casus, per tot discrimina rerum,' but returned
loaded with the treasures of oral tradition. The
principal result of our enquiries has been a complete
and perfect copy of ' Maitland with his Auld Berd
Graie,' referred to by Douglas in his ' Palice of
Honour,' along with John the Reef and other popular characters, and celebrated also in the poems from
the Maitland MS. You may guess the surprise of
Leyden and myself when this was presented to us,
copied down from the recitation of an old shepherd,

by a country farmer, and with no greater corruptions than might be supposed to be introduced by
the lapse of time, and the ignorance of reciters. I
don't suppose it was originally composed later than
the days of Blind Harry. Many of the old words
are retained, which neither the reciter nor the copyer
understood. Such are the military engines *sowies*,
springwalls (springalds), and many others. Though
the poetical merit of this curiosity is not striking,
yet it has an odd energy and dramatic effect."

A few weeks later, he thus answers Ellis's enquiries
as to the progress of the Sir Tristrem : — " The
worthy knight is still in embryo, though the whole
poetry is printed. The fact is, that a second edition
of the Minstrelsy has been demanded more suddenly
than I expected, and has occupied my immediate
attention. I have also my third volume to compile
and arrange ; for the Minstrelsy is now to be completed altogether independent of the *preux chevalier*,
who might hang heavy upon its skirts. I assure
you my *Continuation* is mere doggrel, not poetry —
it is *argued in the same division* with Thomas's
own production, and therefore not worth sending.
However, you may depend on having the whole long
before publication. I have derived much information from Turner : he combines the knowledge of
the Welsh and northern authorities, and, in despite

of a most detestable *Gibbonism*, his book is interesting.*   I intend to study the Welsh triads before
I finally commit myself on the subject of Border
poetry. . . . . As for Mr Ritson, he and I still continue on decent terms ; and, in truth, he makes *patte
de velours ;* but I dread I shall see ' a whisker first
and then a claw' stretched out against my unfortunate lucubrations. Ballantyne, the Kelso printer,
who has a book of his in hand, groans in spirit over
the peculiarities of his orthography, which, sooth to
say, hath seldom been equalled since the days of
Elphinstone, the ingenious author of the mode of
spelling according to the pronunciation, which he
aptly termed ' Propriety ascertained in her Picture.'
I fear the remark of Festus to St Paul might be
more justly applied to this curious investigator of
antiquity, and it is a pity such research should be
rendered useless by the infirmities of his temper.   I
have lately had from him *a copie* of ' Ye litel wee
Mon,' of which I think I can make some use.   In
return, I have sent him a sight of Auld Maitland,
the original MS.   If you are curious, I dare say you
may easily see it.   Indeed, I might easily send you
a transcribed copy, — but I wish him to see it *in
puris naturalibus.*"

* The first part of Mr Sharon Turner's History of the Anglo-
Saxons was published in 1799 ; the second in 1801.

Ritson had visited Lasswade in the course of this autumn, and his conduct had been such as to render the precaution here alluded to very proper in the case of one who, like Scott, was resolved to steer clear of the feuds and heartburnings that gave rise to such scandalous scenes among the other antiquaries of the day.   Leyden met Ritson at the cottage, and, far from imitating his host's forbearance, took a pleasure of tormenting the half-mad pedant by every means in his power.   Among other circumstances, Scott delighted to detail the scene that occurred when his two uncouth allies first met at dinner.   Well knowing Ritson's holy horror of all animal food, Leyden complained that the joint on the table was overdone.   " Indeed, for that matter," cried he, " meat can never be too little done, and raw is best of all."   He sent to the kitchen accordingly for a plate of literally raw beef, and manfully ate it up, with no sauce but the exquisite ruefulness of the Pythagorean's glances.

Mr Robert Pierce Gillies, a gentleman of the Scotch bar, well known, among other things, for some excellent translations from the German, was present at the cottage another day, when Ritson was in Scotland.   He has described the whole scene in the second section of his " Recollections of Sir Walter Scott,"—a set of papers in which many inaccurate statements occur, but which convey, on

the whole, a lively impression of the persons introduced.* " In approaching the cottage," he says,
" I was struck with the exceeding air of neatness
that prevailed around. The hand of tasteful culti-
vation had been there, and all methods employed to
convert an ordinary thatched cottage into a handsome and comfortable abode. The doorway was in
an angle formed by the original old cabin and the
additional rooms which had been built to it. In a
moment I had passed through the lobby, and found
myself in the presence of Mr and Mrs Scott, and
Mr William Erskine. At this early period, Scott
was more like the portrait, by Saxon, engraved for
the first edition of the Lady of the Lake, than to
any subsequent picture. He retained in features
and form an impress of that elasticity and youthful
vivacity, which he used to complain wore off after
he was forty, and by *his own* account was exchanged
for the plodding heaviness of an operose student.
He had now, indeed, somewhat of a boyish gaiety of
look, and in person was tall, slim, and extremely
active. On my entrance, he was seated at a table
near the window, and occupied in transcribing from
an old MS. volume into his commonplace book. As
to costume, he was carelessly attired in a widely-

* These papers appeared in Fraser's Magazine for September,
November, and December 1835, and January 1836.

made shooting-dress, with a coloured handkerchief round his neck; the very antithesis of style usually adopted either by student or barrister. ' Hah!' he exclaimed, ' welcome, thrice welcome! for we are just proposing to have lunch, and then a long, long walk through wood and wold, in which I am sure you will join us. But no man can thoroughly appreciate the pleasure of such a life who has not known what it is to rise spiritless in a morning, and *daidle* out half the day in the Parliament House, where we must all *compear* within another fortnight; then to spend the rest of one's time in applying proofs to *condescendences*, and hauling out papers to bamboozle judges, most of whom are *daized* enough already. What say you, Counsellor Erskine? Come — *alla guerra* — rouse, and say whether you are for a walk to-day.'—' Certainly, in such fine weather I don't see what we can propose better. It is the last I shall see of the country this vacation.'—' Nay, say not so, man; we shall all be merry twice and once yet before the evil days arrive.'—' I'll tell you what I have thought of this half-hour: it is a plan of mine to rent a cottage and a cabbage-garden — not here, but somewhere farther out of town, and never again, after this one session, to enter the Parliament House.'—' And you'll ask Ritson, perhaps,' said Scott, ' to stay with you, and help to consume the cabbages. Rest as-

sured we shall both sit on the bench one day; but,
heigho! we shall both have become very old and
philosophical by that time.' — ' Did you not expect
Lewis here this morning?'—' Lewis, I venture to
say, is not up yet, for he dined at Dalkeith yesterday, and of course found the wine very good.   Besides, you know, I have entrusted him with *Finella*
till his own steed gets well of a sprain, and he could
not join our walking excursion. — I see you are
admiring that broken sword,' he added, addressing
me, ' and your interest would increase if you knew
how much labour was required to bring it into my
possession.   In order to grasp that mouldering
weapon, I was obliged to drain the well at the Castle
of Dunnottar.   But it is time to set out; and here
is one *friend*' (addressing himself to a large dog)
' who is very impatient to be in the field.   He tells
me he knows where to find a hare in the woods
of Mavisbank.   And here is another' (caressing a
terrier), ' who longs to have a battle with the
weazels and water-rats, and the foumart that *wons*
near the caves of Gorthy: so let us be off.'"

Mr Gillies tells us, that in the course of their
walk to Rosslyn, Scott's foot slipped, as he was
scrambling towards a cave on the edge of a precipitous bank, and that, " had there been no trees in
the way, he must have been killed, but midway he
was stopped by a large root of hazel, when, instead of

struggling, which would have made matters greatly
worse, he seemed perfectly resigned to his fate, and
slipped through the tangled thicket till he lay flat on
the river's brink. He rose in an instant from his
recumbent attitude, and with a hearty laugh called
out, ' Now, let me see who else will do the like.'
He scrambled up the cliff with alacrity, and entered
the cave, where we had a long dialogue."

Even after he was an old and hoary man, he con-
tinually encountered such risks with the same reck-
lessness. The extraordinary strength of his hands
and arms was his great reliance in all such difficulties,
and if he could see any thing to lay hold of, he was
afraid of no leap, or rather hop, that came in his way.
Mr Gillies says, that when they drew near the famous chapel of Rosslyn, Erskine expressed a hope
that they might, as habitual visitors, escape hearing
the usual endless story of the silly old woman that
showed the ruins; but Scott answered, " There is a
pleasure in the song which none but the songstress
knows, and by telling her we know it all already, we
should make the poor devil unhappy."

On their return to the cottage, Scott enquired for
the learned cabbage-eater, meaning Ritson, who had
been expected to dinner. " Indeed," answered his
wife, " you may be happy he is not here, he is so
very disagreeable. Mr Leyden, I believe, frightened
him away." It turned out that it was even so.

When Ritson appeared, a round of cold beef was on
the luncheon-table, and Mrs Scott, forgetting his
peculiar creed, offered him a slice. " The antiquary,
in his indignation, expressed himself in such outra-
geous terms to the lady, that Leyden first tried to
correct him by ridicule, and then, on the madman
growing more violent, became angry in his turn, till
at last he threatened, that if he were not silent, he
would *thraw his neck*.   Scott shook his head at this
recital, which Leyden observing, grew vehement in
his own justification. Scott said not a word in reply,
but took up a large bunch of feathers fastened to a
stick, denominated *a duster*, and shook it about the
student's ears till he laughed — then changed the
subject."

All this is very characteristic of the parties.
Scott's playful aversion to dispute was a trait in his
mind and manners that could alone have enabled him
to make use at one and the same time, and for the
same purpose, of two such persons as Ritson and
Leyden.

To return to Ellis. In answer to Scott's letter
last quoted, he urged him to make Sir Tristrem
volume fourth of the Minstrelsy. " As to his hanging heavy on hand," says he, " I admit, that as a
separate publication he may do so, but the Minstrelsy
is now established as a library book, and in this
bibliomaniac age, no one would think it perfect with-

out the *preux chevalier,* if you avow the said chevalier as your adopted son.   Let him, at least, be
printed in the same size and paper, and then I am
persuaded our booksellers will do the rest fast enough,
upon the credit of your reputation."   Scott replies
(November), that it is now too late to alter the fate
of Sir Tristrem.   " Longman, of Paternoster Row,
has been down here in summer, and purchased the
copyright of the Minstrelsy.   Sir Tristrem is a
separate property, but will be on the same scale in
point of size."

The next letter introduces to Ellis's personal acquaintance Leyden, who had by this time completed
his medical studies, and taken his degree as a physician.   In it Scott says, " At length I write to you
per favour of John Leyden.   I presume Heber has
made you sufficiently acquainted with this original
(for he is a true one), and therefore I will trust to
your own kindness, should an opportunity occur of
doing him any service in furthering his Indian plans.
You will readily judge, from conversing with him,
that with a very uncommon stock of acquired knowledge, he wants a good deal of another sort of knowledge — which is only to be gleaned from an early
intercourse with polished society.   But he dances
his bear with a good confidence, and the bear itself
is a very good-natured and well-conditioned animal.
All his friends are much interested about him, as

the qualities both of his heart and head are very uncommon." He adds —" My third volume will appear as soon after the others as the despatch of the printers will admit. Some parts will, I think, interest you; particularly the preservation of the entire Auld Maitland by oral tradition, probably from the reign of Edward II. or III. As I have never met with such an instance, I must request you to enquire all about it of Leyden, who was with me when I received my first copy. In the third volume I intend to publish *Cadyow Castle*, a historical sort of a ballad upon the death of the Regent Murray, and besides this, a long poem of my own. It will be a kind of romance of Border chivalry, in a light-horseman sort of stanza."

He appears to have sent a copy of *Cadyow Castle* by Leyden, whose reception at Mr Ellis's villa, near Windsor, is thus described in the next letter of the correspondence:—" Let me thank you," says Ellis, " for your poem, which Mrs E. has *not* received, and which, indeed, I could not help feeling glad, in the first instance (though we now begin to grow very impatient for it), that she did not receive. Leyden would not have been your Leyden if he had arrived like a careful citizen, with all his packages carefully docketed in his portmanteau. If on the point of leaving for many years, perhaps for ever, his country and the friends of his youth, he had not deferred to

the last, and till it was too late, all that could be
easily done, and that stupid people find time to do—
if he had not arrived with all his ideas perfectly bewildered—and tired to death, and sick—and without any settled plans for futurity, or any accurate
recollection of the past—we should have felt much
more disappointed than we were by the non-arrival
of your poem, which he assured us he remembered to
have left somewhere or other, and therefore felt very
confident of recovering.   In short, his whole air and
countenance told us, ‘ I am come to be one of your
friends,’ and we immediately took him at his word.”

By the “ romance of Border chivalry,” which was
designed to form part of the third volume of the
Minstrelsy, the reader is to understand the first
draught of The Lay of the Last Minstrel; and the
author's description of it as being “ in a light-horseman sort of stanza,” was probably suggested by the
circumstances under which the greater part of that
original draught was composed.   He has told us, in
his Introduction of 1830, that the poem originated
in a request of the young and lovely Countess of
Dalkeith, that he would write a ballad on the legend
of Gilpin Horner: that he began it at Lasswade, and
read the opening stanzas, as soon as they were written, to his friends, Erskine and Cranstoun: that
their reception of these was apparently so cold as to
discourage him, and disgust him with what he had

done; but that finding, a few days afterwards, that
the stanzas had nevertheless excited their curiosity,
and haunted their memory, he was encouraged to resume the undertaking. The scene and date of this
resumption I owe to the recollection of the then
Cornet of the Edinburgh light-horse. While the
troop were on permanent duty at Musselburgh, in
the autumnal recess of 1802, the Quarter-master,
during a charge on Portobello sands, received a kick
of a horse, which confined him for three days to his
lodgings. Mr Skene found him busy with his pen;
and he produced before these three days expired the
first canto of the Lay, very nearly, if his friend's
memory may be trusted, in the state in which it was
ultimately published. That the whole poem was
sketched and filled in with extraordinary rapidity,
there can be no difficulty in believing. He himself
says (in the Introduction of 1830), that after he
had once got fairly into the vein, it proceeded at the
rate of about a canto in a week. The Lay, however, like the Tristrem, soon outgrew the dimensions
which he had originally contemplated; the design of
including it in the third volume of the Minstrelsy
was of course abandoned; and it did not appear
until nearly three years after that fortunate mishap
on the beach of Portobello.

To return to Scott's correspondence:—it shows
that Ellis had, although involved at the time in se-

rious family afflictions, exerted himself strenuously
and effectively in behalf of Leyden; a service which
Scott acknowledges most warmly. His friend writes,
too, at great length, about the completion of the
Minstrelsy, urging, in particular, the propriety of
prefixing to it a good map of the Scottish Border —
" for, in truth," he says, " I have never been able to
find even *Ercildoune* on any map in my possession."
The poet answers (January 30, 1803) — " The idea
of a map pleases me much, but there are two strong
objections to its being prefixed to this edition. *First*,
we shall be out in a month, within which time it
would be difficult, I apprehend, for Mr Arrowsmith,
labouring under the disadvantages which I am about
to mention, to complete the map. *Secondly*, you
are to know that I am an utter stranger to geometry,
surveying, and all such *inflammatory* branches of
study, as Mrs Malaprop calls them. My education
was unfortunately interrupted by a long indisposi-
tion, which occasioned my residing for about two
years in the country with a good maiden aunt, who
permitted and encouraged me to run about the fields,
as wild as any buck that ever fled from the face of
man. Hence my geographical knowledge is merely
practical, and though I think that in the *South
country*, ' I could be a guide worth ony twa that
may in Liddesdale be found,' yet I believe Hobby
Noble, or Kinmont Willie, would beat me at laying

down a map. I have, however, sense enough to see
that our mode of executing maps in general is any
thing but perfect. The country is most inaccurately
defined, and had your General (Wade) marched
through Scotland by the assistance of Ainslie's map,
his flying artillery would soon have stuck fast among
our morasses, and his horse broke their knees among
our cairns. Your system of a bird's-eye view is
certainly the true principle." He goes on to mention some better maps than Ellis seemed to have
consulted, and to inform him where he may discover
Ercildoune, under its modern form of Earlston, upon
the river Leader; and concludes, " the map then
must be deferred until the *third* edition, about which,
I suppose, Longman thinks courageously." He then
adds—" I am almost glad Cadyow Castle is miscar-
ried, as I have rather lost conceit of it at present,
being engaged on what I think will be a more generally interesting legend. I have called it the ' Lay
of the Last Minstrel,' and put it in the mouth of an
old bard, who is supposed to have survived all his
brethren, and to have lived down to 1690. The
thing itself will be very long, but I would willingly
have sent you the *Introduction*, had you been still
in possession of your senatorial privilege;—but
double postage would be a strange innovation on the
established price of ballads, which have always sold
at the easy rate of one halfpenny."

I must now give part of a letter in which Leyden
recurs to the kindness, and sketches the person and
manners of George Ellis, in a highly characteristic
fashion. He says to Scott (January 25, 1803)—
" You were, no doubt, surprised, my dear sir, that I
gave you so little information about my movements ;
but it is only this day I have been able to speak of
them with any precision.   Such is the tardiness in
every thing connected with the India House, that a
person who is present in the character of spectator is
quite amazed ; but if we consider it as the centre of
a vast commercial concern, in comparison of which
Tyre and Sidon, and the Great Carthage itself, must
inevitably dwindle into huckster shops, we are induced to think of them with more patience.   Even
yet I cannot answer you exactly—being very uncertain whether I am to sail on the 18th of next month,
or the 28th.

1.

" Now shal i telen to ye, i wis,
Of that kind Squeyere Ellis,
That wonnen in this cité ;
Courtess he is, by God almizt !
That he nis nought ymaked knizt
It is the more pitie.

2.

" He konnen better eche glewe
Than I konnen to ye shewe,
Baith maist and least.

So wel he wirketh in eche thewe
That where he commen, I tell ye trewe,
   He is ane welcome guest.

3.

" His eyen graye as glas ben,
And his looks ben also kene,
   Loveliche to paramour.
Brown as acorn ben his faxe,
His face is thin as bettel axe
   That dealeth dintis doure.

4.

" His wit ben both keene and sharpe,
To kniзt or dame that carll can carpe
   Either in hall or bower ;
And had I not this squeyere yfonde,
I had been at the se-gronde,
   Which had been great doloure.

5.

" In him Ich finden non other euil,
Save that his nostril so doth snivel,
   It is not myche my choice.
But than his wit ben so perquire,
That thai who can his carpynge here
   Thai thynke not of his voice.

6.

" To speake not of his gentel dame
Ich wis it war bothe sin and shame
   Lede is not to layne ;

She is a ladye of rich pryce,
To loven in that dame's service
Meni wer ful fain.

7.

" Hir wit is ful kene and queynt,
And hir stature smale and gent,
    Semeleche to be seene ;
Armes, houdes, and fingres smale,
Of pearl beth eche fingre nale ;
    She mixt be ferys Quene.

8.

" That lady she wil giv a scarf
To him that wold ykillen a dwarf
    Charle of Paynim kinde ;
That dwarf he is so fell of mode
Tho ye shold drynk his hert blode,
    Gode wold ze never finde.

9.

" That dwarf he ben beardless and bare
And weasselblowen ben al his hair,
    Like an ympe or elfe ;
And in this world beth al and hale
Ben nothynge that he loveth an dele
    Safe his owen selfu" . . . . .

The fourth of these verses refers to the loss of
the Hindostan, in which ship Leyden, but for Mr
Ellis's interference, must have sailed, and which
foundered in the Channel.   The dwarf is, of course,
Ritson.

After various letters of the same kind, I find one, dated Isle of Wight, April the 1st (1803), the morning before Leyden finally sailed. " I have been two days on board," he writes, " and you may conceive what an excellent change I made from the politest society of London to the brutish skippers of Portsmouth. Our crew consists of a very motley party ; but there are some of them very ingenious, and Robert Smith, Sydney's brother, is himself a host. He is almost the most powerful man I have met with. My money concerns I shall consider you as trustee of ; and all remittances, as well as dividends from Longman, will be to your direction. These, I hope, we shall soon be able to adjust very accurately. Money may be paid, but kindness never. Assure your excellent Charlotte, whom I shall ever recollect with affection and esteem, how much I regret that I did not see her before my departure, and say a thousand pretty things, for which my mind is too much agitated, being in the situation of Coleridge's devil and his grannam, ' expecting and hoping the trumpet to blow.'* And now, my dear Scott, adieu. Think of me with indulgence, and be certain, that wherever, and in whatever situation, John Leyden is, his heart is unchanged by place, and his soul by time."

* This is a line of Coleridge's *jeu d' esprit* on Mackintosh.

This letter was received by Scott, not in Edinburgh, but in London. He had hurried up to town as soon as the Court of Session rose for the spring vacation, in hopes of seeing his friend once more before he left England; but he came too late. He had, however, done his part: he had sent Leyden £50, through Messrs Longman, a week before; and on the back of that bill there is the following memorandum:—" Dr Leyden's total debt to me £150; he also owes £50 to my uncle."

He thus writes to Ballantyne, on the 21st April 1803:—" I have to thank you for the accuracy with which the Minstrelsy is thrown off. Longman and Rees are delighted with the printing. Be so good as to disperse the following presentation copies, with ' From the Editor' on each:—

James Hogg, Ettrick House, care of Mr Oliver, Hawick—by the carrier—a complete set.
Thomas Scott (my brother), ditto.
Colin Mackenzie, Esq., Prince's Street, third volume only.
Mrs Scott, George Street, ditto.
Dr Rutherford, York Place, ditto.
Captain Scott, Rosebank, ditto.

I mean all these to be ordinary paper. Send one set fine paper to Dalkeith House, addressed to the

Duchess ; another, by the Inverary carrier, to Lady Charlotte Campbell ; the remaining *ten*, fine paper, with any of Vol. III. which may be on fine paper, to be sent to me by sea. I think they will give you some *eclat* here, where printing is so much valued. I have settled about printing an edition of the Lay, 8vo, with vignettes, provided I can get a draughts-man whom I think well of. We may throw off a few superb in quarto. To the Minstrelsy I mean this note to be added, by way of advertisement : — ' In the press, and will speedily be published, The Lay of the Last Minstrel, by Walter Scott, Esq., Editor of the Minstrelsy of the Scottish Border. Also, Sir Tristrem, a Metrical Romance, by Thomas of Ercildoune, called the Rhymer, edited from an ancient MS., with an Introduction and Notes, by Walter Scott, Esq.' Will you cause such a thing to be appended in your own way and fashion ?"

This letter is dated " No. 15, Piccadilly West," — he and Mrs Scott being there domesticated under the roof of the late M. Charles Dumergue, a man of very superior abilities and of excellent education, well known as surgeon-dentist to the royal family — who had been intimately acquainted with the Charpentiers in his own early life in France, and had warmly be-friended Mrs Scott's mother on her first arrival in England. M. Dumergue's house was, throughout the whole period of the emigration, liberally opened

to the exiles of his native country; nor did some of
the noblest of those unfortunate refugees scruple to
make a free use of his purse, as well as of his hospitality.   Here Scott met much highly interesting
French society, and until a child of his own was
established in London, he never thought of taking
up his abode any where else, as often as he had
occasion to be in town.

The letter is addressed to " Mr James Ballantyne, printer, Abbey-hill, Edinburgh ;" which shows,
that before the third volume of the Minstrelsy passed
through the press, the migration recommended two
years earlier had at length taken place.   " It was
about the end of 1802," says Ballantyne in his Memorandum, " that I closed with a plan so congenial
to my wishes.   I removed, bag and baggage, to
Edinburgh, finding accommodation for two presses,
and a proof one, in the precincts of Holyrood-house,
then deriving new lustre and interest from the recent arrival of the royal exiles of France.   In these
obscure premises some of the most beautiful productions of what we called *The Border Press* were
printed."   The Memorandum states, that Scott
having renewed his hint as to pecuniary assistance,
so soon as the printer found his finances straitened,
" a liberal loan was advanced accordingly."   Of
course Scott's interest was constantly exerted in
procuring employment, both legal and literary, for
his friend's types.

Heber, and Mackintosh then at the height of his
reputation as a conversationist, and daily advancing
also at the Bar, had been ready to welcome Scott in
town as old friends; and Rogers, William Stewart
Rose, and several other men of literary eminence,
were at the same time added to the list of his acquaintance. His principal object, however — having
missed Leyden — was to peruse and make extracts
from some MSS. in the library of John Duke of
Roxburghe, for the illustration of the Tristrem; and
he derived no small assistance in other researches of
the like kind from the collections which the indefatigable and obliging Douce placed at his disposal.
Having completed these labours, he and Mrs Scott
went, with Heber and Douce, to Sunninghill, where
they spent a happy week, and Mr and Mrs Ellis
heard the first two or three cantos of the Lay of
the Last Minstrel read under an old oak in Windsor
Forest.

I should not omit to say, that Scott was attended
on this trip by a very large and fine bull-terrier, by
name Camp, and that Camp's master, and mistress
too, were delighted by finding that the Ellises cordially sympathized in their fondness for this animal,
and indeed for all his race. At parting, Scott promised to send one of Camp's progeny, in the course
of the season, to Sunninghill.

From thence they proceeded to Oxford, accom-

panied by Heber; and it was on this occasion, as I
believe, that Scott first saw his friend's brother,
Reginald, in afterdays the apostolic Bishop of Calcutta. He had just been declared the successful
competitor for that year's poetical prize, and read to
Scott at breakfast, in Brazen Nose College, the MS.
of his " Palestine." Scott observed that, in the
verses on Solomon's Temple, one striking circumstance had escaped him, namely, that no tools were
used in its erection. Reginald retired for a few
minutes to the corner of the room, and returned with
the beautiful lines,—

> " No hammer fell, no ponderous axes rung,
> Like some tall palm the mystic fabric sprung.
> Majestic silence," &c. *

After inspecting the University and Blenheim,
under the guidance of the Hebers, Scott returned to
London, as appears from the following letter to Miss
Seward, who had been writing to him on the subject
of her projected biography of Dr Darwin.   The
conclusion and date are lost :—

" I have been for about a fortnight in this huge
and bustling metropolis, when I am agreeably sur-

* See " Life of Bishop Heber, by his Widow," edition 1830,
vol. i. p. 30.

prised by a packet from Edinburgh, containing Miss
Seward's letter.   I am truly happy at the information
it communicates respecting the life of Dr Darwin,
who could not have wished his fame and character
intrusted to a pen more capable of doing them ample,
and, above all, discriminating justice.   Biography,
the most interesting perhaps of every species of composition, loses all its interest with me, when the
shades and lights of the principal character are not
accurately and faithfully detailed ; nor have I much
patience with such exaggerated daubing as Mr Hayley
has bestowed upon poor Cowper.   I can no more
sympathize with a mere eulogist, than I can with a
ranting hero upon the stage ; and it unfortunately
happens that some of our disrespect is apt, rather
unjustly, to be transferred to the subject of the
panegyric in the one case, and to poor Cato in the
other.   Unapprehensive that even friendship can bias
Miss Seward's duty to the public, I shall wait most
anxiously for the volume her kindness has promised
me.

" As for my third volume, it was very nearly
printed when I left Edinburgh, and must, I think,
be ready for publication in about a fortnight, when
it will have the honour of travelling to Lichfield.
I doubt you will find but little amusement in it, as
there are a good many old ballads, particularly those
of ' the Covenanters,' which, in point of composi-

tion, are mere drivelling trash. They are, however, curious in an historical point of view, and have enabled me to slide in a number of notes about that dark and bloody period of Scottish history. There is a vast convenience to an editor in a tale upon which, without the formality of adapting the notes very precisely to the shape and form of the ballad, he may hang on a set like a herald's coat without sleeves, saving himself the trouble of taking measure, and sending forth the tale of ancient time, ready equipped from the Monmouth Street warehouse of a commonplace book. Cadyow Castle is to appear in volume third.

" —— I proceeded thus far about three weeks ago, and shame to tell, have left my epistle unfinished ever since ; yet I have not been wholly idle, about a fortnight of that period having been employed as much to my satisfaction as any similar space of time during my life. I was, the first week of that fortnight, with my invaluable friend George Ellis, and spent the second week at Oxford, which I visited for the first time. I was peculiarly fortunate in having for my patron at Oxford, Mr Heber, a particular friend of mine, who is intimately acquainted with all, both animate and inanimate, that is worth knowing at Oxford. The time, though as much as I could possibly spare, has, I find, been too short to convey to me separate and distinct ideas of all the variety of

wonders which I saw.   My memory only at present
furnishes a grand but indistinct picture of towers,
and chapels, and oriels, and vaulted halls, and libraries, and paintings.   I hope, in a little time, my
ideas will develope themselves a little more distinctly,
otherwise I shall have profited little by my tour.
I was much flattered by the kind reception and
notice I met with from some of the most distinguished inhabitants of the halls of Isis, which was
more than such a truant to the classic page as myself was entitled to expect at the source of classic
learning.

   " On my return, I find an apologetic letter from
my printer, saying the third volume will be despatched in a day or two.   There has been, it seems,
a meeting among the printers' devils ; also among
the paper-makers.   I never heard of authors *striking
work*, as the mechanics call it, until their masters
the booksellers should increase their pay ; but if such
a combination could take place, the revolt would
now be general in all branches of literary labour.
How much sincere satisfaction would it give me
could I conclude this letter (as I once hoped), by
saying I should visit Lichfield, and pay my personal
respects to my invaluable correspondent in my way
northwards ; but as circumstances render this impossible, I shall depute the poetry of the olden time
in the editor's stead.   My ' Romance' is not yet

finished. I prefer it much to any thing I have done of the kind." . . . .

He was in Edinburgh by the middle of May; and thus returns to his view of Oxford in a letter to his friend at Sunninghill:—

" *To George Ellis, Esq., &c. &c.*

"Edinburgh, 25th May 1803.

" My Dear Ellis,

" . . . . I was equally delighted with that venerable seat of learning, and flattered by the polite attention of Heber's friends. I should have been enchanted to have spent a couple of months among the curious libraries. What stores must be reserved for some painful student to bring forward to the public! Under the guidance and patronage of our good Heber, I saw many of the literary men of his Alma Mater, and found matters infinitely more active in every department than I had the least previous idea of. Since I returned home, my time has been chiefly occupied in professional labours; my truant days spent in London having thrown me a little behind; but now, I hope, I shall find spare moments to resume Sir Tristrem — and the Lay, which has acquired additional value in my estimation from its pleasing you. How often do Charlotte and I think of the little paradise at Sunninghill and its kind in-

habitants; and how do we regret, like Dives, the
gulf which is placed betwixt us and friends, with
whom it would give us such pleasure to spend much
of our time.   It is one of the vilest attributes of the
best of all possible worlds, that it contrives to split
and separate and subdivide every thing like congenial pursuits and habits, for the paltry purpose, one
would think, of diversifying every little spot with a
share of its various productions.   I don't know why
the human and vegetable departments should differ so
excessively.   Oaks and beeches, and ashes and elms,
not to mention cabbages and turnips, are usually arrayed *en masse*; but where do we meet a town of
antiquaries, a village of poets, or a hamlet of philo-
sophers?   But, instead of fruitless lamentations, we
sincerely hope Mrs Ellis and you will unrivet your-
selves from your forest, and see how the hardy blasts
of our mountains will suit you for a change of climate. . . . . . . The new edition of ' Minstrelsy' is
published here, but not in London as yet, owing to
the embargo on our shipping.   An invasion is expected from Flushing, and no measures of any kind
taken to prevent or repel it.   Yours ever faithfully,
                                  W. SCOTT."

    This letter enclosed a sheet of extracts from For-
dun, in Scott's handwriting; the subject being the
traditional marriage of one of the old Counts of

Anjou with a female demon, by which the Scotch chronicler accounts for all the crimes and misfortunes of the English Plantagenets.

Messrs Longman's new edition of the first two volumes of the Minstrelsy consisted of 1000 copies — of volume third there were 1500. A complete edition of 1250 copies followed in 1806; a fourth, also of 1250, in 1810; a fifth, of 1500, in 1812; a sixth, of 500, in 1820; and since then it has been incorporated in various successive editions of Scott's Collected Poetry—to the extent of at least 15,000 copies more. Of the Continental and American editions I can say nothing, except that they have been very numerous. The book was soon translated into German, Danish, and Swedish; and, the structure of those languages being very favourable to the undertaking, the Minstrelsy of the Scottish Border has thus become widely naturalized among nations themselves rich in similar treasures of legendary lore. Of the extraordinary accuracy and felicity of the German version of Schubart, Scott has given some specimens in the last edition which he himself superintended — that of 1830.

He speaks, in the Essay to which I have referred, as if the first reception of the Minstrelsy on the south of the Tweed had been cold. "The curiosity of the English," he says, "was not much awakened by poems in the rude garb of antiquity, accompanied

with notes referring to the obscure feuds of barbarous clans, of whose very names civilized history was
ignorant." In writing those beautiful Introductions
of 1830, however, Scott, as I have already had occasion to hint, trusted entirely to his recollection of
days long since gone by, and he has accordingly let
fall many statements, which we must take with some
allowance. His impressions as to the reception of
the Minstrelsy were different, when, writing to his
brother-in-law, Charles Carpenter, on the 3d March
1803, for the purpose of introducing Leyden, he
said—" I have contrived to turn a very slender portion of literary talents to some account, by a publication of the poetical antiquities of the Border, where
the old people had preserved many ballads descrip-
tive of the manners of the country during the wars
with England. This trifling collection was so well
received by a *discerning public*, that, after receiving
about £100 profit for the first edition, which my
vanity cannot omit informing you went off in six
months, I have sold the copyright for £500 more."
This is not the language of disappointment; and
though the edition of 1803 did not move off quite so
rapidly as the first, and the work did not perhaps
attract much notice beyond the more cultivated
students of literature, until the Editor's own genius
blazed out in full splendour in the Lay, and thus lent
general interest to whatever was connected with his

name, I suspect there never was much ground for
accusing the English public of regarding the Minstrelsy with more coldness than the Scotch — the
population of the Border districts themselves being,
of course, excepted. Had the sale of the original
edition been chiefly Scotch, I doubt whether Messrs
Longman would have so readily offered £500, in
those days of the trade a large sum, for the second.
Scott had become habituated, long before 1830, to a
scale of bookselling transactions, measured by which
the largest editions and copy-monies of his own early
days appeared insignificant ; but the evidence seems
complete that he was well contented at the time.   '

He certainly had every reason to be so as to the
impression which the Minstrelsy made on the minds
of those entitled to think for themselves upon such a
subject. The ancient ballads in his collection, which
had never been printed at all before, were in number
forty-three ; and of the others — most of which were
in fact all but new to the modern reader — it is
little to say that his editions were superior in all respects to those that had preceded them.   He had, I
firmly believe, interpolated hardly a line or even an
epithet of his own ; but his diligent zeal had put him
in possession of a variety of copies in different stages
of preservation ; and to the task of selecting a standard text among such a diversity of materials, he
brought a knowledge of old manners and phraseology,

and a manly simplicity of taste, such as had never
before been united in the person of a poetical antiquary. From among a hundred corruptions he
seized, with instinctive tact, the primitive diction and
imagery; and produced strains in which the un-
broken energy of half-civilized ages, their stern and
deep passions, their daring adventures and cruel
tragedies, and even their rude wild humour, are
reflected with almost the brightness of a Homeric
mirror, interupted by hardly a blot of what deserves
to be called vulgarity, and totally free from any ad-
mixture of artificial sentimentalism. As a picture
of manners, the Scottish Minstrelsy is not surpassed,
if equalled, by any similar body of poetry preserved
in any other country; and it unquestionably owes its
superiority in this respect over Percy's Reliques, to
the Editor's conscientious fidelity, on the one hand,
which prevented the introduction of any thing new
—to his pure taste, on the other, in the balancing of
discordant recitations. His introductory essays and
notes teemed with curious knowledge, not hastily
grasped for the occasion, but gradually gleaned and
sifted by the patient labour of years, and presented
with an easy, unaffected propriety and elegance of
arrangement and expression, which it may be doubted
if he ever materially surpassed in the happiest of his
imaginative narrations. I well remember, when
Waverley was a new book, and all the world were

puzzling themselves about its authorship, to have
heard the Poet of " the Isle of Palms " exclaim im-
patiently — " I wonder what all these people are perplexing themselves with : have they forgotten the
prose of the Minstrelsy ?"   Even had the Editor
inserted none of his own verse, the work would have
contained enough, and more than enough, to found a
lasting and graceful reputation.

It is not to be denied, however, that the Minstrelsy of the Scottish Border has derived a very
large accession of interest from the subsequent career
of its Editor.   One of the critics of that day said
that the book contained " the elements of a hundred
historical romances ;"—and this critic was a prophe-
tic one.   No person who has not gone through its
volumes for the express purpose of comparing their
contents with his great original works, can have
formed a conception of the endless variety of inci
dents and images now expanded and emblazoned by
his mature art, of which the first hints may be found
either in the text of those primitive ballads, or in
the notes, which the happy rambles of his youth
had gathered together for their illustration.   In the
edition of the Minstrelsy published since his death,
not a few such instances are pointed out; but the
list might have been extended far beyond the limits .
which such an addition allowed.   The taste and
fancy of Scott appear to have been formed as early as

his moral character; and he had, before he passed
the threshold of authorship, assembled about him, in
the uncalculating delight of native enthusiasm, almost
all the materials on which his genius was destined to
be employed for the gratification and instruction of
the world.

CHAPTER XII.

Contributions to the Edinburgh Review — Progress of the Tristrem — and of the Lay of the Last Minstrel — Visit of Wordsworth — Publication of ." Sir Tristrem."

1803–1804.

SHORTLY after the complete " Minstrelsy" issued from the press, Scott made his first appearance as a reviewer.   The Edinburgh Review had been commenced in October 1802, under the superintendence of the Rev. Sydney Smith, with whom, during his short residence in Scotland, he had lived on terms of great kindness and familiarity.   Mr Smith soon resigned the editorship to Mr Jeffrey, who had by this time been for several years among the most valued of Scott's friends and companions at the bar ; and, the new journal being far from committing itself to violent politics at the outset, he appreciated

the brilliant talents regularly engaged in it far too
highly, not to be well pleased with the opportunity
of occasionally exercising his pen in its service.
His first contribution was an article on Southey's
Amadis of Gaul, included in the number for October 1803.   Another, on Sibbald's Chronicle of
Scottish Poetry, appeared in the same number:—
a third, on Godwin's Life of Chaucer; a fourth, on
Ellis's Specimens of Ancient English Poetry; and a
fifth, on the Life and Works of Chatterton, followed
in the course of 1804.*

During the summer of 1803, however, his chief
literary labour was still on the Tristrem; and I
shall presently give some further extracts from his
letters to Ellis, which will amply illustrate the spirit
in which he continued his researches about the Seer
of Ercildoune, and the interruptions which these
owed to the prevalent alarm of French invasion.
Both as Quartermaster of the Edinburgh Light-
horse, and as Sheriff of The Forest, he had a full
share of responsibility in the warlike arrangements
to which the authorities of Scotland had at length
been roused; nor were the duties of his two offices
considered as strictly compatible by Francis Lord
Napier, then Lord-Lieutenant of Selkirkshire; for

* Scott's contributions to our periodical literature have been,
with some trivial exceptions, included in the recent collection of
his Miscellaneous Prose Writings.

I find several letters in which his Lordship complains that the incessant drills and musters of Musselburgh and Portobello prevented the Sheriff from
attending county meetings held at Selkirk in the
course of this summer and autumn, for the purpose
of organizing the trained bands of the Forest, on a
scale hitherto unattempted.   Lord Napier strongly
urges the propriety of his resigning his connexion
with the Edinburgh troop, and fixing his summer
residence somewhere within the limits of his proper
jurisdiction; nay, he goes so far as to hint, that if
these suggestions should be neglected, it must be his
duty to state the case to the Government.   Scott
could not be induced (least of all by a threat), while
the fears of invasion still prevailed, to resign his
place among his old companions of " the voluntary
band;" but he seems to have presently acquiesced
in the propriety of the Lord-Lieutenant's advice
respecting a removal from Lasswade to Ettrick
Forest.

The following extract is from a letter written at
Musselburgh during this summer or autumn :—

" Miss Seward's acceptable favour reaches me in
a place, and at a time, of great bustle, as the corps
of voluntary cavalry to which I belong is quartered
for a short time in this village, for the sake of
drilling and discipline.   Nevertheless, had your letter announced the name of the gentleman who took

the trouble of forwarding it, I would have made it
my business to find him out, and to prevail on him,
if possible, to spend a day or two with us in quarters. We are here assuming a very military appearance. Three regiments of militia, with a formidable
park of artillery, are encamped just by us. The
Edinburgh troop, to which I have the honour to be
quartermaster, consists entirely of young gentlemen
of family, and is, of course, admirably well mounted
and armed. There are other four troops in the regiment, consisting of yeomanry, whose iron faces and
muscular forms announce the hardness of the climate
against which they wrestle, and the powers which
nature has given them to contend with and subdue
it. These corps have been easily raised in Scotland,
the farmers being in general a high-spirited race of
men, fond of active exercises, and patient of hard-
ship and fatigue. For myself, I must own that to
one who has, like myself, *la tête un peu exaltée*, the
‘ pomp and circumstance of war’ gives, for a time, a
very poignant and pleasing sensation. The imposing
appearance of cavalry, in particular, and the rush
which marks their onset, appear to me to partake
highly of the sublime. Perhaps I am the more
attached to this sort of sport of swords, because my
health requires much active exercise, and a lameness
contracted in childhood renders it inconvenient for
me to take it otherwise than on horseback. I have,

too, a hereditary attachment to the animal—not, I
flatter myself, of the common jockey cast, but because I regard him as the kindest and most generous
of the subordinate tribes. I hardly even except the
dogs; at least they are usually so much better treated,
that compassion for the steed should be thrown into
the scale when we weigh their comparative merits.
My wife (a foreigner) never sees a horse ill-used
without asking what that poor horse has done in his
state of pre-existence? I would fain hope they have
been carters or hackney-coachmen, and are only experiencing a retort of the ill-usage they have formerly
inflicted. What think you?"

It appears that Miss Seward had sent Scott some
obscure magazine criticism on his "Minstrelsy," in
which the censor had condemned some phrase as
naturally suggesting a low idea. The lady's letter
not having been preserved, I cannot explain farther
the sequel of that from which I have been quoting.
Scott says, however —

" I am infinitely amused with your sagacious
critic. God wot, I have often admired the vulgar
subtlety of such minds as can with a depraved ingenuity attach a mean or disgusting sense to an epithet capable of being otherwise understood, and more
frequently, perhaps, used to express an elevated
idea. In many parts of Scotland the word *virtue* is
limited entirely to *industry;* and a young divine who

preached upon the moral beauties of virtue was considerably surprised at learning that the whole discourse was supposed to be a panegyric upon a particular damsel who could spin fourteen spindles of yarn in the course of a week. This was natural; but your literary critic has the merit of going very far a-field to fetch home his degrading association."

To return to the correspondence with Ellis — Scott writes thus to him in July:—" I cannot pretend immediately to enter upon the serious discussion which you propose respecting the age of ' Sir Tristrem;' but yet, as it seems likely to strip Thomas the Prophet of the honours due to the author of the English ' Tristrem,' I cannot help hesitating before I can agree to your theory;—and here my doubt lies. Thomas of Ercildoune, called the Rhymer, is a character mentioned by almost every Scottish historian, and the date of whose existence is almost as well known as if we had the parish register. Now, his great reputation, and his designation of *Rymour*, could only be derived from his poetical performances; and in what did these consist excepting in the romance of ' Sir Tristrem,' mentioned by Robert de Brunne? I hardly think, therefore, we shall be justified in assuming the existence of an earlier *Thomas*, who would be, in fact, merely the creature of our system. I own I am not prepared to take this step, if I can escape

otherwise from you and M. de la Ravaillere — and
thus I will try it. M. de la R. barely informs us
that the history of Sir Tristrem was known to
Chretien de Troys in the end of the twelfth century,
and to the King of Navarre in the beginning of the
thirteenth. Thus far his evidence goes, and I think
not one inch farther — for it does not establish the
existence either of the metrical romance, as you
suppose, or of the prose romance, as M. de la R.
much more erroneously supposes, at that very early
period. If the *story* of Sir Tristrem was founded
in fact, and if, which I have all along thought, a
person of this name really swallowed a dose of
cantharides intended to stimulate the exertions of
his uncle, a petty monarch of Cornwall, and involved
himself of course in an intrigue with his aunt, these
facts must have taken place during a very early
period of English history, perhaps about the time of
the Heptarchy. Now, if this be once admitted, it
is clear that the raw material from which Thomas
wove his web, must have been current long before
his day, and I am inclined to think that Chretien
and the King of Navarre refer, not to the special
metrical romance contained in Mr Douce's fragments, but to the general story of Sir Tristrem,
whose love and misfortunes were handed down by
tradition as a historical fact. There is no difficulty
in supposing a tale of this kind to have passed from

the Armoricans, or otherwise, into the mouths of
the French; as, on the other hand, it seems to have
been preserved among the Celtic tribes of the Border, from whom, in all probability, it was taken by
their neighbour, Thomas of Ercildoune. If we
suppose, therefore, that Chretien and the King
allude only to the general and well-known *story* of
Tristrem, and not to the particular edition of which
Mr Douce has some fragments — (and I see no
evidence that any such special allusion to these
fragments is made) — it will follow that *they* may
be as late as the end of the thirteenth century, and
that the Thomas mentioned in them may be *the*
Thomas of whose existence we have historical evidence. In short, the question is, shall Thomas be
considered as a landmark by which to ascertain the
antiquity of the fragments, or shall the *supposed*
antiquity of the fragments be held a sufficient reason
for *supposing* an earlier Thomas? For aught yet
seen, I incline to my former opinion, that those
fragments are coeval with the *ipsissimus Thomas.*
I acknowledge, the internal evidence, of which you
are so accurate a judge, weighs more with me than
the reference to the King of Navarre; but, after all,
the extreme difficulty of judging of style, so as to
bring us within sixty or seventy years, must be fully
considered. Take notice, I have never pleaded the
matter so high as to say, that the Auchinleck MS.

contains· the very words devised by Thomas the
Rhymer.   On the contrary, I have always thought
it one of the spurious copies in *queint Inglis,* of
which Robert de Brunne so heavily complains.   But
this will take little from the curiosity, perhaps little
from the antiquity, of the romance.   Enough of Sir
T. for the present.—How happy it will make us
if you can fulfil the expectation you hold out of a
northern expedition.   Whether in the cottage or
at Edinburgh, we will be equally happy to receive
you, and show you all the lions of our vicinity.
Charlotte is hunting out music for Mrs E., but I
intend to add *Johnson's* collection, which, though
the tunes are simple, and often bad sets, contains
much more original Scotch music than any other."

About this time, Mr and Mrs Ellis, and their
friend Douce, were preparing for a tour into the
North of England; and Scott was invited and
strongly tempted to join them at various points of
their progress, particularly at the Grange, near
Rotherham, in Yorkshire, a seat of the Earl of
Effingham.   But he found it impossible to escape
again from Scotland, owing to the agitated state of
the country.— On returning to the cottage from an
excursion to his Sheriffship, he thus resumes :—

" To George Ellis, Esq.

"Lasswade, August 27, 1803.

" Dear Ellis,

" My conscience has been thumping me as hard
as if it had studied under Mendoza, for letting your
kind favour remain so long unanswered. Nevertheless, in this it is, like Launcelot Gobbo's, but a
hard kind of conscience, as it must know how much
I have been occupied with Armies of Reserve, and
Militia, and Pikemen, and Sharpshooters, who are
to descend from Ettrick Forest to the confusion of
all invaders.   The truth is, that this country has for
once experienced that the pressure of external danger
may possibly produce internal unanimity; and so
great is the present military zeal, that I really wish
our rulers would devise some way of calling it into
action, were it only on the economical principle of
saving so much good courage from idle evaporation.
— I am interrupted by an extraordinary accident,
nothing less than a volley of small shot fired through
the window, at which my wife was five minutes
before arranging her flowers.   By Camp's assistance,
who run the culprit's foot like a Liddesdale bloodhound, we detected an unlucky sportsman, whose
awkwardness and rashness might have occasioned
very serious mischief — so much for interruption.

— To return to Sir Tristrem. As for Mr Thomas's
name, respecting which you state some doubts,[*] I
request you to attend to the following particulars :
— In the first place, surnames were of very late
introduction into Scotland, and it would be difficult
to show that they became in general a hereditary
distinction, until after the time of Thomas the
Rhymer; previously they were mere personal distinctions peculiar to the person by whom they were
borne, and dying along with him. Thus the children of *Alan Durward* were not called *Durward*,
because they were not *Ostiarii*, the circumstance
from which he derived the name. When the surname was derived from property, it became naturally
hereditary at a more early period, because the distinction applied equally to the father and the son.
The same happened with *patronymics*, both because
the name of the father is usually given to the son ;
so that Walter Fitzwalter would have been my son's
name in those times as well as my own; and also
because a clan often takes a sort of general patro-
nymic from one common ancestor, as Macdonald,
&c. &c. But though these classes of surnames
become hereditary at an early period, yet, in the
natural course of things, epithets merely personal

* Mr Ellis had hinted that " *Rymer* might not more necessarily
indicate an actual poet, than the name of *Taylor* does in modern
times an actual knight of the thimble."

are much longer of becoming a family distinction.* But I do not trust, by any means, to this general argument; because the charter quoted in the Minstrelsy contains written evidence, that the epithet of *Rymour* was peculiar to our Thomas, and was dropped by his son, who designs himself simply, *Thomas of Erceldoune, son of Thomas the Rymour of Erceldoune;* which I think is conclusive upon the subject. In all this discussion, I have scorned

* The whole of this subject has derived much illustration from the recent edition of the " Ragman's Roll," a contribution to the Bannatyne Club of Edinburgh by two of Sir Walter Scott's most esteemed friends, the Lord Chief Commissioner Adam and Sir Samuel Shepherd. That record of the oaths of fealty tendered to Edward I., during his Scotch usurpation, furnishes, indeed, very strong confirmation of the views which the Editor of " Sir Tristrem" had thus early adopted concerning the origin of surnames in Scotland. The landed gentry, over most of the country, seem to have been generally distinguished by the surnames still borne by their descendants—it is wonderful how little the land seems to have changed hands in the course of so many centuries. But the towns' people have, with few exceptions, designations apparently indicating the actual trade of the individual; and in many instances, there is distinct evidence that the plan of transmitting such names had not been adopted; for example, Thomas the Tailor is described as son of Thomas the Smith, or *vice versâ.* The chief magistrates of the burghs appear, however, to have been, in most cases, younger sons of the neighbouring gentry, and have of course their hereditary designations. This singular document, so often quoted and referred to, was never before printed *in extenso.*

to avail myself of the tradition of the country, as
well as the suspicious testimony of Boece, Dempster,
&c., grounded probably upon that tradition, which
uniformly affirms the name of Thomas to have been
Learmont or Leirmont, and that of the Rhymer a
personal epithet. This circumstance may induce us,
however, to conclude that some of his descendants
had taken that name—certain it is that his castle
is called Leirmont's Tower, and that he is as well
known to the country people by that name, as by
the appellation of the Rhymer.

" Having cleared up this matter, as I think, to
every one's satisfaction, unless to those resembling
not Thomas himself, but his namesake the Apostle,
I have, secondly, to show that my Thomas is the
Tomas of Douce's MS. Here I must again refer to
the high and general reverence in which Thomas
appears to have been held, as is proved by Robert
de Brunne ; but above all, as you observe, to the
extreme similarity betwixt the French and English
poems, with this strong circumstance, that the *mode*
of telling the story approved by the French minstrel,
under the authority of his Tomas, is the very mode
in which my Thomas has told it. Would you desire
better sympathy?

" I lately met by accident a Cornish gentleman,
who had taken up his abode in Selkirkshire for the
sake of fishing—and what should his name be but

Caerlion? You will not doubt that this interested
me very much.   He tells me that there is but one
family of the name in Cornwall, or as far as ever he
heard any where else, and that they are of great antiquity.   Does not this circumstance seem to prove
that there existed in Cornwall a place called Caerlion, giving name to that family?   Caerlion would
probably be *Castrum Leonense*, the chief town of
Liones, which in every romance is stated to have
been Tristrem's country, and from which he derived
his surname of Tristrem *de Liones*.   This district,
as you notice in the notes on the *Fabliaux*, was
swallowed up by the sea.   I need not remind you
that all this tends to illustrate the *Caerlioun* mentioned by Tomas, which I always suspected to be a
very different place from Caerlion on Uske—which
is no seaport.   How I regret the number of leagues
which prevented my joining you and the sapient
Douce, and how much ancient lore I have lost.
Where I have been, the people talked more of the
praises of Ryno and Fillan (not Ossian's heroes, but
two Forest greyhounds which I got in a present)
than, I verily believe, they would have done of the
prowesses of Sir Tristrem, or of Esplandian, had
either of them appeared to lead on the levy *en
masse.*   Yours ever,   W. Scott."

Ellis says in reply—" My dear Scott, I must be-

gin by congratulating you on Mrs Scott's escape;
Camp, if he had had no previous title to immortality,
would deserve it, for his zeal and address in detecting
the stupid marksman, who, while he took aim at a
bird on a tree, was so near shooting your fair ' bird
in bower.' If there were many such shooters, it
would become then a sufficient excuse for the reluctance of Government to furnish arms indifferently to
all volunteers.   In the next place, I am glad to hear
that you are disposed to adopt my channel for transmitting the tale of Tristrem to Chretien de Troye.
The more I have thought on the subject, the more
I am convinced that the Normans, long before the
Conquest, had acquired from the Britons of Armo-
rica a considerable knowledge of our old British
fables, and that this led them, after the Conquest, to
enquire after such accounts as were to be found in
the country where the events are supposed to have
taken place.   I am satisfied, from the internal evidence of Geoffrey of Monmouth's History, that it
must have been fabricated in Bretagne, and that he
did, as he asserts, only *translate* it.   Now, as *Marie*,
who lived about a century later, *certainly* translated
also from the Breton a series of lays relating to
Arthur and his knights, it will follow that the first
poets who wrote *in France*, such as Chretien, &c.,
must have acquired their knowledge of our traditions
from Bretagne.   Observe, that the pseudo-Turpin,

who is supposed to have been anterior to Geoffrey, and who, on that supposition, cannot have borrowed from him, mentions, among Charlemagne's heroes, Hoel (the hero of Geoffrey also), ' de quo canitur cantilena usque ad hodiernum diem.' Now, if Thomas was able to establish his story as the most *authentic*, even by the avowal of the French themselves, and if the *sketch* of that story was previously known, it must have been because he wrote in the country which his hero was supposed to have inhabited; and on the same grounds the Norman minstrels here, and even their English successors, were allowed to fill up, with as many circumstances as they thought proper, the tales of which the Armorican Bretons probably furnished the first imperfect outline.

" What you tell me about your Cornish fisherman is very curious; and I think with you that little reliance is to be placed on our Welsh geography—and that Caerlion on Uske is by no means *the* Caerlion of Tristrem. Few writers or readers have hitherto considered sufficiently, that from the moment when Hengist first obtained a settlement in the Isle of Thanet, that settlement became *England*, and all the rest of the country became *Wales;* that these divisions continued to represent different proportions of the island at different periods; but that Wales, during the whole Heptarchy, and for a long time after, comprehended the whole western coast very nearly from Cornwall to Dunbretton; and that this whole tract, of which the eastern frontier may be easily traced for each particular period, preserved most probably to the age of Thomas a community of language, of manners, and traditions.

" As your last volume announces your *Lay*, as well as *Sir Tristrem*, as *in the press*, I begin, in common with all your friends, to be uneasy about the future disposal of your time. Having nothing but a very active profession, and your military pursuits, and your domestic occupations to think of, and Leyden having monopolized Asiatic lore, you will presently be quite an idle man! You are, however, still in time to learn Erse, and it is, I am afraid, very necessary that you should do so, in order to stimulate my laziness, which has hitherto made no progress whatever in Welsh.

" Your ever faithful,   G. E.

" P. S.—*Is Camp married yet ?*"

Ellis had projected some time before this an edition of the Welsh *Mabinogion*,* in which he was to be assisted by Mr Owen, the author of the " Welsh and English Dictionary," " Cambrian Biography," &c. " I am very sorry," Scott says (September 14), " that you flag over those wild and interesting tales. I hope, if you will not work yourself (for which you

* The Mabinogion have at last been translated, and are now in the course of publication, in a very beautiful form, by the Lady Charlotte Guest. [1839.]

have so little excuse, having both the golden talents
and the golden leisure necessary for study), you will
at least keep Owen to something that is rational —
I mean to *iron horses*, and *magic cauldrons*, and
Bran the Blessed, with the music of his whole army
upon his shoulders, and, in short, to something more
pleasing and profitable than old apophthegms, triads,
and ' blessed burdens of the womb of the isle of
Britain.'   Talking of such burdens, Camp has been
regularly wedded to a fair dame in the neighbourhood, but notwithstanding the Italian policy of lock-
ing the lady in a stable, she is suspected of some
inaccuracy; but we suspend judgment, as Othello
ought in all reason to have done, till we see the
produce of the union.   As for my own employment,
I have yet much before me, and as the beginning of
letting out ink is like the letting out of water, I
daresay I shall go on scribbling one nonsense or
another to the end of the chapter.   People may say
this and that of the pleasure of fame or of profit as
a motive of writing.   I think the only pleasure is
in the actual exertion and research, and I would no
more write upon any other terms than I would hunt
merely to dine upon hare-soup.   At the same time,
if credit and profit came unlooked for, I would no
more quarrel with them than with the soup.   I
hope this will find you and Mrs Ellis safely and
pleasantly settled

' " — By the way, while you are in his neighbourhood, I hope you will not fail to enquire into the
history of the valiant Moor of Moorhall and the
Dragon of Wantley. As a noted burlesque upon
the popular romance, the ballad has some curiosity
and merit. — Ever yours,   W. S."

Mr Ellis received this letter where Scott hoped
it would reach him, at the seat of Lord Effingham;
and he answers, on the 3d of October — " The
beauty of this part of the country is such as to
indemnify the traveller for a few miles of very indifferent road, and the tedious process of creeping
up and almost sliding down a succession of high
hills; and in the number of picturesque landscapes
by which we are encompassed, the den of the dragon
which you recommended to our attention is the
most superlatively beautiful and romantic. You are,
I suppose, aware that this same den is the very spot
from whence Lady Mary Wortley Montague wrote
many of her early letters; and it seems that an old
housekeeper, who lived there till last year, remembered to have seen her, and dwelt with great pleasure
on the various charms of her celebrated mistress;
so that its wild scenes have an equal claim to vene-
ration from the admirers of wit and gallantry, and
the far-famed investigators of remote antiquity. With
regard to the original Dragon, I have met with two

different traditions.   One of these (which I think
is preserved by Percy) states him to have been a
wicked attorney, a relentless persecutor of the poor,
who was at length, fortunately for his neighbours,
ruined by a law-suit which he had undertaken against
his worthy and powerful antagonist Moor of Moorhall.   The other legend, which is current in the
Wortley family, states him to have been a most
formidable drinker, whose powers of inglutition,
strength of stomach, and stability of head, had procured him a long series of triumphs over common
visitants, but who was at length fairly drunk dead
by the chieftain of the opposite moors.   It must be
confessed that the form of the den, a cavern cut in
the rock, and very nearly resembling a wine or ale
cellar, tends to corroborate this tradition; but I am
rather tempted to believe that both the stories were
invented *apres coup*, and that the supposed dragon
was some wolf or other destructive animal, who
was finally hunted down by Moor of Moorhall, after
doing considerable mischief to the flocks and herds
of his superstitious neighbours.

" The present house appears to have grown to
its even now moderate size by successive additions
to a very small *logge* (lodge), built by ' a gentle
knight, Sir Thomas Wortley,' in the time of Henry
VIII., for the pleasure, as an old inscription in the
present scullery testifies, of ' listening to the Hartes

hell.' Its site is on the side of a very high rocky hill, covered with oaks (the weed of the country), and overhanging the river Don, which in this place is little more than a mountain torrent, though it becomes navigable a few miles lower at Sheffield. A great part of the road from hence (which is seven miles distant) runs through forest ground, and I have no doubt that the whole was at no distant period covered with wood, because the modern improvements of the country, the result of flourishing manufactories, have been carried on almost within our own time in consequence of the abundance of coal which here breaks out in many places even on the surface. On the opposite side of the river begin almost immediately the extensive moors which strike along the highest land of Yorkshire and Derbyshire, and following the chain of hills, probably communicated not many centuries ago with those of Northumberland, Cumberland, and Scotland. I therefore doubt whether the general face of the country is not better evidence as to the nature of the monster than the particular appearance of the cavern; and am inclined to believe that Moor of Moorhall was a hunter of wild beasts, rather than of attorneys or hard drinkers.

" You are unjust in saying that I flag over the Mabinogion — I have been very constantly employed upon my preface, and was proceeding to the last

section when I set off for this place — so you see I
am perfectly exculpated, and all over as white as
snow.　Anne being a true aristocrat, and considering
purity of blood as essential to lay the foundation of
all the virtues she expects to call out by a laborious
education of a true son of Camp — she highly ap-
proves the strict and even prudish severity with
which you watch over the morals of his bride, and
expects you, inasmuch as all the good knights she
has read of have been remarkable for their incom-
parable beauty, not to neglect that important re-
quisite in selecting her future guardian.　We possess
a vulgar dog (a pointer), to whom it is intended to
commit the charge of our house during our absence,
and to whom I mean to give orders to repel by force
any attempts of our neighbours during the times
that I shall be occupied in preparing *hare-soup ;*
but Fitz-Camp will be *her* companion, and she trusts
that you will strictly examine him while yet a varlet,
and only send him up when you think him likely to
become a true knight.　*Adieu — mille choses.*

G. E."

Scott tells Ellis in reply (October 14), that he
was "infinitely gratified with his account of Wortley Lodge and the Dragon," and refers him to the
article " Kempion," in the Minstrelsy, for a similar
tradition respecting an ancestor of the noble house

of Somerville. The reader can hardly need to be
reminded that the gentle knight, Sir Thomas Wortley's, love of hearing the deer *bell* was often alluded
to in Scott's subsequent writings. He goes on to
express his hope, that next summer will be " a more
propitious season for a visit to Scotland. The necessity of the present occasion," he says, " has kept
almost every individual, however insignificant, to his
post. God has left us entirely to our own means
of defence, for we have not above one regiment of
the line in all our ancient kingdom. In the mean
while, we are doing the best we can to prepare ourselves for a contest, which, perhaps, is not far distant. A beacon light, communicating with that of
Edinburgh Castle, is just erecting in front of our
quiet cottage. My field equipage is ready, and I want
nothing but a pipe and a *schnurbärtchen* to convert
me into a complete hussar." Charlotte, with the
infantry (of the household troops, I mean), is to
beat her retreat into Ettrick Forest, where, if the
Tweed is in his usual wintry state of flood, she may
weather out a descent from Ostend. Next year I

* *Schnurbärtchen* is German for mustachio. It appears from
a page of an early note-book previously transcribed, that Scott
had been sometimes a smoker of tobacco in the first days of his
light-horsemanship. He had laid aside the habit at the time
when this letter was written; but he twice again resumed it,
though he never carried the indulgence to any excess.

hope all this will be over, and that not only I shall
have the pleasure of receiving you in peace and quiet,
but also of going with you through every part of
Caledonia, in which you can possibly be interested.
Friday se'ennight our corps takes the field for ten
days — for the second time within three months —
which may explain the military turn of my epistle.

" Poor Ritson is no more. All his vegetable soups
and puddings have not been able to avert the evil
day, which, I understand, was preceded by madness.
It must be worth while to enquire who has got his
MSS., — I mean his own notes and writings. The
' Life of Arthur,' for example, must contain many
curious facts and quotations, which the poor defunct
had the power of assembling to an astonishing degree, without being able to combine any thing like a
narrative, or even to deduce one useful inference
— witness his ' Essay on Romance and Minstrelsy,'
which reminds one of a heap of rubbish, which had
either turned out unfit for the architect's purpose,
or beyond his skill to make use of. The ballads he
had collected in Cumberland and Northumberland,
too, would greatly interest me. If they have fallen
into the hands of any liberal collector, I dare say I
might be indulged with a sight of them. Pray enquire about this matter.

" Yesterday Charlotte and I had a visit which we
owe to Mrs E. A rosy lass, the sister of a bold

yeoman in our neighbourhood, entered our cottage,
towing in a monstrous sort of bulldog, called em-
phatically Cerberus, whom she came on the part of
her brother to beg our acceptance of, understanding
we were anxious to have a son of Camp. Cerberus
was no sooner loose (a pleasure which, I suspect, he
had rarely enjoyed) than his father *(supposé)* and
he engaged in a battle which might have been celebrated by the author of the ' Unnatural Combat,' and
which, for aught I know, might have turned out a
combat *à l'outrance,* if I had not interfered with a
horse-whip, instead of a baton, as *juge de Camp.*
The odds were indeed greatly against the stranger
knight—two fierce Forest greyhounds having arrived,
and, contrary to the law of arms, stoutly assailed
him. I hope to send you a puppy instead of this
redoubtable Cerberus. Love to Mrs E.—W. S."

After giving Scott some information about Ritson's
literary treasures, most of which, as it turned out, had
been disposed of by auction shortly before his death,
Mr Ellis (10th November) returns to the charge
about Tristrem and True Thomas. " You appear,"
he says, " to have been for some time so military,
that I am afraid the most difficult and important part
of your original plan, viz. your History of Scottish
poetry, will again be postponed, and must be kept
for some future publication. I am, at this moment,
much in want of two such assistants as you and

Leyden. It seems to me, that if I had some local knowledge of that wicked Ettrick Forest, I could extricate myself tolerably—but as it is, although I am convinced that my general idea is tolerably just, I am unable to guide my elephants in that quiet and decorous step-by-step march which the nature of such animals requires through a country of which I don't know any of the roads. My comfort is, that you cannot publish Tristrem without a preface,—that you can't write one without giving me some assistance,—and that you must finish the said preface long before I go to press with my Introduction."

This was the Introduction to Ellis's " Specimens of Ancient English Romances," in which he intended to prove, that as Valentia was, during several ages, the exposed frontier of Roman Britain towards the unsubdued tribes of the North, and as two whole legions were accordingly usually quartered there, while one besides sufficed for the whole southern part of the island, the manners of Valentia, which included the district of Ettrick Forest, must have been greatly favoured by the continued residence of so many Roman troops. " It is probable, therefore," he says, in another letter, " that the civilisation of the northern part became gradually the most perfect. That country gave birth, as you have observed, to Merlin, and to Aneurin,—who was probably the same as the historian Gildas. It seems to have given

education to Taliessin—it was the country of Bede
and Adonnan."

I shall not quote more on this subject, as the reader
may turn to the published essay for Mr Ellis's matured opinions respecting it. To return to his letter
of November 10th 1803, he proceeds—" And now
let me ask you about the Lay of the Last Minstrel.
That, I think, may go on as well in your tent,
amidst the clang of trumpets and the dust of the
field, as in your quiet cottage—perhaps indeed still
better—nay, I am not sure whether a *real* invasion
would not be, as far as your poetry is concerned, a
thing to be wished."

It was in the September of this year that Scott
first saw Wordsworth. Their common acquaintance,
Stoddart, had so often talked of them to each other,
that they met as if they had not been strangers; and
they parted friends.

Mr and Miss Wordsworth had just completed that
tour in the Highlands, of which so many incidents
have since been immortalized, both in the poet's verse
and in the hardly less poetical prose of his sister's
Diary. On the morning of the 17th of September,
having left their carriage at Rosslyn, they walked
down the valley to Lasswade, and arrived there before
Mr and Mrs Scott had risen. " We were received,"
Mr Wordsworth has told me, " with that frank cor-

diality which, under whatever circumstances I afterwards met him, always marked his manners; and,
indeed, I found him then in every respect — except,
perhaps, that his animal spirits were somewhat higher
— precisely the same man that you knew him in
later life; the same lively, entertaining conversation,
full of anecdote, and averse from disquisition; the
same unaffected modesty about himself; the same
cheerful and benevolent and hopeful views of man
and the world. He partly read and partly recited,
sometimes in an enthusiastic style of chant, the first
four cantos of the Lay of the Last Minstrel; and
the novelty of the manners, the clear picturesque
descriptions, and the easy glowing energy of much
of the verse, greatly delighted me."

After this he walked with the tourists to Rosslyn,
and promised to meet them in two days at Melrose.
The night before they reached Melrose they slept at
the little quiet inn of Clovenford, where, on mentioning his name, they were received with all sorts
of attention and kindness, — the landlady observing
that Mr Scott, "who was a very clever gentleman,"
was an old friend of the house, and usually spent a
good deal of time there during the fishing season;
but, indeed, says Mr Wordsworth, "wherever we
named him, we found the word acted as an *open
sesamum;* and I believe, that in the character of the

Sheriff's friends, we might have counted on a hearty welcome under any roof in the Border country."

He met them at Melrose on the 19th, and escorted them through the Abbey, pointing out all its beauties, and pouring out his rich stores of history and tradition. They then dined and spent the evening together at the inn; but Miss Wordsworth observed that there was some difficulty about arranging matters for the night, " the landlady refusing to settle any thing until she had ascertained from *the Sheriff himself* that he had no objection to sleep in the same room with *William*." Scott was thus far on his way to the Circuit Court at Jedburgh, in his capacity of Sheriff, and there his new friends again joined him; but he begged that they would not enter the court, " for," said he " I really would not like you to see the sort of figure I cut there." They did see him casually, however, in his cocked hat and sword, marching in the Judge's procession to the sound of one cracked trumpet, and were then not surprised that he should have been a little ashamed of the whole ceremonial. He introduced to them his friend William Laidlaw, who was attending the court as a juryman, and who, having read some of Wordsworth's verses in a newspaper, was exceedingly anxious to be of the party, when they explored at leisure, all the law-business being over, the beau-

tiful valley of the Jed, and the ruins of the Castle of
Fernieherst, the original fastness of the noble family
of Lothian.   The grove of stately ancient elms about
and below the ruin was seen to great advantage in
a fine, grey, breezy autumnal afternoon; and Mr
Wordsworth happened to say, " What life there is
in trees!"—" How different," said Scott, " was the
feeling of a very intelligent young lady, born and
bred in the Orkney Islands, who lately came to
spend a season in this neighbourhood!   She told
me nothing in the mainland scenery had so much
disappointed her as woods and trees.   She found
them so dead and lifeless, that she could never help
pining after the eternal motion and variety of the
ocean.   And so back she has gone, and I believe
nothing will ever tempt her from *the wind-swept
Orcades* again."

Next day they all proceeded together up the
Teviot to Hawick, Scott entertaining his friends
with some legend or ballad connected with every
tower or rock they passed.   He made them stop for
a little to admire particularly a scene of deep and
solemn retirement, called *Horne's Pool,* from its
having been the daily haunt of a contemplative
schoolmaster, known to him in his youth; and at
Kirkton he pointed out the little village schoolhouse,
to which his friend Leyden had walked six or eight
miles every day across the moors " when a poor

barefooted boy." From Hawick, where they spent the night, he led them next morning to the brow of a hill, from which they could see a wide range of the Border mountains, Ruberslaw, the Carter, and the Cheviots; and lamented that neither their engagements nor his own would permit them to make at this time an excursion into the wilder glens of Liddesdale, " where," said he, " I have strolled so often and so long, that I may say I have a home in every farm-house." " And, indeed," adds Mr Wordsworth, " wherever we went with him, he seemed to know every body, and every body to know and like him." Here they parted—the Wordsworths to pursue their journey homeward by Eskdale—he to return to Lasswade.

The impression on Mr Wordsworth's mind was, that on the whole he attached much less importance to his literary labours or reputation than to his bodily sports, exercises, and social amusements; and yet he spoke of his profession as if he had already given up almost all hope of rising by it; and some allusion being made to its profits, observed that " he was sure he could, if he chose, get more money than he should ever wish to have from the booksellers."*

* I have drawn up the account of this meeting from my recollection partly of Mr Wordsworth's conversation—partly from that of his sister's charming " Diary," which he was so kind as to read over to me on the 16th May 1836.

This confidence in his own literary resources appeared to Mr Wordsworth remarkable—the more so, from the careless way in which its expression dropt from him. As to his despondence concerning the bar, I confess his *fee-book* indicates much less ground for such a feeling than I should have expected to discover there. His practice brought him, as we have seen, in the session of 1796–7, £144 : 10s.; its proceeds fell down, in the first year of his married life, to £79 : 17s.; but they rose again, in 1798–9, to £135 : 9s.; amounted, in 1799–1800, to £129 : 13s.; in 1800–1, to £170; in 1801–2, to £202 : 12s.; and in the session that had just elapsed (which is the last included in the record before me), to £228 : 18s.

On reaching his cottage in Westmoreland, Wordsworth addressed a letter to Scott, from which I must quote a few sentences. It is dated Grasmere, October 16, 1803. " We had a delightful journey home, delightful weather, and a sweet country to travel through. We reached our little cottage in high spirits, and thankful to God for all his bounties. My wife and child were both well, and as I need not say, we had all of us a happy meeting. . . . . . We passed Dranxholme—your Branxholme, we supposed—about four miles on this side of Hawick. It looks better in your poem than in its present realities. The situation, however, is delightful, and makes

amends for an ordinary mansion. The whole of the
Teviot and the pastoral steeps about Mosspaul
pleased us exceedingly. The Esk below Langholm
is a delicious river, and we saw it to great advantage.
We did not omit noticing Johnnie Armstrong's
Keep; but his hanging place, to our great regret, we
missed. We were, indeed, most truly sorry that we
could not have you along with us into Westmoreland.
The country was in its full glory—the verdure of
the valleys, in which we are so much superior to you
in Scotland, but little tarnished by the weather, and
the trees putting on their most beautiful looks. My
sister was quite enchanted, and we often said to each
other, What a pity Mr Scott is not with us! . . . . .
I had the pleasure of seeing Coleridge and Southey
at Keswick last Sunday. Southey, whom I never
saw much of before, I liked much: he is very pleasant in his manner, and a man of great reading in
old books, poetry, chronicles, memoirs, &c. &c., particularly Spanish and Portuguese. . . . . My sister
and I often talk of the happy days that we spent in
your company. Such things do not occur often in
life. If we live we shall meet again; that is my
consolation when I think of these things. Scotland
and England sound like division, do what ye can;
but we really are but neighbours, and if you were
no farther off, and in Yorkshire, we should think so.
Farewell. God prosper you, and all that belongs to

you. Your sincere friend, for such I will call myself,
though slow to use a word of such solemn meaning
to any one,— W. WORDSWORTH."

The poet then transcribes his noble sonnet on
Neidpath Castle, of which Scott had, it seems, requested a copy.   In the MS. it stands somewhat
differently from the printed edition; but in that
original shape Scott always recited it, and few
lines in the language were more frequently in his
mouth.

I have already said something of the beginning of
Scott's acquaintance with " the Ettrick Shepherd."
Shortly after their first meeting, Hogg, coming into
Edinburgh with a flock of sheep, was seized with a
sudden ambition of seeing himself in type, and he
wrote out that same night " Willie and Katie," and
a few other ballads, already famous in the Forest,
which some obscure bookseller gratified him by
printing accordingly; but they appear to have
attracted no notice beyond their original sphere.
Hogg then made an excursion into the Highlands,
in quest of employment as overseer of some extensive sheep-farm; but, though Scott had furnished
him with strong recommendations to various friends, .
he returned without success.   He printed an account
of his travels, however, in a set of letters in the
Scots Magazine, which, though exceedingly rugged

and uncouth, had abundant traces of the native
shrewdness and genuine poetical feeling of this
remarkable man. These also failed to excite attention; but, undeterred by such disappointments, the
Shepherd no sooner read the third volume of the
" Minstrelsy," than he made up his mind that the
Editor's " Imitations of the Ancients" were by no
means what they should have been. " Immediately,"
he says, in one of his many Memoirs of himself, " I
chose a number of traditional facts, and set about
imitating the manner of the ancients myself." These
imitations he transmitted to Scott, who warmly
praised the many striking beauties scattered over
their rough surface. The next time that Hogg's
business carried him to Edinburgh, he waited upon
Scott, who invited him to dinner in Castle Street,
in company with William Laidlaw, who happened
also to be in town, and some other admirers of the
rustic genius. When Hogg entered the drawing-
room, Mrs Scott, being at the time in a delicate
state of health, was reclining on a sofa. The Shepherd, after being presented, and making his best
bow, forthwith took possession of another sofa placed
opposite to hers, and stretched himself thereupon at
all his length; for, as he said afterwards, " I thought
I could never do wrong to copy the lady of the
house." As his dress at this period was precisely
that in which any ordinary herdsman attends cattle

to the market, and as his hands, moreover, bore
most legible marks of a recent sheep-smearing, the
lady of the house did not observe with perfect equa-
nimity the novel usage to which her chintz was
exposed. The Shepherd, however, remarked nothing
of all this — dined heartily and drank freely, and, by
jest, anecdote, and song, afforded plentiful merri-
ment to the more civilized part of the company.
As the liquor operated, his familiarity increased and
strengthened; from " Mr Scott," he advanced to
" Sherra," and thence to " Scott," " Walter," and
" Wattie,"—until, at supper, he fairly convulsed the
whole party by addressing Mrs Scott as " Charlotte."

The collection entitled " The Mountain Bard"
was eventually published by Constable, in consequence of Scott's recommendation, and this work did
at last afford Hogg no slender share of the popular
reputation for which he had so long thirsted. It is
not my business, however, to pursue the details of
his story. What I have written was only to render
intelligible the following letter :—

" *To Walter Scott. Esq., Advocate, Castle Street,*
Edinburgh.

" Ettrick-House, December 24, 1803.
" Dear Mr Scott,

" I have been very impatient to hear from you.

There is a certain affair of which you and I talked a
little in private, and which must now be concluded,
that naturally increaseth this.

"I am afraid that I was at least half-seas over
the night I was with you, for I cannot, for my life,
recollect what passed when it was late; and, there
being certainly a small vacuum in my brain, which,
when empty, is quite empty, but is sometimes supplied with a small distillation of intellectual matter
— this must have been empty that night, or it never
could have been taken possession of by the fumes
of the liquor so easily. If I was in the state in
which I suspect that I was, I must have spoke a
very great deal of nonsense, for which I beg ten
thousand pardons. I have the consolation, however,
of remembering that Mrs Scott kept in company all
or most of the time, which she certainly could not
have done, had I been very rude. I remember,
too, of the filial injunction you gave at parting,
cautioning me against being ensnared by the loose
women in town. I am sure I had not reason enough
left at that time to express either the half of my
gratitude for the kind hint, or the utter abhorrence
I inherit at those seminaries of lewdness.

"You once promised me your best advice in the
first lawsuit in which I had the particular happiness of being engaged. I am now going to ask it
seriously in an affair, in which, I am sure, we will

both take as much pleasure. It is this:—I have
as many songs beside me, which are certainly the
worst of my productions, as will make about one
hundred pages close printed, and about two hundred,
printed as the Minstrelsy is.   Now, although I will
not proceed without your consent and advice, yet I
would have you to understand that I expect it, and
have the scheme much at heart at present.   The
first thing that suggested it, was their extraordinary
repute in Ettrick and its neighbourhood, and being
everlastingly plagued with writing copies, and promising scores which I never meant to perform.   As
my last pamphlet was never known, save to a few
friends, I wish your advice what pieces of it are
worth preserving.   The ' Pastoral' I am resolved
to insert, as I am ' Sandy Tod.'   As to my manu-
scripts, they are endless ; and as I doubt you will
disapprove of publishing them wholesale, and letting
the good help off the bad, I think you must trust
to my discretion in the selection of a few.   I wish
likewise to know if you think a graven image on the
first leaf is any recommendation ; and if we might
front the songs with a letter to you, giving an
impartial account of my manner of life and education, and, which if you pleased to transcribe, putting
He for I.   Again, there is no publishing a book
without a patron, and I have one or two in my eye,
and of which I will, with my wonted assurance to

you, give you the most free choice. The first is
Walter Scott, Esq., Advocate, Sheriff-depute of
Ettrick Forest, which, if permitted, I will address
you in a dedication singular enough. The next is
Lady Dalkeith, which, if you approved of, you must
become the Editor yourself; and I shall give you
my word for it, that neither word nor sentiment in
it shall offend the most delicate ear. You will not
be in the least jealous, if, alongst with my services
to you, I present my kindest compliments to the
sweet little lady whom you call Charlotte. As for
Camp and Walter (I beg pardon for this pre-emi-
nence), they will not mind them if I should exhaust
my eloquence in compliments. Believe me, Dear
Walter, your most devoted servant,

                                   JAMES HOGG."

The reader will, I doubt not, be particularly
amused with one of the suggestions in this letter;
namely, that Scott should transcribe the Shepherd's
narrative *in fore* of his life and education, and
merely putting " He" for " I," adopt it as his own
composition. James, however, would have had no
hesitation about offering a similar suggestion either
to Scott, or Wordsworth, or Byron, at any period
of their renown. To say nothing about modesty, his
notions of literary honesty were always exceedingly
loose; but, at the same time, we must take into

account his peculiar notions, or rather no notions, as to the proper limits of a joke.

Literature, like misery, makes men acquainted with strange bed-fellows. Let us return from the worthy Shepherd of Ettrick to the courtly wit and scholar of Sunninghill. In the last quoted of his letters, he expresses his fear that Scott's military avocations might cause him to publish the Tristrem unaccompanied by his " Essay on the History of Scottish Poetry." It is needless to add that no such Essay ever was completed; but I have heard Scott say that his plan had been to begin with the age of Thomas of Ercildoune, and bring the subject down to his own, illustrating each stage of his progress by a specimen of verse — imitating every great master's style, as he had done that of the original Sir Tristrem in his " *Conclusion*." Such a series of pieces from his hand would have been invaluable, merely as bringing out in a clear manner the *gradual* divarication of the two great dialects of the English tongue; but seeing by his " Verses on a Poacher," written many years after this in professed imitation of Crabbe, with what happy art he could pour the poetry of his own mind into the mould of another artist, it is impossible to doubt that we have lost better things than antiquarian illumination by the non-completion of a design in which he should have embraced successively the tone and measure of Douglas, Dunbar, Lindesay, Montgomerie, Hamilton, Ramsay, Fergusson, and Burns.

The Tristrem was now far advanced at press. He says to Ellis, on the 19th March 1804—" As I had a world of things to say to you, I have been culpably, but most naturally silent. When you turn a bottle with its head downmost, you must . have remarked that the extreme impatience of the contents to get out all at once greatly impedes their getting out at all. I have, however, been forming the resolution of sending a grand packet with Sir Tristrem, who will kiss your hands in about a fortnight. I intend uncastrated copies for you, Heber, and Mr Douce, who, I am willing to hope, will accept this mark of my great respect and warm remembrance of his kindness while in London.— Pray send me without delay the passage referring to *Thomas* in the French ' Hornchild.' Far from being daunted with the position of the enemy, I am resolved to carry it at the point of the bayonet, and, like an able general, to attack where it would be difficult to defend. Without metaphor or parable, I am determined not only that my Tomas *shall* be the author of Tristrem, but that he shall be the author of Hornchild also. I must, however, read over the romance, before I can make my arrangements. Holding, with Ritson, that the copy in *his* collection is translated from the French, I do not see

why we should not suppose that the French had been
originally a version from our Thomas. The date does
not greatly frighten me, as I have extended Thomas
of Ercildoune's life to the three-score and ten years
of the Psalmist, and consequently removed back the
date of " Sir Tristrem" to 1250. The French translation might be written for that matter within a few
days after Thomas's work was completed — and I
can allow a few years. He lived on the Border,
already possessed by Norman families, and in the
vicinity of Northumberland, where there were many
more. Do you think the minstrels of the Percies,
the Vescies, the Morells, the Grais, and the De
Vaux, were not acquainted with honest Thomas,
their next door neighbour, who was a poet, and
wrote excellent tales — and, moreover, a *laird*, and
gave, I dare be sworn, good dinners? And would
they not anxiously translate, for the amusement of
their masters, a story like Hornchild, so intimately
connected with the lands in which they had settled?
And do you not think, from the whole structure of
Hornchild, however often translated and retrans-
lated, that it must have been originally of northern
extraction? I have not time to tell you certain sus-
picions I entertain that Mr Douce's fragments are
the work of one Raoull de Beauvais, who flourished
about the middle of the thirteenth century, and for
whose accommodation principally I have made Tho-

mas, to use a military phrase, *dress backwards* for
ten years."

All this playful language is exquisitely characteristic of Scott's indomitable adherence to his own
views. But his making *Thomas dress backwards* —
and resolving that, if necessary, he *shall be* the author
of Hornchild, as well as Sir Tristrem — may perhaps
remind the reader of Don Quixote's method of re-
pairing the headpiece which, as originally constructed,
one blow had sufficed to demolish : — " Not altogether approving of his having broken it to pieces
with so much ease, to secure himself from the like
danger for the future, he made it over again, fencing
it with small bars of iron within, in such a manner,
that *he rested satisfied of its strength — and, without caring to make a fresh experiment on it, he
approved and looked upon it as a most excellent
helmet."*

Ellis having made some observations on Scott's
article upon Godwin's Life of Chaucer, which implied a notion that he had formed a regular connexion
with the Edinburgh Review, he in the same letter
says — " I quite agree with you as to the general
conduct of the Review, which savours more of a
wish to display than to instruct ; but as essays, many
of the articles are invaluable, and the principal con-
ductor is a man of very acute and universal talent.
I am not regularly connected with the work, nor

have I either inclination or talents to use the critical
scalping knife, unless as in the case of Godwin,
where flesh and blood succumbed under the temptation.
I don't know if you have looked into his tomes, of
which a whole edition has vanished—I was at a loss
to know how, till I conjectured that, as the heaviest
materials to be come at, they have been sent on the
secret expedition, planned by Mr Phillips and adopted
by our sapient Government, for blocking up the
mouth of our enemy's harbours.   They should have
had my free consent to take Phillips and Godwin,
and all our other lumber, literary and political, for
the same beneficial purpose.   But in general, I think
it ungentlemanly to wound any person's feelings
through an anonymous publication, unless where
conceit or false doctrine strongly calls for reproba-
tion.   Where praise can be conscientiously mingled
in a larger proportion than blame, there is always
some amusement in throwing together our ideas upon
the works of our fellow-labourers, and no injustice in
publishing them.   On such occasions, *and in our
way*, I may possibly, once or twice a-year, furnish
my critical friends with an article."

" Sir Tristrem" was at length published on the
2d of May 1804, by Constable, who, however, expected so little popularity for the work that the
edition consisted only of 150 copies.   These were
sold at a high price (two guineas), otherwise they

would not have been enough to cover the expenses
of paper and printing. Mr Ellis, and Scott's other
antiquarian friends, were much dissatisfied with these
arrangements; but I doubt not that Constable was
a better judge than any of them. The work, however, partook in due time of the favour attending its
editor's name. In 1806, 750 copies were called for;
and 1000 in 1811. After that time Sir Tristrem
was included in the collective editions of Scott's
poetry; but he had never parted with the copyright,
merely allowing his general publishers to insert it
among his other works, whenever they chose to do
so, as a matter of courtesy. It was not a performance
from which he had ever anticipated any pecuniary
profit, but it maintained at least, if it did not raise,
his reputation in the circle of his fellow-antiquaries;
and his own *Conclusion*, in the manner of the
original romance, must always be admired as a remarkable specimen of skill and dexterity.

As to the arguments of the Introduction, I shall
not in this place attempt any discussion.* Whether the story of Tristrem was first told in Welsh,
Armorican, French, or English verse, there can, I

---

* The critical reader will find all the learning on the subject
brought together with much ability in the Preface to " The Poetical Romances of Tristan, in French, in Anglo-Norman, and in
Greek, composed in the Twelfth and Thirteenth Centuries —
Edited by Francisque Michel," 2 vols. London, 1835.

think, be no doubt that it had been told in verse,
with such success as to obtain very general renown,
by Thomas of Ercildoune, and that the copy edited
by Scott was either the composition of one who had
heard the old Rhymer recite his lay, or the identical
lay itself. The introduction of Thomas's name in
the third person, as not the author, but the author's
authority, appears to have had a great share in con-
vincing Scott that the Auchinleck MS. contained
not the original, but the copy of an English admirer
and contemporary. This point seems to have been
rendered more doubtful by some quotations in the
recent edition of Warton's History of English Poetry;
but the argument derived from the enthusiastic ex-
clamation " God help Sir Tristrem the knight — he
fought for England," still remains; and stronger
perhaps even than that, in the opinion of modern
philologists, is the total absence of any Scottish or
even Northumbrian peculiarities in the diction.

All this controversy may be waived here. Scott's
object and delight was to revive the fame of the
Rhymer, whose traditional history he had listened
to while yet an infant among the crags of Smailholme.
He had already celebrated him in a noble ballad; *
he now devoted a volume to elucidate a fragment
supposed to be substantially his work; and we shall

* See the Minstrelsy (Edition 1833), vol. iv. p. 110.

find that thirty years after, when the lamp of his own genius was all but spent, it could still revive and throw out at least some glimmerings of its original brightness at the name of Thomas of Ercildoune.*

* See Castle Dangerous. — Waverley Novels, vol. xlvii.

•

CHAPTER XIIL

*Removal to Ashestiel—Death of Captain Robert
Scott—Mungo Park—Completion and Publication of the Lay of the Last Minstrel.*

1804-1805.

IT has been mentioned, that in the course of the preceding summer, the Lord-Lieutenant of Selkirkshire
complained of Scott's military zeal as interfering
sometimes with the discharge of his shrieval functions,
and took occasion to remind him, that the law, re-
quiring every Sheriff to reside at least four months
in the year within his own .jurisdiction, had not
hitherto been complied with.   It appears that Scott
received this communication with some displeasure,
being conscious that no duty of any importance had
ever been neglected by him; well knowing that the
law of residence was not enforced in the cases of
many of his brother sheriffs; and, in fact, ascribing

his Lord-Lieutenant's complaint to nothing but a
certain nervous fidget as to all points of form, for
which that respectable nobleman was notorious, as
well became, perhaps, an old High Commissioner to
the General Assembly of the Kirk.   Scott, however,
must have been found so clearly in the wrong, had
the case been submitted to the Secretary of State,
and Lord Napier conducted the correspondence with
such courtesy, never failing to allege as a chief argument the pleasure which it would afford himself and
the other gentlemen of Selkirkshire to have more
of their Sheriff's society, that, while it would have
been highly imprudent to persist, there could be no
mortification in yielding.   He flattered himself that
his active habits would enable him to maintain his
connexion with the Edinburgh Cavalry as usual;
and, perhaps, he also flattered himself, that residing
for the summer in Selkirkshire would not interfere
more seriously with his business as a barrister, than
the occupation of the cottage at Lasswade had hitherto done.

While he was seeking about, accordingly, for some
" lodge in the Forest," his kinsman of Harden suggested that the tower of Auld Wat might be refit-
ted, so as to serve his purpose; and he received the
proposal with enthusiastic delight.   On a more careful inspection of the localities, however, he became
sensible that he would be practically at a greater

distance from county business of all kinds at Harden,
than if he were to continue at Lasswade. Just at
this time, the house of Ashestiel, situated on the
southern bank of the Tweed, a few miles from Selkirk, became vacant by the death of its proprietor, ·
Colonel Russell, who had married a sister of Scott's
mother, and the consequent dispersion of the family.
The young laird of Ashestiel, his cousin, was then
in India; and the Sheriff took a lease of the house
and grounds, with a small farm adjoining.   On the
4th May, two days after the Tristrem had been published, he says to Ellis — " I have been engaged in
travelling backwards and forwards to Selkirkshire
upon little pieces of business, just important enough
to prevent my doing any thing to purpose.   One
great matter, however, I have achieved, which is.
procuring myself a place of residence, which will
save me these teasing migrations in future, so that
though I part with my sweet little cottage on the
banks of the Esk, you will find me this summer in
the very centre of the ancient Reged, in a decent
farm-house overhanging the Tweed, and situated in
a wild pastoral country."   And again, on the 19th,
he thus apologizes for not having answered a letter
of the 10th: — " For more than a month my head
was fairly tenanted by ideas, which, though strictly
pastoral and rural, were neither literary nor poetical.
Long sheep, and *short sheep*, and *tups*, and *gimmers*,

and *hogs*, and *dinmonts*, had made a perfect sheep-
fold of my understanding, which is hardly yet cleared
of them.*—I hope Mrs Ellis will clap a bridle on
her imagination. Ettrick Forest boasts finely shaped
hills and clear romantic streams; but, alas! they
are bare, to wildness, and denuded of the beautiful

---

* Describing his meeting with Scott in the summer of 1801,
James Hogg says—"During the sociality of the evening, the
discourse ran very much on the different breeds of sheep, that
curse of the community of Ettrick Forest. The original black-
faced Forest breed being always called *the short sheep*, and the
Cheviot breed *the long sheep*, the disputes at that period ran very
high about the practicable profits of each. Mr Scott, who had
come into that remote district to preserve what fragments remained of its legendary lore, was rather bored with everlasting
questions of the long and the short sheep. So at length, putting
on his most serious, calculating face, he turned to Mr Walter
Bryden, and said, ' I am rather at a loss regarding the merits of
this very important question. How long must a sheep actually
measure to come under the denomination of *a long sheep* ?' Mr
Bryden, who, in the simplicity of his heart, neither perceived the
quiz nor the reproof, fell to answer with great sincerity. ' It's
the woo [wool], sir—it's the woo' that makes the difference. The
lang sheep ha'e the short woo', and the short sheep ha'e the lang
thing, and these are just kind o' names we gi'e them, like.' Mr
Scott could not preserve his grave face of strict calculation: it
went gradually awry, and a hearty guffaw" [*i. e.* horselaugh]
"followed. When I saw the very same words repeated near the
beginning (p. 4) of the ' Black Dwarf,' how could I be mistaken
of the author?"—*Autobiography* prefixed to Hogg's *Altrive
Tales.*

natural wood with which they were formerly shaded.
It is mortifying to see that, though wherever the
sheep are excluded, the copse has immediately sprung
up in abundance, so that enclosures only are wanting
to restore the wood wherever it might be useful or
ornamental, yet hardly a proprietor has attempted to
give it fair play for a resurrection. . . . You see we
reckon positively on you—the more because our
arch-critic Jeffrey tells me that he met you in London, and found you still inclined for a northern trip.
All our wise men in the north are rejoiced at the
prospect of seeing George Ellis. If you delay your
journey till July, I shall then be free of the Courts
of Law, and will meet you upon the Border, at
whatever side you enter."

The business part of these letters refers to Scott's
brother Daniel, who, as he expresses it, " having
been bred to the mercantile line, had been obliged,
by some untoward circumstances, particularly an
imprudent connexion with an artful woman, to leave
Edinburgh for Liverpool, and now to be casting his
eyes towards Jamaica." Scott requests Ellis to help
him if he can, by introducing him to some of his
own friends or agents in that island: and Ellis
furnishes him accordingly with letters to Mr Black-
burne, a friend and brother proprietor, who appears
to have paid Daniel Scott every possible attention,
and soon provided him with suitable employment on

a healthy part of his estates. But the same low tastes and habits which had reduced the unfortunate young man to the necessity of expatriating himself, recurred after a brief season of penitence and order, and continued until he had accumulated great affliction upon all his family.

On the 10th of June 1804, died, at his seat of Rosebank, Captain Robert Scott, the affectionate uncle whose name has often occurred in this narrative.* " He was," says his nephew to Ellis, on the 18th, " a man of universal benevolence, and great kindness towards his friends, and to me individually. His manners were so much tinged with the habits of celibacy as to render them peculiar, though by no means unpleasingly so, and his profession (that of a seaman) gave a high colouring to the whole. The loss is one which, though the course of nature led me to expect it, did not take place at last without considerable pain to my feelings. The arrangement of his affairs, and the distribution of his small fortune among his relations, will devolve in a great measure upon me. He has distinguished me by leaving me a beautiful little villa on the banks of the Tweed, with every possible

* In the obituary of the Scots Magazine for this month I find:
— " Universally regretted, Captain Robert Scott of Rosebank, a gentleman whose life afforded an uniform example of unostentatious charity and extensive benevolence."

convenience annexed to it, and about thirty acres of
the finest land in Scotland.   Notwithstanding, however, the temptation that this bequest offers, I continue to pursue my Reged plan, and expect to be
settled at Ashestiel in the course of a month.   Rosebank is situated so near the village of Kelso as
hardly to be sufficiently a country residence; besides, it is hemmed in by hedges and ditches, not to
mention Dukes and Lady Dowagers, which are bad
things for little people.   It is expected to sell to
great advantage.   I shall buy a mountain farm with
the purchase-money, and be quite the Laird of the
Cairn and the Scaur."

Scott sold Rosebank in the course of the year for
£5000; his share (being a ninth) of his uncle's other
property, amounted, I believe, to about £500; and
he had besides a legacy of £100 in his quality of
trustee.   This bequest made an important change
in his pecuniary position, and influenced accordingly
the arrangements of his future life.   Independently
of practice at the bar, and of literary profits, he was
now, with his little patrimony, his Sheriffship, and
about £200 per annum arising from the stock ultimately settled on his wife, in possession of a fixed
revenue of nearly, if not quite, £1000 a-year.

On the 1st of August he writes to Ellis from
Ashestiel — " Having had only about a hundred
and fifty things to do, I have scarcely done any

thing, and yet could not give myself leave to suppose that I had leisure to write letters. 1*st*, I had
this farm-house to furnish from sales, from brokers'
shops, and from all manner of hospitals for incurable
furniture. 2*dly*, I had to let my cottage on the
banks of the Esk. 3*dly*, I had to arrange matters
for the sale of Rosebank. 4*thly*, I had to go into
quarters with our cavalry, which made a very idle
fortnight in the midst of all this business. Last of
all, I had to superintend a removal, or what we call
a *flitting*, which, of all bores under the cope of Heaven, is bore the most tremendous. After all these
storms, we are now most comfortably settled, and
have only to regret deeply our disappointment at
finding your northern march blown up. We had
been projecting about twenty expeditions, and were
pleasing ourselves at Mrs Ellis's expected surprise
on finding herself so totally built in by mountains,
as I am at the present writing hereof. We are seven
miles from kirk and market. We rectify the last in-
convenience by killing our own mutton and poultry ;
and as to the former, finding there was some chance
of my family turning pagans, I have adopted the
goodly practice of reading prayers every Sunday, to
the great edification of my household. Think of
this, you that have the happiness to be within two
steps of the church, and commiserate those who
dwell in the wilderness. I showed Charlotte yester-

day *the Catrail,* and told her that to inspect that
venerable monument was one main object of your
intended journey to Scotland. She is of opinion
that ditches must be more scarce in the neighbourhood of Windsor Forest than she had hitherto had
the least idea of."

Ashestiel will be visited by many for his sake, as
long as Waverley and Marmion are remembered. A
more beautiful situation for the residence of a poet
could not be conceived. The house was then a small
one, but, compared with the cottage at Lasswade,
its accommodations were amply sufficient. You approached it through an old-fashioned garden, with
holly hedges, and broad, green, terrace walks. On
one side, close under the windows, is a deep ravine,
clothed with venerable trees, down which a mountain rivulet is heard, more than seen, in its progress
to the Tweed. The river itself is separated from
the high bank on which the house stands only by a
narrow meadow of the richest verdure. Opposite,
and all around, are the green hills. The valley
there is narrow, and the aspect in every direction is
that of perfect pastoral repose. The heights immediately behind are those which divide the Tweed
from the Yarrow; and the latter celebrated stream
lies within an easy ride, in the course of which the
traveller passes through a variety of the finest mountain scenery in the south of Scotland. No town is

within seven miles but Selkirk, which was then still smaller and quieter than it is now; there was hardly even a gentleman's family within visiting distance, except at Yair, a few miles lower on the Tweed, the ancient seat of the Pringles of Whytbank, and at Bowhill, between the Yarrow and Ettrick, where the Earl of Dalkeith used occasionally to inhabit a small shooting-lodge, which has since grown into a magnificent ducal residence. The country all around, with here and there an insignificant exception, belongs to the Buccleuch estate; so that, whichever way he chose to turn, the bard of the clan had ample room and verge enough, and all appliances to boot, for every variety of field sport that might happen to please his fancy; and being then in the prime vigour of manhood, he was not slow to profit by these advantages. ⁻ Meantime, the concerns of his own little farm, and the care of his absent relation's woods, gave him healthful occupation in the intervals of the chase; and he had long, solitary evenings for the uninterrupted exercise of his pen; perhaps, on the whole, better opportunities of study than he had ever enjoyed before, or was to meet with elsewhere in later days.

When he first examined Ashestiel, with a view to being his cousin's tenant, he thought of taking home James Hogg to superintend the sheep-farm, and keep watch over the house also during the win-

ter. I am not able to tell exactly in what manner
this proposal fell to the ground. In January 1804,
the Shepherd writes to him:—" I have no intention of waiting for so distant a prospect as that of
being manager of your farm, though I have no
doubt of our joint endeavour proving successful,
nor yet of your willingness to employ me in that
capacity. His grace the Duke of Buccleuch hath at
present a farm vacant in Eskdale, and I have been
importuned by friends to get a letter from you and
apply for it. You can hardly be conscious what
importance your protection hath given me already,
not only in mine own eyes, but even in those of
others. You might write to him, or to any of the
family you are best acquainted with, stating that
such and such a character was about leaving his
native country for want of a residence in the farm-
ing line." I am very doubtful if Scott — however
willing to encounter the risk of employing Hogg as
his own *grieve* or bailiff — would have felt himself
justified at this, or, indeed, at any time, in recommending him as the tenant of a considerable farm
on the Duke of Buccleuch's estate. But I am also
quite at a loss to comprehend how Hogg should
have conceived it possible, at this period, when he
certainly had no capital whatever, that the Duke's
Chamberlain should agree to accept him for a tenant,
on any attestation, however strong, as to the excel-

lence of his character and intentions. Be that as it
may, if Scott made the application which the Shepherd suggested, it failed. So did a negotiation which
he certainly did enter upon about the same time with
the late Earl of Caernarvon (then Lord Porchester),
through that nobleman's aunt, Mrs Scott of Harden,
with the view of obtaining for Hogg the situation of
bailiff on one of his Lordship's estates in the west
of England; and such, I believe, was the result of
several other attempts of the same kind with landed
proprietors nearer home. Perhaps the Shepherd
had already set his heart so much on taking rank as
a farmer in his own district, that he witnessed the
failure of any such negotiations with indifference.
As regards the management of Ashestiel, I find no
trace of that proposal having ever been renewed.

In truth, Scott had hardly been a week in possession of his new domains, before he made acquaintance
with a character much better suited to his purpose
than James Hogg ever could have been. I mean
honest Thomas Purdie, his faithful servant — his
affectionately devoted humble friend from this time
until death parted them. Tom was first brought
before him, in his capacity of Sheriff, on a charge of
poaching, when the poor fellow gave such a touching
account of his circumstances, — a wife, and I know
not how many children depending on his exertions
— work scarce and grouse abundant, — and all this

with a mixture of odd sly humour, — that the She-riff's heart was moved. Tom escaped the penalty of the law — was taken into employment as shepherd, and showed such zeal, activity, and shrewdness in that capacity, that Scott never had any occasion to repent of the step he soon afterwards took, in pro-moting him to the position which had been originally offered to James Hogg.

It was also about the same time that he took into his service as coachman Peter Mathieson, brother-in-law to Thomas Purdie, another faithful servant, who never afterwards left him, and still survives his kind master. Scott's awkward management of the little phaeton had exposed his wife to more than one perilous overturn, before he agreed to set up a close carriage, and call in the assistance of this steady charioteer.

During this autumn Scott formed the personal acquaintance of Mungo Park, the celebrated victim of African discovery. On his return from his first expedition, Park endeavoured to establish himself as a medical practitioner in the town of Hawick, but the drudgeries of that calling in such a district soon exhausted his ardent temper, and he was now living in seclusion in his native cottage at Fowlsheils on the Yarrow, nearly opposite Newark Castle. His brother, Archibald Park (then tenant of a large farm on the Buccleuch estate), a man remarkable for

strength both of mind and body, introduced the
traveller to the Sheriff. They soon became much
attached to each other; and Scott supplied some
interesting anecdotes of their brief intercourse, to Mr
Wishaw, the editor of Park's posthumous Journal,
with which I shall blend a few minor circumstances,
gathered from him in conversation long afterwards.
" On one occasion," he says, " the traveller communicated to him some very remarkable adventures
which had befallen him in Africa, but which he
had not recorded in his book." On Scott's asking
the cause of this silence, Mungo answered, " That
in all cases where he had information to communicate, which he thought of importance to the public,
he had stated the facts boldly, leaving it to his
readers to give such credit to his statements as they
might appear justly to deserve; but that he would
not shock their faith, or render his travels more
marvellous, by introducing circumstances, which,
however true, were of little or no moment, as they
related solely to his own personal adventures and
escapes." This reply struck Scott as highly characteristic of the man; and though strongly tempted to
set down some of these marvels for Mr Wishaw's
use, he on reflection abstained from doing so, holding
it unfair to record what the adventurer had deliberately chosen to suppress in his own narrative.
He confirms the account given by Park's biographer,

of his cold and reserved manners to strangers; and in particular, of his disgust with the *indirect* questions which curious visitors would often put to him upon the subject of his travels. " This practice," said Mungo, " exposes me to two risks; either that I may not understand the questions meant to be put, or that my answers to them may be misconstrued;" and he contrasted such conduct with the frankness of Scott's revered friend, Dr Adam Ferguson, who, the very first day the traveller dined with him at Hallyards, ·spread a large map of Africa on the table, and made him trace out his progress thereupon, inch by inch, questioning him minutely as to every step he had taken. " Here, however," says Scott, " Dr F. was using a privilege to which he was well entitled by his·venerable age and high literary character, but which could not have been exercised with propriety by any common stranger."

Calling one day at Fowlsheils, and not finding Park at home, Scott walked in search of him along the banks of the Yarrow, which in that neighbourhood passes over various ledges of rock, forming deep pools and eddies between them. Presently he discovered his friend standing alone on the bank, plunging one stone after another into the water, and watching anxiously the bubbles as they rose to the surface. " This," said Scott, " appears but an idle amusement for one who has seen so much stirring adventure." " Not so idle, perhaps, as you suppose," answered Mungo: — " This was the manner in which I used to ascertain the depth of a river in Africa before I ventured to cross it — judging whether the attempt would be safe, by the time the bubbles of air took to ascend." At this time Park's intention of a second expedition had never been revealed to Scott; but he instantly formed the opinion that these experiments on Yarrow were connected with some such purpose.

His thoughts had always continued to be haunted with Africa. He told Scott, that whenever he awoke suddenly in the night, owing to a nervous disorder with which he was troubled, he fancied himself still a prisoner in the tent of Ali; but when the poet expressed some surprise that he should design again to revisit those scenes, he answered, that he would rather brave Africa and all its horrors, than wear out his life in long and toilsome rides over the hills of Scotland, for which the remuneration was hardly enough to keep soul and body together.

Towards the end of the autumn, when about to quit his country for the last time, Park paid Scott a farewell visit, and slept at Ashestiel. Next morning his host accompanied him homewards over the wild chain of hills between the Tweed and the Yarrow. Park talked much of his new scheme, and mentioned his determination to tell his family that he had some

business for a day or two in Edinburgh, and send
them his blessing from thence, without returning to
take leave.   He had married, not long before, a
pretty and amiable woman ; and when they reached
the *Williamhope ridge*, " the autumnal mist floating
heavily and slowly down the valley of the Yarrow,"
presented to Scott's imagination " a striking em-
blem of the troubled and uncertain prospect which
his undertaking afforded."   He remained, however,
unshaken, and at length they reached the spot at
which they had agreed to separate.   A small ditch
divided the moor from the road, and, in going over
it, Park's horse stumbled, and nearly fell.   " I am
afraid, Mungo," said the Sheriff, " that is a bad
omen."   To which he answered, smiling, " *Freits*
(omens) follow those who look to them."   With this
expression Mungo struck the spurs into his horse,
and Scott never saw him again.   His parting proverb, by the way, was probably suggested by one of
the Border ballads, in which species of lore he was
almost as great a proficient as the Sheriff himself ;
for we read in " Edom o' Gordon," —

> " Them look to freits, my master dear,
>   Then freits will follow them."

    I must not omit that George Scott, the unfor-
tunate companion of Park's second journey, was the
son of a tenant on the Buccleuch estate, whose skill

in drawing having casually attracted the Sheriff's attention, he was recommended by him to the protection of the family, and by this means established in a
respectable situation in the Ordnance department of
the Tower of London; but the stories of his old acquaintance Mungo Park's discoveries, had made such
an impression on his fancy, that nothing could prevent his accompanying him on the fatal expedition
of 1805.

The brother of Mungo Park remained in Scott's
neighbourhood for some years, and was frequently his
companion in his mountain rides. Though a man
of the most dauntless temperament, he was often
alarmed at Scott's reckless horsemanship. " The
de'il's in ye, Sherra," he would say, " ye'll never halt
till they bring you hame, with your feet foremost."
He rose greatly in favour, in consequence of the
gallantry with which he assisted the Sheriff in seizing
a gipsy, accused of murder, from amidst a group of
similar desperadoes, on whom they had come unex-
pectedly in a desolate part of the country.

To return to The Lay of the Last Minstrel: —
Ellis, understanding it to be now nearly ready for
the press, writes to Scott, urging him to set it forth
with some engraved illustrations — if possible, after
Flaxman, whose splendid designs from Homer had
shortly before made their appearance. He answers,
August 21 — " I should have liked very much to

have had appropriate embellishments.   Indeed, we
made some attempts of the kind, but they did not
succeed.   I should fear Flaxman's genius is too
classic to stoop to body forth my Gothic Borderers.
Would there not be some risk of their resembling
the antique of Homer's heroes, rather than the iron
race of Salvator?   After all, perhaps, nothing is
more difficult than for a painter to adopt the author's
ideas of an imaginary character, especially when it is
founded on traditions to which the artist is a stranger.
I should like at least to be at his elbow when at
work.   I wish very much I could have sent you the
Lay while in MS., to have had the advantage of your
opinion and corrections.   But Ballantyne galled my
kibes so severely during an unusual fit of activity,
that I gave him the whole story in a sort of pet both
with him and with it. . . . . I have lighted upon a
very good amanuensis for copying such matters as
the *Lay le Frain*, &c.   He was sent down here by
some of the London booksellers in a half starved
state, but begins to pick up a little. . . . I am just
about to set out on a grand expedition of great importance to my comfort in this place.   You must
know that Mr Plummer, my predecessor in this
county, was a good antiquary, and left a valuable collection of books, which he entailed with the estate,
the first successors being three of his sisters, at
least as old and musty as any Caxton or Wynkyn

de Worde in his library.   Now I must contrive to
coax those watchful dragons to give me admittance
into this garden of the Hesperides.   I suppose they
trouble the volumes as little as *the* dragon did the
golden pippins ; but they may not be the more easily
soothed on that account.   However, I set out on my
quest, like a *preux chevalier,* taking care to leave
Camp, for dirtying the carpet, and to carry the greyhounds with me, whose appearance will indicate that
hare soup may be forthcoming in due season.   By
the way, did I tell you that Fitz-Camp is dead, and
another on the stocks ?   As our stupid postman
might mistake *Reged,* address, as per date, Ashestiel,
Selkirk, by Berwick."

I believe the spinsters of Sunderland hall proved
very generous dragons ; and Scott lived to see them
succeeded in the guardianship of Mr Plummer's literary treasures by an amiable young gentleman of his
own name and family.   The half-starved amanuensis
of this letter was *Henry Weber,* a laborious German, of whom we shall hear more hereafter.   With
regard to the pictorial embellishments contemplated
for the first edition of the Lay of the Last Minstrel,
I believe the artist in whose designs the poet took
the greatest interest was Mr Masquerier, now of
Brighton, with whom he corresponded at some length
on the subject ; but his distance from that ingenious

gentleman's residence was inconvenient, and the booksellers were probably impatient of delay, when the MS. was once known to be in the hands of the printer.

There is a circumstance which must already have struck such of my readers as knew the author in his latter days, namely, the readiness with which he seems to have communicated this poem, in its progress, not only to his own familiar friends, but to new and casual acquaintances. We shall find him following the same course with his Marmion—but not, I think, with any of his subsequent works. His determination to consult the movements of his own mind alone in the conduct of his pieces, was probably taken before he began the Lay; and he soon resolved to trust for the detection of minor inaccuracies to two persons only—James Ballantyne and William Erskine. The printer was himself a man of considerable literary talents: his own style had the incurable faults of pomposity and affectation, but his eye for more venial errors in the writings of others was quick, and, though his personal address was apt to give a stranger the impression of insincerity, he was in reality an honest man, and conveyed his mind on such matters with equal candour and delicacy during the whole of Scott's brilliant career. In the vast majority of instances he found his friend acquiesce at once in the propriety of his suggestions; nay, there

certainly were cases, though rare, in which his advice
to alter things of much more consequence than a
word or a rhyme, was frankly tendered, and on deliberation adopted by Scott.   Mr Erskine was the
referee whenever the poet hesitated about taking the
hints of the zealous typographer; and his refined
taste and gentle manners rendered his critical alliance highly valuable. With two such faithful friends
within his reach, the author of the Lay might safely
dispense with sending his MS. to be revised even by
George Ellis.

Before he left Ashestiel for the winter session, the
printing of the poem had made considerable progress.
Ellis writes to him on the 10th November, com-
plaining of bad health, and adds — " Tu quid agis ?
I suppose you are still an inhabitant of Reged, and
being there it is impossible that your head should
have been solely occupied by the ten -thousand cares
which you are likely to have in common with other
mortals, or even by the *Lay,* which must have been
long since completed, but must have started during
the summer new projects sufficient to employ the
lives of half-a-dozen patriarchs.   Pray tell me all
about it, for as the present state of my frame pre-
cludes me from much activity, I want to enjoy that
of my friends."   Scott answers from Edinburgh : —
" I fear you fall too much into the sedentary habits
incident to a literary life, like my poor friend

Plummer, who used to say that a walk from the
parlour to the garden once a-day was sufficient
exercise for any rational being, and that no one but
a fool or a fox-hunter would take more. I wish
you could have had a seat on Hassan's tapestry, to
have brought Mrs Ellis and you soft and fair to
Ashestiel, where, with farm mutton at 4 P.M., and
goat's whey at 6 A.M., I think we could have re-
established as much *embonpoint* as ought to satisfy
a poetical antiquary. As for my country amusements, I have finished the Lay, with which and its
accompanying notes the press now groans; but I
have started nothing except some scores of hares,
many of which my gallant greyhounds brought to
the ground."

Ellis had also touched upon a literary feud then
raging between Scott's allies of the Edinburgh
Review, and the late Dr Thomas Young, illustrious
for inventive genius, displayed equally in physical
science and in philological literature. A northern
critic, whoever he was, had treated with merry
contempt certain discoveries in natural philosophy
and the mechanical arts, more especially that of the
undulating theory of light, which ultimately conferred
on Young's name one of its highest distinctions.
" He had been for some time," says Ellis, " lecturer
at the Royal Institution ; and having determined to
publish his lectures, he had received from one of the

booksellers the offer of £1000 for the copyright.
He was actually preparing for the press, when the
bookseller came to him, and told him that the ridicule thrown by the Edinburgh Review on some
. papers of his in the Philosophical Transactions, had
so frightened the whole *trade* that he must request
to be released from his bargain.   This consequence,
it is true, could not have been foreseen by the
reviewer, who, however, appears to have written
from feelings of private animosity; and I still continue to think, though I greatly admire the good
taste of the literary essays, and the perspicuity of
the dissertations on political economy, that an
apparent want of candour is too generally the character of a work which, from its independence on
the interests of booksellers, might have been expected
to be particularly free from this defect."   Scott
rejoins — " I am sorry for the very pitiful catastrophe of Dr Young's publication, because, although
I am altogether unacquainted with the merits of the
controversy, one must always regret so very serious
a consequence of a diatribe.   The truth is, that these
gentlemen reviewers ought often to read over the
fable of the boys and frogs, and should also remember it is much more easy to destroy than to build,
to criticise than to compose.   While on this subject
I kiss the rod of my critic in the Edinburgh, on the
subject of the price of Sir Tristrem ; it was not my

fault, however, that the public had it not cheap
enough, as I declined taking any copy-money, or
share in the profits; and *nothing*, surely, was as
reasonable a charge as I could make."

On the 30th December he resumes—" The *Lay*
is now ready, and will probably be in Longman and
Rees's hands shortly after this comes to yours. I
have charged them to send you a copy by the first
conveyance, and shall be impatient to know whether
you think the entire piece corresponds to that which
you have already seen. I would also fain send a
copy to Gifford, by way of introduction.— My
reason is that I understand he is about to publish
an edition of Beaumont and Fletcher, and I think
I could offer him the use of some miscellaneous
notes, which I made long since on the margin of
their works.* Besides, I have a good esteem of
Mr Gifford as a manly English poet, very different
from most of our modern versifiers.— We are so
fond of Reged, that we are just going to set out for
our farm in the middle of a snow-storm; all that
we have to comfort ourselves with is, that our march

* It was his *Massinger* that Gifford had at this time in hand.
His *Ben Jonson* followed, and then his *Ford.* Some time later,
he projected editions, both of *Beaumont and Fletcher*, and of
Shakspeare; but, to the grievous misfortune of literature, died
without having completed either of them. We shall see presently
what became of Scott's Notes on *Beaumont and Fletcher.*

has been ordered with great military talent — a
detachment of minced pies and brandy having preceded us. In case we are not buried in a snow-
wreath, our stay will be but short. Should that
event happen, we must wait the thaw."

Ellis, not having as yet received the new poem,
answers, on the 9th January 1805 — " I look daily
and with the greatest anxiety for the Last Minstrel
—of which I still hope to see a future edition de-
corated with designs *à la Flaxman*, as the Lays of
Homer have already been. I think you told me
that Sir Tristrem had not excited much sensation
in Edinburgh. As I have not been in London this
age, I can't produce the contrary testimony of our
metropolis. But I can produce one person, and
that one worth a considerable number, who speaks
of it with rapture, and says, ' I am only sorry that
Scott has not (and I am sure he has not) told us
the whole of his creed on the subject of Tomas, and
the other early Scotch Minstrels. I suppose he was
afraid of the critics, and determined to say very little
more than he was able to establish by incontestable
proofs. I feel infinitely obliged to him for what
he has told us, and I have no hesitation in saying,
that I consider Sir T. as by far the most interesting
work that has as yet been published on the subject
of our earliest poets, and, indeed, such a piece of
literary antiquity as no one could have, *a priori*,

supposed to exist.' This is Frere—our ex-ambas-
sador for Spain, whom you would delight to know,
and who would delight to know you. It is remarkable that *you* were, I believe, the *most ardent* of all
the admirers of his old English version of the Saxon
Ode;* and he is, *per contra*, the warmest pane-
gyrist of your *Conclusion*, which he can repeat by
heart, and affirms to be the very best imitation of
old English at present existing. I think I can trust
you for having concluded the Last Minstrel with as
much spirit as it was begun — if you have been
capable of any thing unworthy of your fame amidst
the highest mountains of Reged, there is an end of
all inspiration."

Scott answers—" Frere is so perfect a master of

* " I have only met, in my researches into these matters,"
says Scott in 1830, " with one poem, which if it had been produced as ancient could not have been detected on internal evidence.
It is the War Song upon the Victory at Brunnanburgh, translated
from the Anglo-Saxon into Anglo-Norman, by the Right Hon.
John Hookham Frere. See Ellis's *Specimens of Ancient English
Poetry*, vol. i. p. 32. The accomplished editor tell us, that this
very singular poem was intended as an imitation of the style and
language of the fourteenth century, and was written during the
controversy occasioned by the poems attributed to Rowley.
Mr. Ellis adds—' The reader will probably hear with some surprise,
that this singular instance of critical ingenuity was the composition
of an Eton schoolboy.'" — *Essay on Imitations of the Ancient
Ballad*, p. 19.

the ancient style of composition, that I would rather
have his suffrage than that of a whole synod of your
vulgar antiquaries.   The more I think on *our* system of the origin of Romance, the more simplicity
and uniformity it seems to possess; and though I
adopted it late and with hesitation, I believe I shall
never see cause to abandon it.   Yet I am aware of
the danger of attempting to *prove*, where proofs
are but scanty, and probable suppositions must be
placed in lieu of them.   I think the Welsh antiquaries have considerably injured their claims to confidence, by attempting to detail very remote events
with all the accuracy belonging to the facts of yesterday.   You will hear one of them describe you the
cut of Llywarch Hen's beard, or the whittle of
Urien Reged, as if he had trimmed the one, or cut
his cheese with the other.   These high pretensions
weaken greatly our belief in the Welsh poems,
which probably contain real treasures.   'Tis a pity
some sober-minded man will not take the trouble to
sift the wheat from the chaff, and give us a good
account of their MSS. and traditions.   Pray, what
is become of the *Mabinogion?*   It is a proverb,
that children and fools talk truth, and I am mistaken
if even the same valuable quality may not sometimes
be extracted out of the tales made to entertain both.
I presume, while we talk of childish and foolish
tales, that the Lay is already with you, although, in

these points, *Long-manum est errare.*   Pray enquire for your copy."

In the first week of January 1805, "The Lay" was published; and its success at once decided that literature should form the main business of Scott's . life.

In his modest *Introduction* of 1830, he had himself told us all that he thought the world would ever desire to know of the origin and progress of this his first great original production.   The present Memoir, however, has already included many minor particulars, for which I believe no student of literature will reproach the compiler.   I shall not mock the reader with many words as to the merits of a poem which has now kept its place for nearly a third of a century; but one or two additional remarks on the history of the composition may be pardoned.

It is curious to trace the small beginnings and gradual developement of his design.   The lovely Countess of Dalkeith hears a wild rude legend of Border *diablerie,* and sportively asks him to make it the subject of a ballad.   He had been already labouring in the elucidation of the "quaint Inglis" ascribed to an ancient seer and bard of the same district, and perhaps completed his own sequel, intending the whole to be included in the third volume of the Minstrelsy.   He assents to Lady Dalkeith's request, and casts about for some new variety of

diction and rhyme, which might be adopted without
impropriety in a closing strain for the same collection.   Sir John Stoddart's casual recitation, a year
or two before, of Coleridge's unpublished Christabel,
. had fixed the music of that noble fragment in his
memory; and it occurs to him, that by throwing the
story of Gilpin Horner into somewhat of a similar
cadence, he might produce such an echo of the later
metrical romance, as would serve to connect his
Conclusion of the primitive Sir Tristrem with his
imitations of the common popular ballad in the Gray
Brother and Eve of St John.   A single scene of
feudal festivity in the hall of Branksome, disturbed
by some pranks of a nondescript goblin, was probably
all that he contemplated; but his accidental con-
finement in the midst of a volunteer camp gave him
leisure to meditate his theme to the sound of the
bugle;—and suddenly there flashes on him the idea
of extending his simple outline, so as to embrace a
vivid panorama of that old Border life of war and
tumult, and all earnest passions, with which his
researches on the " Minstrelsy" had by degrees fed
his imagination, until every the minutest feature
had been taken home and realized with unconscious
intenseness of sympathy; so that he had won for
himself in the past, another world, hardly less complete or familiar than the present.   Erskine or
Cranstoun suggests that he would do well to divide

the poem into cantos, and prefix to each of them a
motto explanatory of the action, after the fashion
of Spenser in the Faery Queen.   He pauses for a
moment—and the happiest conception of the frame-
work of a picturesque narrative that ever occurred
to any poet—one that Homer might have envied—
the creation of the ancient harper, starts to life.   By
such steps did the " Lay of the Last Minstrel" grow
out of the " Minstrelsy of the Scottish Border."

A word more of its felicitous machinery.   It was
at Bowhill that the Countess of Dalkeith requested
a ballad on Gilpin Horner.   The ruined castle of
Newark closely adjoins that seat, and is now indeed
included within its *pleasance.*   Newark had been the
chosen residence of the first Duchess of Buccleuch,
and he accordingly shadows out his own beautiful
friend in the person of her lord's ancestress, the last
of the original stock of that great house; himself
the favoured inmate of Bowhill, introduced certainly
to the familiarity of its circle in consequence of his
devotion to the poetry of a bypast age, in that of an
aged minstrel, " the last of all the race," seeking
shelter at the gate of Newark, in days when many
an adherent of the fallen cause of Stewart,—his own
bearded ancestor, *who had fought at Killiekrankie,*
among the rest,—owed their safety to her who

> " In pride of power, in beauty's bloom,
> Had wept o'er Monmouth's bloody tomb."

The arch allusions which run through all these *Introductions*, without in the least interrupting the truth and graceful pathos of their main impression, seem to me exquisitely characteristic of Scott, whose delight and pride was to play with the genius which nevertheless mastered him at will.   For, in truth, what is it that gives to all his works their unique and marking charm, except the matchless effect which sudden effusions of the purest heart-blood of nature derive from their being poured out, to all appearance involuntarily, amidst diction and sentiment cast equally in the mould of the busy world, and the seemingly habitual desire to dwell on nothing but what might be likely to excite curiosity, without too much disturbing deeper feelings, in the saloons of polished life? Such outbursts come forth dramatically in all his writings; but in the interludes and passionate parentheses of the Lay of the Last Minstrel we have the poet's own inner soul and temperament laid bare and throbbing before us. Even here, indeed, he has a mask, and he trusts it — but fortunately it is a transparent one.

Many minor personal allusions have been explained in the notes to the last edition of the " Lay."   It was hardly necessary even then to say that the choice of the hero had been dictated by the poet's affection for the living descendants of the Baron of Cranstoun; and now — none who have perused the preceding

pages can doubt that he had dressed out his Margaret
of Branksome in the form and features of his own
first love. This poem may be considered as the
" bright consummate flower" in which all the dearest
dreams of his youthful fancy had at length found
expansion for their strength, spirit, tenderness, and
beauty.

In the closing lines —

> " Hush'd is the harp—the Minstrel gone ;
> And did he wander forth alone ?
> Alone, in indigence and age,
> To linger out his pilgrimage ?
> No !— close beneath proud Newark's tower
> Arose the Minstrel's humble bower," &c.—

— in these charming lines he has embodied what
was, at the time when he penned them, the chief
day-dream of Ashestiel. From the moment that his
uncle's death placed a considerable sum of ready
money at his command, he pleased himself, as we
have seen, with the idea of buying a mountain farm,
and becoming not only the " sheriff" (as he had in
former days delighted to call himself), but " the
laird of the cairn and the scaur." While he was
" labouring doucement at the Lay" (as in one of his
letters he expresses it), during the recess of 1804,
circumstances rendered it next to certain that the
small estate of Broadmeadows, situated just over

against the ruins of Newark, on the northern bank
of the Yarrow, would soon be exposed to sale; and
many a time did he ride round it in company with
Lord and Lady Dalkeith,

> " When summer smiled on sweet Bowhill,"

surveying the beautiful little domain with wistful
eyes, and anticipating that

> " *There* would he sing achievement high
> And circumstance of chivalry,
> Till the 'rapt traveller would stay,
> Forgetful of the closing day ;
> And noble youths, the strain to hear,
> Forget the hunting of the deer;
> And Yarrow, as he rolled along,
> Dear burden to the Minstrel's song."

I consider it as, in one point of view, the greatest misfortune of his life that this vision was not
realized ; but the success of the poem itself changed
" the spirit of his dream." The favour which it at
once attained had not been equalled in the case of any
one poem of considerable length during at least two
generations : it certainly had not been approached
in the case of any narrative poem since the days of
Dryden. Before it was sent to the press it had received warm commendation from the ablest and most
influential critic of the time; but when Mr Jeffrey's
reviewal appeared, a month after publication, lauda-

tory as its language was, it scarcely came up to the
opinion which had already taken root in the public
mind.   It, however, quite satisfied the author; and
were I at liberty to insert some letters which passed
between them in the course of the summer of 1805,
it would be seen that their feelings towards each
other were those of mutual confidence and gratitude.
Indeed, a severe domestic affliction which about this
time befell Mr Jeffrey, called out the expression of
such sentiments on both sides in a very touching
manner.

I abstain from transcribing the letters which
conveyed to Scott the private opinions of persons
themselves eminently distinguished in poetry; but I
think it just to state, that I have not discovered in
any of them—no, not even in those of Wordsworth
or Campbell—a strain of approbation higher on the
whole than that of the chief professional reviewer of
the period.   When the happy days of youth are over,
even the most genial and generous of minds are
seldom able to enter into the strains of a new poet
with that full and open delight which he awakens
in the bosoms of the rising generation about him.
Their deep and eager sympathies have already been
drawn upon to an extent of which the prosaic part
of the species can never have any conception; and
when the fit of creative inspiration has subsided,
they are apt to be rather cold critics even of their

own noblest appeals to the simple primary feelings
of their kind.   Miss Seward's letter, on this occasion, has been since included in the printed collection
of her correspondence; but perhaps the reader may
form a sufficient notion of its tenor from the poet's
answer — which, at all events, he will be amused to
compare with the Introduction of 1830 :—

" To Miss Seward, Lichfield.

"Edinburgh, 21st March 1805.

" My Dear Miss Seward,

    " I am truly happy that you found any amuse-
ment in the Lay of the Last Minstrel.   It has great
faults, of which no one can be more sensible than I
am myself.   Above all, it is deficient in that sort of
continuity which a story ought to have, and which,
were it to write again, I would endeavour to give it.
But I began and wandered forward, like one in a
pleasant country, getting to the top of one hill to
see a prospect, and to the bottom of another to
enjoy a shade, and what wonder if my course has
been devious and desultory, and many of my excursions altogether unprofitable to the advance of my
journey? The Dwarf Page is also an excrescence,
and I plead guilty to all the censures concerning
him.   The truth is, he has a history, and it is this :
The story of Gilpin Horner was told by an old gen-

tleman to Lady Dalkeith, and she, much diverted
with his actually believing so grotesque a tale, insisted that I should make it into a Border ballad.
I don't know if ever you saw my lovely chieftainess
— if you have, you must be aware that it is *impossible* for any one to refuse her request, as she
has more of the angel in face and temper than any
one alive; so that if she had asked me to write a
ballad on a broomstick, I must have attempted it.
I began a few verses, to be called the Goblin Page;
and they lay long by me, till the applause of some
friends whose judgment I valued induced me to resume the poem; so on I wrote, knowing no more
than the man in the moon how I was to end.   At
length the story appeared so uncouth, that I was
fain to put it into the mouth of my old minstrel —
lest the nature of it should be misunderstood, and I
should be suspected of setting up a new school of
poetry, instead of a feeble attempt to imitate the old.
In the process of the romance, the page, intended to
be a principal person in the work, contrived (from
the baseness of his natural propensities I suppose) to
slink down stairs into the kitchen, and now he must
e'en abide there.

   " I mention these circumstances to you, and to
any one whose applause I value, because I am unwilling you should suspect me of trifling with the public
in *malice prepense*.   As to the herd of critics, it is

impossible for me to pay much·attention to them;
for, as they do not understand what I call poetry,
we talk in a foreign language to each other. Indeed,
many of these gentlemen appear to me to be a sort
of tinkers, who, unable to *make* pots and pans, set
up for *menders* of them, and, God knows, often
make two holes in patching one. The sixth canto
is altogether redundant; for the poem should certainly have closed with the union of the lovers, when
the interest, if any, was at an end. But what could
I do? I had my book and my page still on my
hands, and must get rid of them at all events.
Manage them as I would, their catastrophe must
have been insufficient to occupy an entire canto;
so I was fain to eke it out with the songs of the
minstrels. I will now descend from the confessional,
which I think I have occupied long enough for the
patience of my fair confessor. I am happy you are
disposed to give me absolution, notwithstanding all
my sins.

· " We have a new poet come forth amongst us—
James Graham, author of a poem called the Sabbath,
which I admire very much. If I can find an opportunity, I will send you a copy. Your affectionate
humble servant,

                              WALTER SCOTT."

Mr Ellis does not seem to have written at any

length on the subject of the Lay, until he had perused the article in the Edinburgh Review.   He then
says — " Though I had previously made up my mind,
or rather perhaps because I had done so, I was very
anxious to compare my sentiments with those of the
Edinburgh critic, and I found that in general we
were perfectly agreed, though there are parts of the
subject which we consider from very different points
of view.   Frere, with whom I had not any previous
communication about it, agrees with me; and trust-
ing very much to the justice of his poetical feelings,
I feel some degree of confidence in my own judgment — though in opposition to Mr Jeffrey, whose
criticism I admire upon the whole extremely, as
being equally acute and impartial, and as exhibiting
the fairest judgment respecting the work that could
be formed by the mere assistance of good sense and
general taste, without that particular sort of taste
which arises from the study of romantic compositions.

" What Frere and myself think, must be stated in
the shape of a *hypercriticism* — that is to say, of a
review of the reviewer.   We say that the Lay of the
Last Minstrel is a work *sui generis*, written with
the *intention* of exhibiting what our old romances do
indeed exhibit in point of fact, but incidentally, and
often without the wish, or rather contrary to the
wish of the author; — viz. the manners of a parti-

cular age; and that therefore, if it does this truly,
and is at the same time capable of keeping the steady
attention of the reader, it is so far perfect.   This is
also a poem, and ought therefore to contain a great
deal of poetical merit.   This indeed it does by the
admission of the reviewer, and it must be admitted
that he has shown much real taste in estimating the
most beautiful passages; but he finds fault with many
of the lines as careless, with some as prosaic, and
contends that the story is not sufficiently full of incident, and that one of the incidents is borrowed
from a merely local superstition, &c. &c.   To this
we answer — 1st, That if the Lay were intended to
give *any* idea of the Minstrel compositions, it would
have been a most glaring absurdity to have rendered
the poetry as perfect and uniform as the works
usually submitted to modern readers — and as in
telling a story, nothing, or very little, would be lost,
though the merely connecting part of the narrative
were in plain prose, the reader is certainly no loser
by the incorrectness of the smaller parts.   Indeed,
who is so unequal as Dryden?   It may be said, that
he was not intentionally so — but to be *very smooth*
is very often to be *tame;* and though this should be
admitted to be a less important fault than inequality
in a common modern poem, there can be no doubt
with respect to the necessity of subjecting yourself
to the latter fault (if it is one) in an imitation of an

ancient model.   2d, Though it is naturally to be
expected that many readers will expect an almost
infinite accumulation of incidents in a romance, this
is only because readers in general have acquired all
their ideas on the subject from the prose romances,
which commonly contained a farrago of metrical
stories.   The *only* thing *essential* to a romance was,
that it should be *believed* by the hearers.   Not only
tournaments, but battles, are indeed accumulated in
some of our ancient romances, because tradition had
of course ascribed to every great conqueror a great
number of conquests, and the minstrel would have
been thought deficient, if, in a warlike age, he had
omitted any military event.   But in other respects
a paucity of incident is the general characteristic of
our minstrel poems.   3d, With respect to the Goblin
Page, it is by no means necessary that the superstition on which this is founded should be universally
or even generally current.   It is quite sufficient that
it should exist somewhere in the neighbourhood of
the castle where the scene is placed; and it cannot
fairly be required, that because the goblin is mis-
chievous, all his tricks should be directed to the
production of general evil.   The old idea of goblins
seems to have been, that they were essentially active,
and careless about the mischief they produced, rather
than providentially malicious.

   " We therefore (*i. e.* Frere and myself) dissent

from all the reviewer's objections to these circumstances in the narrative; but we entertain some
doubts about the propriety of dwelling so long on
the Minstrel songs in the last canto. I say we
doubt, because we are not aware of your having
ancient authority for such a practice; but though
the attempt was a bold one, inasmuch as it is not
usual to add a whole canto to a story which is
already finished, we are far from wishing that you
had left it unattempted. I must tell you the answer
of a philosopher (Sir Henry Englefield) to a friend
of his who was criticising the obscurity of the language used in the Minstrel. ' I read little poetry,
and often am in doubt whether I exactly understand
the poet's meaning; but I found, after reading the
Minstrel three times, that I understood it all perfectly.' ' Three times?' replied his friend. ' Yes, certainly; the first time I discovered that there was a
great deal of meaning in it; a second would have
cleared it all up, but that I was run away with by the
beautiful passages, which distracted my attention;
the third time I skipped over these, and only attended
to the scheme and structure of the poem, with which
I am delighted.' At this conversation I was present,
and though I could not help smiling at Sir Henry's
mode of reading poetry, was pleased to see the degree
of interest which he took in the narrative."

Mr Morritt informs me, that he well remembers

the dinner where this conversation occurred, and
thinks Mr Ellis has omitted in his report the best
thing that Sir Harry Englefield said, in answer to
one of the *Dii Minorum Gentium*, who made himself conspicuous by the severity of his censure on the
verbal inaccuracies and careless lines of The Lay.
" My dear sir," said the Baronet, " you remind me
of a lecture on sculpture, which M. Falconet delivered at Rome, shortly after completing the model
of his equestrian statue of Czar Peter, now at Peters-
burg. He took for his subject the celebrated horse
of Marcus Aurelius in the Capitol, and pointed out
as many faults in it as ever a jockey did in an animal he was about to purchase. But something came
over him, vain as he was, when he was about to conclude the harangue. He took a long pinch of snuff,
and eying his own faultless model, exclaimed with a
sigh — *Cependant, Messieurs, il faut avouer que
cette vilaine bête là est vivante, et que la mienne est
morte.*"

To return to Ellis's letter, I fancy most of my
readers will agree with me in thinking that Sir
Henry Englefield's method of reading and enjoying
poetry was more to be envied than smiled at; and
in doubting whether posterity will ever dispute about
the " *propriety*" of the Canto which includes the
Ballad of Rosabelle and the Requiem of Melrose.
The friendly *hypercritics* seem, I confess, to have

judged the poem on principles not less pedantic,
though of another kind of pedantry, than those which
induced the *critic* to pronounce that its great pre-
vailing blot originated in " those local partialities
of the author," which had induced him to expect
general interest and sympathy for such personages as
his " Johnstones, Elliots, and Armstrongs."   " Mr
Scott," said Jeffrey, " must either sacrifice his Border prejudices, or offend his readers in the other
parts of the empire."   It might have been answered
by Ellis or Frere, that these Border clans figured
after all on a scene at least as wide as the Troad;
and that their chiefs were not perhaps inferior, either
in rank or power, to the majority of the Homeric
kings; but even the most zealous of its admirers
among the professed literators of the day would hardly
have ventured to suspect that the Lay of the Last
Minstrel might have no prejudices to encounter but
their own.   It was destined to charm not only the
British empire, but the whole civilized world; and
had, in fact, exhibited a more Homeric genius than
any regular epic since the days of Homer.

   " It would be great affectation," says the Introduction of 1830, " not to own that the author
expected some success from the Lay of the Last
Minstrel.   The attempt to return to a more simple
and natural poetry was likely to be welcomed, at
a time when the public had become tired of heroic

hexameters, with all the buckram and binding that
belong to them in modern days. But whatever might
have been his expectations, whether moderate or un-
reasonable, the result left them far behind ; for among
those who smiled on the adventurous minstrel were
numbered the great names of William Pitt and
Charles Fox. Neither was the extent of the sale
inferior to the character of the judges who received
the poem with approbation. Upwards of 30,000
copies were disposed of by the trade ; and the author
had to perform a task difficult to human vanity, when
called upon to make the necessary deductions from
his own merits, in a calm attempt to account for its
popularity."

Through what channel or in what terms Fox
made known his opinion of the Lay, I have failed to
ascertain. Pitt's praise, as expressed to his niece,
Lady Hester Stanhope, within a few weeks after the
poem appeared, was repeated by her to Mr William
Stewart Rose, who, of course, communicated it forthwith to the author ; and not long after, the Minister,
in conversation with Scott's early friend the Right
Hon. William Dundas, signified that it would give
him pleasure to find some opportunity of advancing
the fortunes of such a writer. " I remember," writes
this gentleman, " at Mr Pitt's table in 1805, the
Chancellor asked me about you and your then situa-

tion, and after I had answered him, Mr Pitt observed
—' He can't remain as he is,' and desired me to
' look to it.' He then repeated some lines from
the Lay, describing the old harper's embarrassment
when asked to play, and said,—' This is a sort of
thing which I might have expected in painting, but
could never have fancied capable of being given
in poetry.' " *

It is agreeable to know that this great statesman
and accomplished scholar awoke at least once from
his supposed apathy as to the elegant literature of
his own time.

. The poet has under-estimated even the patent and
tangible evidence of his success. The first edition
of the Lay was a magnificent quarto, 750 copies;
but this was soon exhausted, and there followed an
octavo impression of 1500; in 1806, two more, one
of 2000 copies, another of 2250; in 1807, a fifth
edition, of 2000, and a sixth, of 3000; in 1808,
3350; in 1809, 3000 — a small edition in quarto
(the ballads and lyrical pieces being then annexed to
it) — and another octavo edition of 3250; in 1811,
3000; in 1812, 3000; in 1816, 3000; in 1823.
1000.   A fourteenth impression of 2000 foolscap
appeared in 1825; and besides all this, before the

* Letter dated April 25th, 1818, and indorsed by Scott,
" *William Dundas — a very kind letter.*"

end of 1836, 11,000 copies had gone forth in the collected editions of his poetical works. Thus, nearly forty-four thousand copies had been disposed of in this country, and by the legitimate trade alone, before he superintended the edition of 1830, to which his biographical introductions were prefixed. In the history of British Poetry nothing had ever equalled the demand for the Lay of the Last Minstrel.

The publishers of the first edition were Longman and Co. of London, and Archibald Constable and Co. of Edinburgh; which last house, however, had but a small share in the adventure. The profits were to be divided equally between the author and his publishers; and Scott's moiety was £169: 6s. Messrs Longman, when a second edition was called for, offered £500 for the copyright; this was accepted, but they afterwards, as the Introduction says " added £100 in their own unsolicited kindness. It was handsomely given to supply the loss of a fine horse which broke down suddenly while the author was riding with one of the worthy publishers." This worthy publisher was Mr Owen Rees, and the gallant steed, to whom a desperate leap in the coursing-field proved fatal, was, I believe, *Captain*, the immediate successor of *Lenore*, as Scott's charger in the volunteer cavalry; *Captain* was replaced by *Lieutenant*. The author's whole share, then, in the profits of the Lay, came to £769: 6s.

Mr Rees' visit to Ashestiel occurred in the autumn. The success of the poem had already been decisive; and fresh negotiations of more kinds than one were at this time in progress between Scott and various booksellers' houses, both of Edinburgh and London.

CHAPTER XIV.

Partnership with James Ballantyne — Literary Projects — Edition of the British Poets — Edition of the Ancient English Chronicles, &c. &c. — Edition of Dryden undertaken — Earl Moira Commander of the Forces in Scotland — Sham Battles — Articles in the Edinburgh Review — Commencement of Waverley — Letter on Ossian — Mr Skene's Reminiscences of Ashestiel — Excursion to Cumberland — Alarm of Invasion — Visit of Mr Southey — Correspondence on Dryden with Ellis and Wordsworth.

1805.

Mr Ballantyne, in his Memorandum, says, that very shortly after the publication of the Lay, he found himself obliged to apply to Mr Scott for an advance of money; his own capital being inadequate

for the business which had been accumulated on his
press, in consequence of the reputation it had acquired for beauty and correctness of execution.   Already, as we have seen, Ballantyne had received " a
liberal loan ;" " and now," says he, " being compelled,
maugre all delicacy, to renew my application, he
candidly answered that he was not quite sure that it
would be prudent for him to comply, but in order to
evince his entire confidence in me, he was willing to
make a suitable advance to be admitted as a third-
sharer of my business."   In truth, Scott now em-
barked in Ballantyne's concern almost the whole of
the capital which he had a few months before designed to invest in the purchase of Broadmeadows.
Dis aliter visum.

I have, many pages back, hinted my suspicion
that he had formed some distant notion of such an
alliance, as early as the date of Ballantyne's projected
removal from Kelso to Edinburgh ; and his Introduction to the Lay, in 1830, appears to leave little
doubt that the hope of ultimately succeeding at the
Bar had waxed very faint, before the third volume
of the Minstrelsy was brought out in 1803.   When
that hope ultimately vanished altogether, perhaps he
himself would not have found it easy to tell.   The
most important of men's opinions, views, and projects, are sometimes taken up in so very gradual a
manner, and after so many pauses of hesitation and'

of inward retractation, that they themselves are at a
loss to trace in retrospect all the stages through
which their minds have passed. We see plainly that
Scott had never been fond of his profession, but
that, conscious of his own persevering diligence, he
ascribed his scanty success in it mainly to the prejudices of the Scotch solicitors against employing, in
weighty causes at least, any barrister supposed to be
strongly imbued with the love of literature; instancing
the career of his friend Jeffrey as almost the solitary
instance within his experience of such prejudices being entirely overcome. Had Scott, to his strong sense
and dexterous ingenuity, his well-grounded knowledge of the jurisprudence of his country, and his
admirable industry, added a brisk and ready talent
for debate and declamation, I can have no doubt
that his triumph over the prejudices alluded to would
have been as complete as Mr Jeffrey's; nor in truth
do I much question that, had one really great and
interesting case been submitted to his sole care and
management, the result would have been to place his
professional character for skill and judgment, and
variety of resource, on so firm a basis, that even his
rising celebrity as a man of letters could not have
seriously disturbed it. Nay, I think it quite possible, that had he been intrusted with one such case
after his reputation was established, and he had been
compelled to do his abilities some measure of justice

in his own secret estimate, he might have displayed
very considerable powers even as a forensic speaker.
But no opportunities of this engaging kind having
ever been presented to him—after he had persisted
for more than ten years in sweeping the floor of the
Parliament House, without meeting with any employment but what would have suited the dullest
drudge, and seen himself termly and yearly more and
more distanced by contemporaries for whose general
capacity he could have had little respect—while, at
the same time, he already felt his own position in the
eyes of society at large to have been signally elevated
in consequence of his extra-professional exertions—
it is not wonderful that disgust should have gradually
gained upon him, and that the sudden blaze and
tumult of renown which surrounded the author of
the Lay should have at last determined him to con-
centrate all his ambition on the pursuits which had
alone brought him distinction.   It ought to be mentioned, that the business in George's Square, once
extensive and lucrative, had dwindled away in the
hands of his brother Thomas, whose varied and
powerful talents were unfortunately combined with
some tastes by no means favourable to the successful
prosecution of his prudent father's vocation; so that
very possibly even the humble employment of which,
during his first years at the bar, Scott had at least
a sure and respectable allowance, was by this time

much reduced.   I have not his fee-books of later
date than 1803 : it is, however, my impression from
the whole tenour of his conversation and correspondence, that after that period he had not only not
advanced as a professional man, but had been re-
trograding in nearly the same proportion that his
literary reputation advanced.

We have seen that, before he formed his contract
with Ballantyne, he was in possession of such a fixed
income as might have satisfied all his desires, had he
not found his family increasing rapidly about him.
Even as that was, with nearly if not quite £1000
per annum, he might perhaps have retired not only
from the Bar, but from Edinburgh, and settled
entirely at Ashestiel or Broadmeadows, without encountering what any man of his station and habits
ought to have considered as an imprudent risk.   He
had, however, no wish to cut himself off from the
busy and intelligent society to which he had been
hitherto accustomed; and resolved not to leave the
Bar until he should have at least used his best efforts
for obtaining, in addition to his Shrievalty, one of
those clerkships of the supreme court at Edinburgh,
which are usually considered as honourable retire-
ments for advocates who, at a certain standing,
finally give up all hopes of reaching the dignity of
the Bench.   " I determined," he says, " that literature should be my staff but not my crutch, and that

the profits of my literary labour, however convenient otherwise, should not, if I could help it, become necessary to my ordinary expenses.   Upon such a post an author might hope to retreat, without any perceptible alteration of circumstances, whenever the time should arrive that the public grew weary of his endeavours to please, or he himself should tire of the pen. I possessed so many friends capable of assisting me in this object of ambition, that I could hardly over-rate my own prospects of obtaining the preferment to which I limited my wishes; and, in fact, I obtained, in no long period, the reversion of a situation which completely met them."*

The first notice of this affair that occurs in his correspondence, is in a note of Lord Dalkeith's, February the 2d, 1805, in which his noble friend says— " My father desires me to tell you that he has had a communication with Lord Melville within these few days, and that he thinks *your business is in a good train, though not certain."* I consider it as clear, then, that he began his negotiations concerning a seat at the clerk's table immediately after the Lay was published; and that their commencement had been resolved upon in the strictest connexion with his embarkation in the printing concern of James Ballantyne and Company. Such matters are seldom

* Introduction to the Lay of the Last Minstrel — 1830.

speedily arranged; but we shall find him in possession of his object before twelve months had elapsed.

Meanwhile, his design of quitting the Bar was
divulged to none but those immediately necessary for
the purposes of his negotiation with the Government;
and the nature of his connexion with the printing
company remained, I believe, not only unknown, but
for some years wholly unsuspected, by any of his
daily companions except Mr Erskine.

The forming of this commercial connexion was
one of the most important steps in Scott's life.   He
continued bound by it during twenty years, and its
influence on his literary exertions and his worldly
fortunes was productive of much good and not a little
evil. Its effects were in truth so mixed and balanced
during the vicissitudes of a long and vigorous career,
that I at this moment doubt whether it ought, on the
whole, to be considered with more of satisfaction or
of regret.

With what zeal he proceeded in advancing the
views of the new copartnership, his correspondence
bears ample evidence.   The brilliant and captivating
genius, now acknowledged universally, was soon discovered by the leading booksellers of the time to be
united with such abundance of matured information
in many departments, and, above all, with such indefatigable habits, as to mark him out for the most
valuable workman they could engage for the fur-

therance of their schemes.   He had, long before
this, cast a shrewd and penetrating eye over the field
of literary enterprise, and developed in his own mind
the outlines of many extensive plans, which wanted
nothing but the command of a sufficient body of able
subalterns to be carried into execution with splendid
success.   Such of these as he grappled with in his
own person were, with rare exceptions, carried to
a triumphant conclusion; but the alliance with Ballantyne soon infected him with the proverbial rashness of mere mercantile adventure — while, at the
same time, his generous feelings for other men of
letters, and his characteristic propensity to over-rate
their talents, combined to hurry him and his friends
into a multitude of arrangements, the results of
which were often extremely embarrassing, and ultimately, in the aggregate, all but disastrous.   It is
an old saying, that wherever there is a secret there
must be something wrong; and dearly did he pay
the penalty for the mystery in which he had chosen
to involve this transaction.   It was his rule, from
the beginning, that whatever he wrote or edited
must be printed at that press; and had he catered
for it only as author and sole editor, all had been
well; but had the booksellers known his direct pecuniary interest in keeping up and extending the
occupation of those types, they would have taken
into account his lively imagination and sanguine

temperament, as well as his taste and judgment, and considered, far more deliberately than they too often did, his multifarious recommendations of new literary schemes, coupled though these were with some dim understanding that, if the Ballantyne press were employed, his own literary skill would be at his friend's disposal for the general superintendence of the undertaking. On the other hand, Scott's suggestions were, in many cases, perhaps in the majority of them, conveyed through Ballantyne, whose habitual deference to his opinion induced him to advocate them with enthusiastic zeal; and the printer, who had thus pledged his personal authority for the merits of the proposed scheme, must have felt himself committed to the bookseller, and could hardly refuse with decency to take a certain share of the pecuniary risk, by allowing the time and method of his own payment to be regulated according to the employer's convenience. Hence, by degrees, was woven a web of entanglement from which neither Ballantyne nor his adviser had any means of escape, except only in that indomitable spirit, the mainspring of personal industry altogether unparalleled, to which, thus set in motion, the world owes its most gigantic monument of literary genius.

The following is the first letter I have found of Scott to his PARTNER. The Mr Foster mentioned in the beginning of it was a literary gentleman who

had proposed to take on himself a considerable share
in the annotation of some of the new *editions* then
on the carpet — among others, one of Dryden.

" *To Mr James Ballantyne, Printer, Edinburgh.*

" Ashiestiel, April 12th, 1805.

" Dear Ballantyne,

" I have duly received your two favours — also
Foster's.   He still howls about the expense of printing, but I think we shall finally settle.   His argument is that you print too fine, *alias* too dear.
I intend to stick to my answer, that I know nothing
of the matter; but that settle it how you and he will,
it must be printed by you, or can be no concern of
mine.   This gives you an advantage in driving the
bargain.   As to every thing else, I think we shall
do, and I will endeavour to set a few volumes agoing
on the plan you propose.

" I have imagined a very superb work.   What
think you of a complete edition of British Poets,
ancient and modern?   Johnson's is imperfect and out
of print; so is Bell's, which is a Lilliputian thing;
and Anderson's, the most complete in point of number, is most contemptible in execution both of the
editor and printer.   There is a scheme for you!   At
least a hundred volumes, to be published at the rate

of ten a-year. I cannot, however, be ready till mid-summer. If the booksellers will give me a decent allowance per volume, say thirty guineas, I shall hold myself well paid on the *writing* hand. This is a dead secret.

" I think it quite right to let Doig* have a share of Thomson ;† but he is hard and slippery, so settle your bargain fast and firm — no loop-holes ! I am glad you have got some elbow-room at last. Cowan will come to, or we will find some fit place in time. If not, we *must* build — necessity has no law. I see nothing to hinder you from doing Tacitus with your correctness of eye, and I congratulate you on the fair prospect before us. When you have time, you will make out a list of the debts to be discharged at Whit-sunday, that we may see what cash we shall have in bank. Our book-keeping may be very simple — an accurate cash-book and ledger is all that is ne-cessary ; and I think I know enough of the matter to assist at making the balance sheet.

" In short, with the assistance of a little cash I have no doubt things will go on *à merveille*. If you could take a little pleasuring, I wish you could come here and see us in all the glories of a Scottish spring. Yours truly,

W. SCOTT."

* A bookseller in Edinburgh.
† A projected edition of the Works of the author of the Seasons.

Scott opened forthwith his gigantic scheme of
the British Poets to Constable, who entered into
it with eagerness. They found presently that Messrs
Cadell and Davies, and some of the other London
publishers, had a similar plan on foot, and after an
unsuccessful negociation with Mackintosh, were now
actually treating with Campbell for the Biographical
prefaces. Scott proposed that the Edinburgh and
London houses should join in the adventure, and
that the editorial task should be shared between
himself and his brother poet. To this both Messrs
Cadell and Mr Campbell warmly assented; but the
design ultimately fell to the ground, in consequence
of the booksellers refusing to admit certain works
which both Scott and Campbell insisted upon. Such,
and from analogous causes, has been the fate of various similar schemes both before and since. But
the public had no trivial compensation upon the
present occasion, since the failure of the original
project led Mr Campbell to prepare for the press
those " Specimens of English Poetry" which he
illustrated with sketches of biography and critical
essays, alike honourable to his learning and taste;
while Scott, Mr Foster ultimately standing off, took
on himself the whole burden of a new edition, as
well as biography, of Dryden. The body of booksellers meanwhile combined in what they still called a
general edition of the English Poets, under the au-

perintendence of one of their own Grub-street vassals, Mr Alexander Chalmers.

Precisely at the time when Scott's poetical ambition had been stimulated by the first outburst of universal applause, and when he was forming those engagements with Ballantyne which involved so large an accession of literary labours, as well as of pecuniary cares and responsibilities, a fresh impetus was given to the volunteer mania in Scotland, by the appointment of the late Earl of Moira (afterwards Marquis of Hastings) to the chief military command in that part of the empire. The Earl had married, the year before, a Scottish Peeress, the Countess of Loudon, and entered with great zeal into her sympathy with the patriotic enthusiasm of her countrymen. Edinburgh was converted into a camp: independently of a large garrison of regular troops, nearly 10,000 fencibles and volunteers were almost constantly under arms. The lawyer wore his uniform under his gown; the shopkeeper measured out his wares in scarlet; in short, the citizens of all classes made more use for several months of the military than of any other dress; and the new commander-in-chief consulted equally his own gratification and theirs, by devising a succession of manœuvres which presented a vivid image of the art of war conducted on a large and scientific scale. In the *sham battles* and *sham sieges* of 1805,

Craigmillar, Gilmerton, Braidhills, and other formidable positions in the neighbourhood of Edinburgh,
were the scenes of many a dashing assault and re-
solute defence; and occasionally the spirits of the
mock combatants — English and Scotch, or Low-
land and Highland—became so much excited that
there was some difficulty in preventing the rough
mockery of warfare from passing into its realities.
The Highlanders, in particular, were very hard to
be dealt with; and once, at least, Lord Moira was
forced to alter at the eleventh hour his programme
of battle, because a battalion of kilted fencibles
could not or would not understand that it was their
duty to be beat.   Such days as these must have
been more nobly spirit - stirring than even the best
specimens of the fox-chase.   To the end of his life,
Scott delighted to recall the details of their coun-
termarches, ambuscades, charges, and pursuits, and
in all of these his associates of the Light-Horse
agree that none figured more advantageously than
himself.   Yet these military interludes seem only to
have whetted his appetite for closet work.   Indeed,
nothing but a complete publication of his letters
could give an adequate notion of the facility with
which he already combined the conscientious magis-
trate, the martinet quartermaster, the speculative
printer, and the ardent lover of literature for its own
sake.   A few specimens must suffice.

To George Ellis, Esq.

"Edinburgh, May 26, 1805.

" My Dear Ellis,

" Your silence has been so long and *opinion-atire*, that I am quite authorized, as a Border ballad-monger, to address you with a — ' Sleep you, or wake you ?' What has become of the " Romances," which I have expected as anxiously as my neighbours around me have watched for the rain, which was to bring the grass, which was to feed the new-calved cows, and to as little purpose, for both Heaven and you have obstinately delayed your favour. After idling away the spring months at Ashestiel, I am just returned to idle away the summer here, and I have lately lighted upon rather an interesting article in your way. If you will turn to Barbour's Bruce (Pinkerton's edition, p. 66), you will find that the Lord of Lorn, seeing Bruce covering the retreat of his followers, compares him to Gow MacMorn (Macpherson's Gaul the son of Morni.) This simi-litude appears to Barbour a disparagement, and he says, the Lord of Lorn might more mannerly have compared the king to Gadefeir de Lawryss, who was with the mighty Duke Betys when he assailed the forayers in Gadderis, and who in the retreat did much execution among the pursuers, overthrowing

Alexander and Thelomier and Danklin, although he
was at length slain; and here, says Barbour, the
resemblance fails. Now, by one of those chances
which favour the antiquary once in an age, a single
copy of the romance alluded to has been discovered,
containing the whole history of this Gadefeir, who
had hitherto been a stumbling-block to the critics.
The book was printed by Arbuthnot, who flourished
at Edinburgh in the seventeenth century. It is a
metrical romance, called ' the Buik of the Most
Noble and Vauliant Conquerour, Alexander the
Grit.' The first part is called the Foray of Gadderis, an incident supposed to have taken place while
Alexander was besieging Tyre; Gadefeir is one of
the principal champions, and after exerting himself
in the manner mentioned by Barbour, unhorsing the
persons whom he named, he is at length slain by
Emynedus, the Earl-Marshal of the Macedonian
conqueror. The second part is called the Avowis
of Alexander, because it introduces the oaths which
he and others made to the peacock in the ' chalmer
of Venus,' and gives an account of the mode in which
they accomplished them. The third is the Great
Battell of Effesoun, in which Porus makes a distinguished figure. This you are to understand is
not *the* Porus of India, but one of his sons. The
work is in decided Scotch, and adds something to
our ancient poetry, being by no means despicable in

point of composition. The author says he translated it from the *Franch*, or *Romance*, and that
he accomplished his work in 1438-9. Barbour must
therefore have quoted from the French Alexander,
and perhaps his praises of the work excited the
Scottish translator. Will you tell me what you
think of all this, and whether any transcripts will
be of use to you? I am pleased with the accident
of its casting up, and hope it may prove the fore-
runner of more discoveries in the dusty and ill-
arranged libraries of our country gentlemen.

" I hope you continue to like the Lay. I have
had a flattering assurance of Mr Fox's approbation,
mixed with a censure of my eulogy on the Vis-
count of Dundee. Although my Tory principles
prevent my coinciding with his political opinions,
I am very proud of his approbation in a literary
sense.

" Charlotte joins me, &c. &c.   W. S."

In his answer, Ellis says — " Longman lately
informed me that you have projected a General
Edition of our Poets. I expressed to him my
anxiety that the booksellers, who certainly can ultimately sell what they please, should for once undertake something calculated to please intelligent
readers, and that they should confine themselves to

the selection of paper, types, &c. (which they possibly may understand), and by no means interfere with the literary part of the business, which, if popularity be the object, they must leave exclusively to you. I am talking, as you perceive, about your plan, without knowing its extent, or any of its details; for these, therefore, I will wait—after confessing that, much as I wish for a *corpus poetarum,* edited as you would edit it, I should like still better another Minstrel Lay by the last and best Minstrel; and the general demand for the poem seems to prove that the public are of my opinion. If, however, you don't feel disposed to take a second ride on Pegasus, why not undertake something far less *infra dig.* than a mere edition of our poets? Why not undertake what Gibbon once undertook — an edition of our historians? I have never been able to look at a volume of the Benedictine edition of the early French historians without envy."

Mr Ellis appears to have communicated all his notions on this subject to Messrs Longman, for Scott writes to Ballantyne (Ashestiel, September 5), "I have had a visit from Rees yesterday. He is anxious about a *corpus historiarum,* or full edition of the Chronicles of England, an immense work. I proposed to him beginning with Holinshed, and I think the work will be secured for your press. I congratulate you on Clarendon, which, under Thomson's direction, will be a glorious publication." [*]

The printing office in the Canongate was by this time in very great request; and the letter I have been quoting contains evidence that the partners had already found it necessary to borrow fresh capital — on the personal security, it need not be added, of Scott himself. He says, " As I have full confidence in your applying the accommodation received from Sir William Forbes in the most convenient and prudent manner, I have no hesitation to return the bonds subscribed as you desire. This will put you in cash for great matters."

But to return. To Ellis himself he says — " I have had booksellers here in the plural number. You have set little Rees's head agog about the Chronicles, which would be an admirable work, but should, I think, be edited by an Englishman who can have access to the MSS. of Oxford and Cambridge, as one cannot trust much to the correctness of printed copies. I will, however, consider the matter, so far as a decent edition of Holinshed is concerned, in case my time is not otherwise taken up. As for the British Poets, my plan was greatly too liberal to stand the least chance of being adopted by the trade at large, as I wished them to begin with Chaucer. The fact

---

[*] An edition of Clarendon had been, it seems, contemplated by Scott's friend, Mr Thomas Thomson.

is, I never expected they would agree to it. The Benedictines had an infinite advantage over us in that *esprit du corps* which led them to set labour and expense at defiance, when the honour of the order was at stake. Would to God your English Universities, with their huge endowments and the number of learned men to whom they give competence and leisure, would but imitate the monks in their literary plans. My present employment is an edition of John Dryden's Works, which is already gone to press. As for riding on Pegasus, depend upon it, I will never again cross him in a serious way, unless I should by some strange accident reside so long in the Highlands, and make myself master of their ancient manners, so as to paint them with some degree of accuracy in a kind of *companion* to the Minstrel Lay. . . . . . . I am interrupted by the arrival of two *gentil bachelors*, whom, like the Count of Artois, I must despatch upon some adventure till dinner time. Thank Heaven, that will not be difficult, for although there are neither dragons nor boars in the vicinity, and men above six feet are not only scarce, but pacific in their habits, yet we have a curious breed of wild-cats who have eaten all Charlotte's chickens, and against whom I have declared a war at *outrance*, in which the assistance of these *gentes demoiseaux* will be fully as valuable as that of Don Quixote to Pentalopin with the naked arm.

So, if Mrs Ellis takes a fancy for cat-skin fur, now
is the time."

Already, then, he was seriously at work on Dryden.   During the same summer, he drew up for the
Edinburgh Review an admirable article on Todd's edition of Spenser; another on Godwin's Fleetwood; a
third, on the Highland Society's Report concerning
the Poems of Ossian; a fourth, on Johnes's Translation of Froissart; a fifth, on Colonel Thornton's
Sporting Tour—and a sixth, on some cookery books
—the two last being excellent specimens of his
humour.   He had, besides, a constant succession of
minor cares in the superintendence of multifarious
works passing through the Ballantyne press.   But
there is yet another important item to be included
in the list of his literary labours of this period.   The
General Preface to his Novels informs us, that
" about 1805" he wrote the opening chapters of
Waverley; and the second title, *'Tis Sixty Years
Since,* selected, as he says, " that the actual date of
publication might correspond with the period in
which the scene was laid," leaves no doubt that he
had begun the work so early in 1805 as to contemplate publishing it before Christmas.*   He adds, in
the same page, that he was induced, by the favour-

* I have ascertained, since this page was written, that a small
part of the MS. of Waverley is on paper bearing the watermark
of 1805—the rest on paper of 1813.

able reception of the Lady of the Lake, to think of
giving some of his recollections of Highland scenery
and customs in prose; but this is only one instance
of the inaccuracy as to matters of date which per-
vades all those delightful Prefaces.   The Lady of
the Lake was not published until five years after the
first chapters of Waverley were written; its success,
therefore, could have had no share in suggesting the
original design of a Highland novel, though no doubt
it principally influenced him to take up that design
after it had been long suspended, and almost forgotten.   Thus early, then, had Scott meditated deeply
such a protraiture of Highland manners as might
" make a sort of companion" to that of the old
Border life in the " Minstrel Lay;" and he had
probably begun and suspended his Waverley, before
he expressed to Ellis his feeling that he ought to
reside for some considerable time in the country to
be delineated, before seriously committing himself in
the execution of such a task.

   " Having proceeded," he says, " as far as I think
the seventh chapter, I showed my work to a critical
friend, whose opinion was unfavourable; and having
then some poetical reputation, I was unwilling to
risk the loss of it by attempting a new style of composition.   I, therefore, then threw aside the work I
had commenced, without either reluctance or remon-
strance.   I ought to add, that though my ingenuous

friend's sentence was afterwards reversed, on an appeal to the public, it cannot be considered as any
imputation on his good taste; for the specimen subjected to his criticism did not extend beyond the
departure of the hero for Scotland, and consequently
had not entered upon the part of the story which
was finally found most interesting." A letter to be
quoted under the year 1810 will, I believe, satisfy
the reader that the first critic of the opening chapters
of Waverley was William Erskine.

The following letter must have been written in
the course of this autumn. It is in every respect a
very interesting one; but I introduce it here as illustrating the course of his reflections on Highland
subjects in general, at the time when the first outlines both of the Lady of the Lake and Waverley
must have been floating about in his mind:—

"To Miss Seward, Lichfield.

" Ashestiel, [1805.]

" My Dear Miss Seward,

" You recall me to some very pleasant feelings
of my boyhood, when you ask my opinion of Ossian.
His works were first put into my hands by old Dr
Blacklock, a blind poet, of whom you may have
heard; he was the worthiest and kindest of human

beings, and particularly delighted in encouraging the
pursuits, and opening the minds, of the young people
by whom he was surrounded.   I, though at the
period of our intimacy a very young boy, was fortunate enough to attract his notice and kindness; and
if I have been at all successful in the paths of literary
pursuit, I am sure I owe much of that success to the
books with which he supplied me, and his own instructions. Ossian and Spencer were two books which
the good old bard put into my hands, and which I
devoured rather than perused. Their tales were for a
long time so much my delight, that I could repeat
without remorse whole Cantos of the one and Duans
of the other; and wo to the unlucky wight who
undertook to be my auditor, for in the height of my
enthusiasm I was apt to disregard all hints that my
recitations became tedious.   It was a natural consequence of progress in taste, that my fondness for these
authors should experience some abatement. Ossian's
poems, in particular, have more charms for youth than
for a more advanced stage.   The eternal repetition
of the same ideas and imagery, however beautiful
in themselves, is apt to pall upon a reader whose
taste has become somewhat fastidious; and, although
I agree entirely with you that the question of their
authenticity ought not to be confounded with that of
their literary merit, yet scepticism on that head takes
away their claim for indulgence as the productions

of a barbarous and remote age; and, what is perhaps
more natural, it destroys that feeling of reality which
we should otherwise combine with our sentiments of
admiration. As for the great dispute, I should be
no Scottishman if I had not very attentively considered it at some period of my studies; and, indeed, I
have gone some lengths in my researches, for I have
beside me translations of some twenty or thirty of
the unquestioned originals of Ossian's poems. After
making every allowance for the disadvantages of a
literal translation, and the possible debasement which
those *now* collected may have suffered in the great
and violent change which the Highlands have under-
gone since the researches of Macpherson, I am compelled to admit that incalculably the greater part of
the English Ossian must be ascribed to Macpherson
himself, and that his whole introductions, notes, &c.
&c. are an absolute tissue of forgeries.

" In all the ballads I ever saw or could hear of,
Fin and Ossin are described as natives of Ireland,
although it is not unusual for the reciters sturdily
to maintain that this is a corruption of the text.
In point of merit, I do not think these Gaelic poems
much better than those of the Scandinavian Scalds;
they are very unequal, often very vigorous and
pointed, often drivelling and crawling in the very
extremity of tenuity. The manners of the heroes
are those of Celtic savages; and I could point out

twenty instances in which Macpherson has very
cunningly adopted the beginning, the names, and
the leading incidents, &c. of an old tale, and dressed.
it up with all those ornaments of sentiment and
sentimental manners, which first excite our surprise,
and afterwards our doubt of its authenticity. The
Highlanders themselves, recognising the leading features of tales they had heard in infancy, with here
and there a tirade really taken from an old poem,
were readily seduced into becoming champions for
the authenticity of the poems. How many people,
not particularly addicted to poetry, who may have
heard Chevy-Chase in the nursery or at school, and
never since met with the ballad, might be imposed
upon by a new Chevy-Chase, bearing no resemblance
to the old one, save in here and there a stanza or
an incident? Besides, there is something in the
severe judgment passed on my countrymen—' that
if they do not prefer Scotland to truth, they will
always prefer it to enquiry.' When once the Highlanders had adopted the poems of Ossian as an article
of national faith, you would far sooner have got them
to disavow the Scripture than to abandon a line of
the contested tales. *Only* they all allow that Macpherson's translation is very unfaithful, and some
pretend to say inferior to the original; by which
they can only mean, if they mean any thing, that
they miss the charms of the rhythm and vernacular

idiom, which pleases the Gaelic natives; for in the real attributes of poetry, Macpherson's version is far superior to any I ever saw of the fragments which he seems to have used.

" The Highland Society have lately set about investigating, or rather, I should say, collecting materials to defend, the authenticity of Ossian. Those researches have only proved that there were no real originals—using that word as is commonly understood—to be found for them. The oldest tale they have found seems to be that of Darthula; but it is perfectly different, both in diction and story, from that of Macpherson. It is, however, a beautiful specimen of Celtic poetry, and shows that it contains much which is worthy of preservation. Indeed how should it be otherwise, when we know that, till about fifty years ago, the Highlands contained a race of hereditary poets? Is it possible to think, that among perhaps many hundreds, who for such a course of centuries have founded their reputation and rank on practising the art of poetry, in a country where the scenery and manners gave such effect and interest and imagery to their productions, there should not have been some who attained excellence? In searching out those genuine records of the Celtic Muse, and preserving them from oblivion, with all the curious information which they must doubtless contain, I humbly think our Highland antiquaries would merit better of their country, than by confining their researches to the fantastic pursuit of a chimera.

" I am not to deny that Macpherson's inferiority in other compositions is a presumption that he did not actually compose these poems. But we are to consider his advantage when on his own ground. Macpherson was a Highlander, and had his imagination fired with the charms of Celtic poetry from his very infancy. We know, from constant experience, that most Highlanders, after they have become complete masters of English, continue to *think* in their own language; and it is to me demonstrable that Macpherson *thought* almost every word of Ossian in Gaelic, although he wrote it down in English. The specimens of his early poetry which remain are also deeply tinged with the peculiarities of the Celtic diction and character; so that, in fact, he might be considered as a Highland poet, even if he had not left us some Earse translations (or originals of Ossian) unquestionably written by himself. These circumstances gave a great advantage to him in forming the style of Ossian, which, though exalted and modified according to Macpherson's own ideas of modern taste, is in great part cut upon the model of the tales of the Sennachies and Bards. In the translation of Homer, he not only lost these advantages, but the circumstances on which they were founded were a great detriment to his undertaking; for al-

though such a dress was appropriate and becoming
for Ossian, few people cared to see their old Grecian
friend disguised in a tartan plaid and philabeg. In
a word, the style which Macpherson had formed,
however admirable in a Highland tale, was not calculated for translating Homer; and it was a great
mistake in him, excited, however, by the general
applause his first work received, to suppose that there
was any thing homogeneous betwixt his own ideas
and those of Homer. Macpherson, in his way, was
certainly a man of high talents, and his poetic powers
as honourable to his country, as the use which he
made of them, and I fear his personal character in
other respects, was a discredit to it.

" Thus I have given you with the utmost sincerity
my creed on the great national question of Ossian;
it has been formed after much deliberation and enquiry. I have had for some time thoughts of writing
a Highland poem, somewhat in the style of the Lay,
giving as far as I can a real picture of what that
enthusiastic race actually were before the destruction
of their patriarchal government. It is true, I have
not quite the same facilities as in describing Border
manners, where I am, as they say, more at home.
But to balance my comparative deficiency in knowledge of Celtic manners, you are to consider that I
have from my youth delighted in all the Highland

traditions which I could pick up from the old Jaco-
bites who used to frequent my father's house; and
this will, I hope, make some amends for my having
less immediate opportunities of research than in the
Border tales.

" Agreeably to your advice, I have actually read
over Madoc a second time, and I confess have seen
much beauty which escaped me in the first perusal.
Yet (which *yet*, by the way, is almost as vile a
monosyllable as *but*) I cannot feel quite the interest
I would wish to do. The difference of character
which you notice, reminds me of what by Ben Jonson and other old comedians were called *humours*,
which consisted rather in the personification of some
individual passion or propensity, than of an actual
individual man. Also, I cannot give up my objection,
that what was strictly true of Columbus becomes
an unpleasant falsehood when told of some one else.
Suppose I was to write a fictitious book of travels,
I should certainly do ill to copy exactly the incidents
which befel Mungo Park or Bruce of Kinnaird.
What was true of them would incontestably prove
at once the falsehood and plagiarism of my supposed
journal. It is not but what the incidents are natural
—but it is their having already happened, which
strikes us when they are transferred to imaginary
persons. Could any one bear the story of a second
city being taken by a wooden horse?

" Believe me, I shall not be within many miles of
Lichfield without paying my personal respects to
you ; and yet I should not do it in prudence, because
I am afraid you have formed a higher opinion of me
than I deserve : you would expect to see a person
who had dedicated himself much to literary pursuits,
and you would find me a rattle-sculled half-lawyer,
half-sportsman, through whose head a regiment of
horse has been exercising since he was five years
old ; half-educated — half-crazy, as his friends sometimes tell him ; half every thing, but *entirely* Miss
Seward's much obliged, affectionate, and faithful
servant,   WALTER SCOTT."

His correspondence shows how largely he was
exerting himself all this while in the service of
authors less fortunate than himself.   James Hogg,
among others, continued to occupy from time to time
his attention ; and he assisted regularly and assiduously throughout this and the succeeding year Mr
Robert Jameson, an industrious and intelligent antiquary, who had engaged in editing a collection of
ancient popular ballads before the third volume of
the Minstrelsy appeared, and who at length published
his very curious work in 1807.   Meantime, Ashestiel,
in place of being less resorted to by literary strangers
than Lasswade cottage had been, shared abundantly
in the fresh attractions of the Lay, and " booksellers

in the plural number" were preceded and followed by
an endless variety of enthusiastic " gentil bachelors,"
whose main temptation from the south had been the
hope of seeing the Borders in company with their
Minstrel. He still writes of himself as " idling
away his hours;" he had already learned to appear
as if he were doing so to all who had no particular
right to confidence respecting the details of his
privacy.

But the most agreeable of all his visitants were
his own old familiar friends, and one of these has
furnished me with a sketch of the autumn life of
Ashestiel, of which I shall now avail myself.   Scott's
invitation was in these terms :—

" *To James Skene, Esq. of Rubislaw.*

" Ashestiel, 16th August 1805.

" Dear Skene,

" I have prepared another edition of the Lay,
1500 strong, moved thereunto by the faith, hope, and
charity of the London booksellers. . . . . . . If you
could, in the interim, find a moment to spend here,
you know the way, and the ford is where it was;
which, by the way, is more than I expected after
Saturday last, the most dreadful storm of thunder
and lightning I ever witnessed. The lightning broke

repeatedly in our immediate vicinity, *i. e.* betwixt us
and the Peel wood. Charlotte resolved to die in bed
like a good Christian. The servants said it was the
preface to the end of the world, and I was the only
person that maintained my character for stoicism,
which I assure you had some merit, as I had no
doubt that we were in real danger. It was accompanied with a flood so tremendous, that I would have
given five pounds you had been here to make a
sketch of it. The little Glenkinnon brook was im-
passable for all the next day, and indeed I have been
obliged to send all hands to repair the ford, which
was converted into a deep pool. Believe me ever
yours affectionately, W. S."

Mr Skene says — " I well remember the ravages of
the storm and flood described in this letter. The
ford of Ashestiel was never a good one, and for some
time after this it remained not a little perilous. He
was himself the first to attempt the passage on his
favourite black horse *Captain*, who had scarcely
entered the river when he plunged beyond his depth,
and had to swim to the other side with his burden.
It requires a good horseman to swim a deep and
rapid stream, but he trusted to the vigour of his
steady trooper, and in spite of his lameness kept his
seat manfully. A cart bringing a new kitchen *range*
(as I believe the grate for that service is technically

called) was shortly after upset in this ugly ford.
The horse and cart were with difficulty got out, but
the grate remained for some time in the middle of
the stream to do duty as a horse-trap, and furnish
subject for many a good joke when Mrs Scott happened to complain of the imperfection of her kitchen
appointments."

Mr Skene soon discovered an important change
which had recently been made in his friend's distribution of his time.   Previously it had been his custom,
whenever professional business or social engagements
occupied the middle part of his day, to seize some
hours for study after he was supposed to have retired
to bed.   His physician suggested that this was very
likely to aggravate his nervous headaches, the only
malady he was subject to in the prime of his manhood ; and, contemplating with steady eye a course
not only of unremitting but of increasing industry,
he resolved to reverse his plan, and carried his purpose into execution with unflinching energy.   In
short, he had now adopted the habits in which, with
very slender variation, he ever after persevered when
in the country.   He rose by five o'clock, lit his own
fire when the season required one, and shaved and
dressed with great deliberation—for he was a very
martinet as to all but the mere coxcombries of the
toilet, not abhorring effeminate dandyism itself so
cordially as the slightest approach to personal sloven-

liness, or even those " bed-gown and slipper tricks,"
as he called them, in which literary men are so apt
to indulge. Arrayed in his shooting-jacket, or whatever dress he meant to use till dinner time, he was
seated at his desk by six o'clock, all his papers arranged before him in the most accurate order, and
his books of reference marshalled around him on the
floor, while at least one favourite dog lay watching
his eye, just beyond the line of circumvallation.
Thus, by the time the family assembled for breakfast
between nine and ten, he had done enough (in his
own language) " *to break the neck of the day's
work.*" After breakfast, a couple of hours more
were given to his solitary tasks, and by noon he was,
as he used to say, " his own man." When the
weather was bad, he would labour incessantly all the
morning; but the general rule was to be out and
on horseback by one o'clock at the latest; while, if
any more distant excursion had been proposed over
night, he was ready to start on it by ten; his occasional rainy days of unintermitted study forming, as
he said, a fund in his favour, out of which he was
entitled to draw for accommodation whenever the sun
shone with special brightness.

It was another rule, that every letter he received
should be answered that same day. Nothing else
could have enabled him to keep abreast with the
flood of communications that in the sequel put his

good nature to the severest test—but already the
demands on him in this way also were numerous;
and he included attention to them among the necessary business which must be despatched before he
had a right to close his writing-box, or as he phrased
it, " to say, *out damned spot*, and be a gentleman."
In turning over his enormous mass of correspondence,
I have almost invariably found some indication that,
when a letter had remained more than a day or two
unanswered, it had been so because he found occasion
for enquiry or deliberate consideration.

I ought not to omit, that in those days Scott was
far too zealous a dragoon not to take a principal
share in the stable duty.   Before beginning his desk-
work in the morning, he uniformly visited his favourite steed, and neither *Captain* nor *Lieutenant*, nor
the Lieutenant's successor, *Brown Adam* (so called
after one of the heroes of the Minstrelsy), liked to be
fed except by him.   The latter charger was indeed
altogether intractable in other hands, though in his
the most submissive of faithful allies.   The moment
he was bridled and saddled, it was the custom to open
the stable door as a signal that his master expected
him, when he immediately trotted to the side of the
leaping-on-stone, of which Scott from his lameness
found it convenient to make use, and stood there,
silent and motionless as a rock, until he was fairly in
his seat, after which he displayed his joy by neighing

triumphantly through a brilliant succession of cur-
vettings. Brown Adam never suffered himself to be
backed but by his master. He broke, I believe, one
groom's arm and another's leg in the rash attempt to
tamper with his dignity.

Camp was at this time the constant parlour dog.
He was very handsome, very intelligent, and naturally ·very fierce, but gentle as a lamb among the
children. As for the more locomotive Douglas and
Percy, he kept one window of his study open, whatever might be the state of the weather, that they
might leap out and in as the fancy moved them. He
always talked to Camp as if he understood what was
said — and the animal certainly did understand not a
little of it; in particular, it seemed as if he perfectly
comprehended on all occasions that his master considered him as a sensible and steady friend, the greyhounds as volatile young creatures whose freaks
must be borne with.

"Every day," says Mr Skene, "we had some
hours of coursing with the greyhounds, or riding at
random over the hills, or of spearing salmon in the
Tweed by sunlight: which last sport, moreover, we
often renewed at night by the help of torches. This
amusement of *burning the water*, as it is called, was
not without some hazard, for the large salmon generally lie in the pools, the depths of which it is not
easy to estimate with precision by torchlight, — so

that not unfrequently, when the sportsman makes a
determined thrust at a fish apparently within reach,
his eye has grossly deceived him, and instead of the
point of the weapon encountering the prey, he finds
himself launched with corresponding vehemence heels
over head into the pool, both spear and salmon gone,
the torch thrown out by the concussion of the boat,
and quenched in the stream, while the boat itself has
of course receded to some distance.   I remember the
first time I accompanied our friend, he went right
over the gunwale in this manner, and had I not ac-
cidentally been close at his side, and made a successful
grasp at the skirt of his jacket as he plunged over-
board, he must at least have had an awkward dive
for it.   Such are the contingencies of *burning the
water.*   The pleasures consist in being penetrated
with cold and wet, having your shins broken against
the stones in the dark, and perhaps mastering one
fish out of every twenty you take aim at."

In all these amusements, but particularly in the
burning of the water, Scott's most regular companion at this time was John Lord Somerville, who
united with many higher qualities a most enthusiastic
love for such sports, and consummate address in the
prosecution of them.   This amiable nobleman then
passed his autumns at his pretty seat of Alwyn, or
the Pavilion, situated on the Tweed, some eight
or nine miles below Ashestiel.   They interchanged

visits almost every week ; and Scott did not fail to
profit largely by his friend's matured and well-known
skill in every department of the science of rural
economy.   He always talked of him, in particular,
as his master in the art of planting.

The laird of Rubislaw seldom failed to spend a
part of the summer and autumn at Ashestiel, as long
as Scott remained there, and during these visits they
often gave a wider scope to their expeditions.   " Indeed," says Mr Skene, " there are few scenes at all
celebrated either in the history, tradition, or romance
of the Border counties, which we did not explore
together in the course of our rambles.   We traversed
the entire vales of the Yarrow and Ettrick, with all
their sweet tributary glens, and never failed to find
a hearty welcome from the farmers at whose houses
we stopped, either for dinner or for the night.   He
was their chief-magistrate, extremely popular in that
official capacity, and nothing could be more gratify-
ing than the frank and hearty reception which every-
where greeted our arrival, however unexpected. —
The exhilarating air of the mountains, and the
healthy exercise of the day, secured our relishing
homely fare, and we found inexhaustible entertainment in the varied display of character which the
affability of *the Sheriff* drew forth on all occasions
in genuine breadth and purity.   The beauty of the
scenery gave full employment to my pencil, with the

free and frequent exercise of which he never seemed
to feel impatient. He was at all times ready and
willing to alight when any object attracted my notice,
and used to seat himself beside me on the brae, to
con over some ballad appropriate to the occasion, or
narrate the tradition of the glen — sometimes, perhaps, to note a passing idea in his pocket-book ; but
this was rare, for in general he relied with confidence
on the great storehouse of his memory. And much
amusement we had, as you may suppose, in talking
over the different incidents, conversations, and traits
of manners that had occurred at the last hospitable
fireside where we had mingled with the natives.
Thus the minutes glided away until my sketch was
complete, and then we mounted again with fresh
alacrity.

    " These excursions derived an additional zest from
the uncertainty that often attended the issue of our
proceedings ; for, following the game started by the
dogs, our unfailing comrades, we frequently got entangled and bewildered among the hills, until we had
to trust to mere chance for the lodging of the night.
Adventures of this sort were quite to his taste, and
the more for the perplexities which on such occasions befell our attendant squires — mine a lanky
Savoyard, his a portly Scotch butler — both of them
uncommonly bad horsemen, and both equally sensi-
tive about their personal dignity, which the rugged-

ness of the ground often made it a matter of some
difficulty for either of them to maintain, but more
especially for my poor foreigner, whose seat re-
sembled that of a pair of compasses astride. Scott's
heavy lumbering *beauffetier* had provided himself
against the mountain showers with a huge cloak,
which, when the cavalcade were at gallop, streamed
at full stretch from his shoulders, and kept flapping
in the other's face, who, having more than enough
to do in preserving his own equilibrium, could not
think of attempting at any time to control the pace
of his steed, and had no relief but fuming and *pest-
ing* at the *sacré manteau*, in language happily un-
intelligible to its wearer. Now and then some ditch
or turf-fence rendered it indispensable to adventure on
a leap, and no farce could have been more amusing
than the display of politeness which then occurred
between these worthy equestrians, each courteously
declining in favour of his friend the honour of the
first experiment, the horses fretting impatient beneath them, and the dogs clamouring encouragement.
The horses generally terminated the dispute by re-
nouncing allegiance, and springing forward without
waiting the pleasure of the riders, who had to settle
the matter with their saddles as they best could.

" One of our earliest expeditions was to visit the
wild scenery of the mountainous tract above Mof-
fat, including the cascade of the Grey Mare's Tail,

and the dark tarn called Loch Skene. In our
ascent to the lake we got completely bewildered in
the thick fog which generally envelopes the rugged
features of that lonely region; and, as we were
groping through the maze of bogs, the ground gave
way, and down went horse and horsemen pell-mell
into a slough of peaty mud and black water, out of
which, entangled as we were with our plaids and
floundering nags, it was no easy matter to get
extricated. Indeed, unless we had prudently left
our gallant steeds at a farm-house below, and borrowed hill ponies for the occasion, the result might
have been worse than laughable. As it was, we rose
like the spirits of the bog, covered *cap-à-pie* with
slime, to free themselves from which, our wily ponies
took to rolling about on the heather, and we had
nothing for it but following their example. At
length, as we approached the gloomy loch, a huge
eagle heaved himself from the margin and rose right
over us, screaming his scorn of the intruders; and
altogether it would be impossible to picture any
thing more desolately savage than the scene which
opened, as if raised by enchantment on purpose to
gratify the poet's eye; thick folds of fog rolling
incessantly over the face of the inky waters, but
rent asunder now in one direction, and then in
another — so as to afford us a glimpse of some
projecting rock or naked point of land, or island

bearing a few scraggy stumps of pine—and then
closing again in universal darkness upon the cheer-
less waste. Much of the scenery of Old Mortality
was drawn from that day's ride.

" It was also in the course of this excursion that
we encountered that amusing personage introduced
into Guy Mannering as ' Tod Gabbie,' though the
appellation by which he was known in the neighbourhood was ' Tod Willie.' He was one of those
itinerants who gain a subsistence among the moor-
land farmers by relieving them of foxes, polecats,
and the like depredators—a half-witted, stuttering,
and most original creature.

" Having explored all the wonders of Moffatdale,
we turned ourselves towards *Blackhouse Tower*, to
visit Scott's worthy acquaintances the Laidlaws, and
reached it after a long and intricate ride, having
been again led off our course by the greyhounds,
who had been seduced by a strange dog that joined
company, to engage in full pursuit upon the tract of
what we presumed to be either a fox or a roe-deer.
The chase was protracted and perplexing, from the
mist that skirted the hill tops; but at length we
reached the scene of slaughter, and were much dis-
tressed to find that a stately old he-goat had been
the victim. He seemed to have fought a stout
battle for his life, but now lay mangled in the midst
of his panting enemies, who betrayed, on our ap-

proach, strong consciousness of delinquency and apprehension of the lash, which was administered accordingly to soothe the manes of the luckless Capricorn — though, after all, the dogs were not so much to blame in mistaking his game flavour, since the fogs must have kept him out of view till the last moment. Our visit to Blackhouse was highly interesting; — the excellent old tenant being still in life, and the whole family group presenting a perfect picture of innocent and simple happiness, while the animated, intelligent, and original conversation of our friend William was quite charming.

" Sir Adam Fergusson and the Ettrick Shepherd were of the party that explored Loch Skene and hunted the unfortunate he-goat.

" I need not tell you that Saint Mary's Loch, and the Loch of the Lowes, were among the most favourite scenes of our excursions, as his fondness for them continued to his last days, and we have both visited them many times together in his company. I may say the same of the Teviot and the Aill, Borthwick-water, and the lonely towers of Buccleuch and Harden, Minto, Roxburgh, Gilnockie, &c. I think it was either in 1805 or 1806 that I first explored the Borthwick with him, when on our way to pass a week at Langholm with Lord and Lady Dalkeith, upon which occasion the otter-hunt, so well described in Guy Mannering, was got

up by our noble host; and I can never forget the
delight with which Scott observed the enthusiasm
of the high-spirited yeomen, who had assembled in
multitudes to partake the sport of their dear young
chief, well mounted, and dashing about from rock
to rock with a reckless ardour which recalled the
alacrity of their forefathers in following the Buc-
cleuchs of former days through adventures of a more
serious order.

" Whatever the banks of the Tweed, from its
source to its termination, presented of interest, we
frequently visited; and I do verily believe there is
not a single ford in the whole course of that river
which we have not traversed together. He had an
amazing fondness for fords, and was not a little adventurous in plunging through, whatever might be
the state of the flood, and this even though there
happened to be a bridge in view. If it seemed possible to scramble through, he scorned to go ten
yards about, and in fact preferred the ford; and it
is to be remarked, that most of the heroes of his
tales seem to have been endued with similar propensities—even the White Lady of Avenel delights in
the ford. He sometimes even attempted them on
foot, though his lameness interfered considerably
with his progress among the slippery stones. Upon
one occasion of this sort I was assisting him through
the Ettrick, and we had both got upon the same

tottering stone in the middle of the stream, when
some story about a *kelpie* occurring to him, he must
needs stop and tell it with all his usual vivacity —
and then laughing heartily at his own joke, he
slipped his foot, or the stone shuffled beneath him,
and down he went headlong into the pool, pulling
me after him.   We escaped, however, with no worse
than a thorough drenching and the loss of his stick,
which floated down the river, and he was as ready
as ever for a similar exploit before his clothes were
half dried upon his back."

About this time Mr and Mrs Scott made a short
excursion to the Lakes of Cumberland and Westmoreland, and visited some of their finest scenery,
in company with Mr Wordsworth.   I have found
no written narrative of this little tour, but I have
often heard Scott speak with enthusiastic delight of
the reception he met with in the humble cottage
which his brother poet then inhabited on the banks
of Gasmere; and at least one of the days they
spent together was destined to furnish a theme for
the verse of each, namely, that which they gave to
the ascent of Helvellyn, where, in the course of the
preceding spring, a young gentleman having lost his
way and perished by falling over a precipice, his
remains were discovered, three months afterwards,
still watched by " a faithful terrier-bitch, his constant attendant during frequent rambles among the

wilds." * This day they were accompanied by an
illustrious philosopher, who was also a true poet —
and might have been one of the greatest of poets
had he chosen; and I have heard Mr Wordsworth
say, that it would be difficult to express the feelings
with which he, who so often had climbed Helvellyn
alone, found himself standing on its summit with
two such men as Scott and Davy.

After leaving Mr Wordsworth, Scott carried his
wife to spend a few days at Gilsland, among the
scenes where they had first met; and his reception
by the company at the wells was such as to make
him look back with something of regret, as well as
of satisfaction, to the change that had occurred in
his circumstances since 1797. They were, however,
enjoying themselves much there, when he received
intelligence which induced him to believe that a
French force was about to land in Scotland: — the
alarm indeed had spread far and wide; and a mighty
gathering of volunteers, horse and foot, from the
Lothians and the Border country, took place in con-

---

* See notice prefixed to the song —

  " I climbed the dark brow of the mighty Helvellyn," &c.
in Scott's *Poetical Works*, edit. 1834, vol. vi. p. 370; and compare the lines —

> " Inmate of a mountain dwelling,
> Thou hast clomb aloft, and gazed
> From the watch-towers of Helvellyn,
> Awed, delighted, and amazed," &c.

Wordsworth's *Poetical Works*, 8vo. edit. vol. III. p. 96.

sequence at Dalkeith.   He was not slow to obey the
summons.   He had luckily chosen to accompany on
horseback the carriage in which Mrs Scott travelled.
His good steed carried him to the spot of rendezvous,
full a hundred miles from Gilsland, within twenty-
four hours; and on reaching it, though, no doubt to
his disappointment, the alarm had already blown over,
he was delighted with the general enthusiasm that
had thus been put to the test — and, above all, by
the rapidity with which the yeomen of Ettrick forest
had poured down from their glens, under the guidance of his good friend and neighbour, Mr Pringle
of Torwoodlee.   These fine fellows were quartered
along with the Edinburgh troop when he reached
Dalkeith and Musselburgh; and after some sham
battling, and a few evenings of high jollity, had
crowned the needless muster of the beacon fires,*
he immediately turned his horse again towards the
south, and rejoined Mrs Scott at Carlisle.

By the way, it was during his fiery ride from
Gilsland to Dalkeith, on the occasion above mentioned, that he composed his Bard's Incantation,
first published six years afterwards in the Edinburgh
Annual Register : —

      " The forest of Glenmore is drear,
        It is all of black pine and the dark oak tree," &c.—

  ───────────────

  * See Note " Alarm of Invasion," Antiquary, vol. ii. p. 338.

and the verses bear the full stamp of the feelings of the moment.

Shortly after he was re-established at Ashestiel, he was visited there by Mr Southey; this being, I believe, their first meeting. It is alluded to in the following letter—a letter highly characteristic in more respects than one: —

" *To George Ellis, Esq., Sunninghill.*

" Ashestiel, 17th October 1805.

" Dear Ellis,

" More than a month has glided away in this busy solitude, and yet I have never sat down to answer your kind letter. I have only to plead a horror of pen and ink with which this country, in fine weather (and ours has been most beautiful) regularly affects me. In recompense, I ride, walk, fish, course, eat and drink, with might and main from morning to night. I could have wished sincerely you had come to Reged this year to partake her rural amusements;—the only comfort I have is, that your visit would have been over, and now I look forward to it as to a pleasure to come. I shall be infinitely obliged to you for your advice and assistance in the course of Dryden. I fear little can be procured for a Life beyond what Malone has compiled, but certainly his facts may be rather better told and arranged. I am at present busy with the dramatic department. This undertaking will make my being in London in spring a matter of absolute necessity.

" And now let me tell you of a discovery which I have made, or rather which Robert Jameson has made, in copying the MS. of ' True Thomas and the Queen of Elfland,' in the Lincoln cathedral. The queen at parting, bestows the gifts of harping and carping upon the prophet, and mark his reply —

> ' To harp and carp, Tomas, where so ever ye gen —
> Thomas take thou these with thee.'—
> ' Harping,' he said, ' ken I nine,
> For Tong is chefe of mynstrelsie.'

If poor Ritson could contradict his own system of materialism by rising from the grave to peep into this MS., he would slink back again in dudgeon and dismay. There certainly cannot be more respectable testimony than that of True Thomas, and you see he describes the tongue, or recitation, as the principal, or at least the most dignified, part of a minstrel's profession.

" Another curiosity was brought here a few days ago by Mr Southey the poet, who favoured me with a visit on his way to Edinburgh. It was a MS. containing sundry metrical romances, and other poetical compositions, in the northern dialect, apparently written about the middle of the 15th century. I had not time to make an analysis of its contents, but some of them seem highly valuable. There is a tale of Sir Gowther, said to be a Breton Lay, which partly resembles the history of Robert the Devil, the hero being begot in the same way; and partly that of Robert of Sicily, the penance imposed on Sir Gowther being the same, as he kept table with the hounds, and was discovered by a dumb lady to be the stranger knight who had assisted her father the emperor in his wars. There is also a MS. of Sir Isunbras; *item* a poem called Sir Amadas — not Amadis of Gaul, but a courteous knight, who, being reduced to poverty, travels to conceal his distress, and gives the wreck of his fortune to purchase the rites of burial for a deceased knight, who had been refused them by the obduracy of his creditors. The rest of the story is the same with that of Jean de Calais, in the Bibliothèque Bleue, and with a vulgar ballad called the Factor's Garland. Moreover there is a merry tale of hunting a hare, as performed by a set of country clowns, with their mastiffs, and curs with ' short legs and never a tail.' The disgraces and blunders of these ignorant sportsmen must have afforded infinite mirth at the table of a feudal baron, prizing himself on his knowledge of the mysteries of the chase performed by these unauthorized intruders.

There is also a burlesque sermon, which informs us
of Peter and Adam journeying together to Babylon,
and how Peter asked Adam *a full great doubtful
question*, saying, ' Adam, Adam, why didst thou eat
the apple unpared ?' This book belongs to a lady. I
would have given something valuable to have had a
week of it. Southey commissioned me to say that
he intended to take extracts from it, and should be
happy to copy, or cause to be copied, any part that
you might wish to be possessed of ; an offer which I
heartily recommend to your early consideration.
Where dwelleth Heber the magnificent, whose library
and cellar* are so superior to all others in the world ?
I wish to write to him about Dryden.   Any word
lately from Jamaica ?   Yours truly,   W. S."

Mr Ellis, in his answer, says — " Heber will, I dare
say, be of service to you in your present undertaking,
if indeed you want any assistance, which I very
much doubt ; because it appears to me that the best
edition which could now be given of Dryden, would be
one which should unite accuracy of text and a handsome appearance, with good critical notes. *Quoad*
Malone, — I should think Ritson himself, could he
rise from the dead, would be puzzled to sift out a

* Ellis had mentioned, in a recent letter, Heber's buying wines
to the value of £1100 at some sale he happened to attend this
autumn.

single additional anecdote of the poet's life; but to
abridge Malone,—and to render his narrative terse,
elegant, and intelligible,—would be a great obligation conferred on the purchasers (I will not say the
readers, because I have doubts whether they exist in
the plural number) of his very laborious compilation.
The late Dr Warton, you may have heard, had a
project of editing Dryden à la Hurd; that is to say,
upon the same principle as the castrated edition of
Cowley. His reason was, that Dryden, having written for bread, became of necessity a most voluminous
author, and poured forth more nonsense of indecency, particularly in his theatrical compositions,
than almost any scribbler in that scribbling age.
Hence, although his transcendent genius frequently
breaks out, and marks the hand of the master, his
comedies seem, by a tacit but general consent, to
have been condemned to oblivion ; and his tragedies,
being printed in such bad company, have shared the
same fate. But Dr W. conceived that, by a judicious selection of these, together with his fables and
prose works, it would be possible to exhibit him in
a much more advantageous light than by a republi-
cation of the whole mass of his writings. Whether
the Doctor (who, by the way, was by no means
scrupulously chaste and delicate, as you will be aware
from his edition of Pope) had taken a just view of
the subject, you know better than I ; but I must

own that the announcement of a *general* edition of Dryden gave me some little alarm.   However, if you can suggest the sort of assistance you are desirous of receiving, I shall be happy to do what I can to promote your views. . . . . . And so you are not disposed to *nibble* at the bait I throw out! Nothing but ' a decent edition of Holinshed'? I confess that my project chiefly related to the later historical works respecting this country — to the union of Gall, Twisden, Camden, Leibnitz, &c. &c. leaving the Chronicles, properly so called, to shift for themselves. . . . . . . I am ignorant when you are to be in Edinburgh, and in that ignorance have not desired Blackburn, who is now at Glasgow, to call on you.   He has the best practical understanding I have ever met with, and I vouch that you would be much pleased with his acquaintance.   And so for the present God bless you.   G. E."

Scott's letter in reply opens thus: — " I will not castrate John Dryden.   I would as soon castrate my own father, as I believe Jupiter did of yore.   What would you say to any man who would castrate Shakspeare, or Massinger, or Beaumont and Fletcher? I don't say but that it may be very proper to select correct passages for the use of boarding schools and colleges, being sensible no improper ideas can be suggested in these seminaries, unless they are intruded or smuggled under the beards and ruffs of our old dramatists. But in making an edition of a man of genius's works for libraries and collections, and such I conceive a complete edition of Dryden to be, I must give my author as I find him, and will not tear out the page, even to get rid of the blot, little as I like it. Are not the pages of Swift, and even of Pope, larded with indecency, and often of the most disgusting kind, and do we not see them upon all shelves and dressing-tables, and in all boudoirs? Is not Prior the most indecent of tale tellers, not even excepting La Fontaine, and how often do we see his works in female hands? In fact, it is not passages of ludicrous indelicacy that corrupt the manners of a people — it is the sonnets which a prurient genius like Master Little sings *virginibus puerisque* — it is the sentimental slang, half lewd, half methodistic, that debauches the understanding, inflames the sleeping passions, and prepares the reader to give way as soon as a tempter appears. At the same time, I am not at all happy when I peruse some of Dryden's comedies: they are very stupid, as well as indelicate; sometimes, however, there is a considerable vein of liveliness and humour, and all of them present extraordinary pictures of the age in which he lived. My critical notes will not be very numerous, but I hope to illustrate the political poems, as Absalom and Achitophel, the Hind and Panther, &c. with some curious annotations. I have already made a complete search among some hundred pamphlets of that pamphlet-writing age, and with considerable success, as I have found several which throw light on my author. I am told that I am to be formidably opposed by Mr Crowe, the Professor of Poetry at Oxford, who is also threatening an edition of Dryden. I don't know whether to be most vexed that some one had not undertaken the task sooner, or that Mr Crowe is disposed to attempt it at the same time with me;—however, I now stand committed, and will not be *crowed* over, if I can help it. The third edition of the Lay is now in the press, of which I hope you will accept a copy, as it contains some trifling improvements or additions. They are, however, very trifling.

" I have written a long letter to Rees, recommending an edition of our historians, both Latin and English; but I have great hesitation whether to undertake much of it myself. What I can I certainly will do; but I should feel particularly delighted if you would join forces with me, when I think we might do the business to purpose. Do, Lord love you, think of this *grande opus.*

" I have not been so fortunate as to hear of Mr Blackburn. I am afraid poor Daniel has been very idly employed — *Cælum non animum.* I am glad you still retain the purpose of visiting Reged. If

you live on mutton and game, we can feast you; for,
as one wittily said, I am not the hare with many
friends, but the friend with many hares.—W. S."

Mr Ellis, in his next letter, says — " I will not
disturb you by contesting any part of your ingenious
apology for your intended *complete* edition of Dryden, whose genius I venerate as much as you do, and
whose negligences, as he was not rich enough to
doom them to oblivion in his own lifetime, it is perhaps incumbent on his editor to transmit to the latest
posterity.   Most certainly I am not so squeamish as
to quarrel with him for his immodesty on any moral
pretence.   Licentiousness in writing, when accompanied by wit, as in the case of Prior, La Fontaine,
&c., is never likely to excite any *passion*, because
every passion is serious; and the grave epistle of
Eloisa is more likely to do moral mischief and convey infection to love-sick damsels, than five hundred
stories of Hans Carvel and Paulo Purgante; but
whatever is in point of expression vulgar—whatever
disgusts the taste—whatever might have been written by any fool, and is therefore unworthy of Dryden
— whatever might have been suppressed, without
exciting a moment's regret in the mind of any of his
admirers—*ought*, in my opinion, to be suppressed by
any editor who should be disposed to make an appeal
to the public taste upon the subject; because a man

who was perhaps the best poet and best prose writer
in the language——but it is foolish to say so much,
after promising to say nothing. Indeed I own *myself*
guilty of possessing all his works in a very indifferent
edition, and I shall certainly purchase a better one
whenever you put it in my power. With regard to
your competitors, I feel perfectly at my ease, because
I am convinced that though you should generously
furnish them with all the materials, they would not
know how to use them: *non cuivis hominum con-
tingit* to write critical notes that any one will read."
Alluding to the regret which Scott had expressed
some time before at the shortness of his visit to the
libraries of Oxford, Ellis says, in another of these
letters:— " A library is like a butcher's shop: it
contains plenty of meat, but it is all raw; no person
living (Leyden's breakfast was only a *tour de force*
to astonish Ritson, and I except the Abyssinians,
whom I never saw) can find a meal in it, till some
good cook (suppose yourself) comes in and says, ' Sir,
I see by your looks that you are hungry; I know
your taste—be patient for a moment, and you shall
be satisfied that you have an excellent appetite.'"

I shall not transcribe the mass of letters which
Scott received from various other literary friends
whose assistance he invoked in the preparation of
his edition of Dryden; but among them there occurs one so admirable, that I cannot refuse myself

the pleasure of introducing it, more especially as the
views which it opens harmonize as remarkably with
some, as they differ from others, of those which Scott
himself ultimately expressed respecting the poetical
character of his illustrious author : —

" My Dear Scott,

  . . " I was much pleased to hear of your engagement with Dryden : not that he is, as a poet,
any great favourite of mine : I admire his talents
and genius highly, but his is not a poetical genius.
The only qualities I can find in Dryden that are
essentially poetical, are a certain ardour and impe-
tuosity of mind, with an excellent ear. It may seem
strange that I do not add to this, great command of
language : *That* he certainly has, and of such language, too, as it is most desirable that a poet should
possess, or rather that he should not be without.
But it is not language that is, in the highest sense of
the word, poetical, being neither of the imagination
nor of the passions ; I mean the amiable, the en-
nobling, or the intense passions. I do not mean to
say that there is nothing of this in Dryden, but as
little, I think, as is possible, considering how much
he has written. You will easily understand my meaning, when I refer to his versification of Palamon and
Arcite, as contrasted with the language of Chaucer.

Dryden had neither a tender heart nor a lofty sense of moral dignity. Whenever his language is poetically impassioned, it is mostly upon unpleasing subjects, such as the follies, vices, and crimes of classes of men or of individuals. That his cannot be the language of imagination, must have necessarily followed from this,—that there is not a single image from nature in the whole body of his works; and in his translation from Virgil, wherever Virgil can be fairly said to have his *eye* upon his object, Dryden always spoils the passage.

" But too much of this; I am glad that you are to be his editor. His political and satirical pieces may be greatly benefited by illustration, and even absolutely require it. A correct text is the first object of an editor—then such notes as explain difficult or obscure passages; and lastly, which is much less important, notes pointing out authors to whom the poet has been indebted, not in the fiddling way of phrase here and phrase there—(which is detestable as a general practice)—but where he has had essential obligations either as to matter or manner.

" If I can be of any use to you, do not fail to apply to me. One thing I may take the liberty to suggest, which is, when you come to the fables, might it not be advisable to print the whole of the tales of Boccace in a smaller type in the original language? If this should look too much like swelling a book, I should certainly make such extracts as would show where Dryden has most strikingly improved upon, or fallen below, his original. I think his translations from Boccace are the best, at least the most poetical, of his poems. It is many years since I saw Boccace, but I remember that Sigismunda is not married by him to Guiscard — (the names are different in Boccace in both tales, I believe — certainly in Theodore, &c.) I think Dryden has much injured the story by the marriage, and degraded Sigismunda's character by it. He has also, to the best of my remembrance, degraded her still more by making her love absolute sensuality and appetite; Dryden had no other notion of the passion. With all these defects, and they are very gross ones, it is a noble poem. Guiscard's answer, when first reproached by Tancred, is noble in Boccace — nothing but this: *Amor può molto più che ne voi ne io possiamo.* This, Dryden has spoiled. He says first very well, ' the faults of love by love are justified,' and then come four lines of miserable rant, quite *à la Maximin.* Farewell, and believe me ever your affectionate friend,

WILLIAM WORDSWORTH."

CHAPTER XV.

*Affair of the Clerkship of Session — Letters to
Ellis and Lord Dalkeith — Visit to London —
Earl Spencer and Mr Fox — Caroline, Prin-
cess of Wales — Joanna Baillie — Appointment
as Clerk of Session — Lord Melville's Trial —
Song on his Acquittal.*

1806.

WHILE the first volumes of his Dryden were passing
through the press, the affair concerning the Clerkship
of the Court of Session, opened nine or ten months
before, had not been neglected by the friends on
whose counsel and assistance Scott had relied.   In
one of his Prefaces of 1830, he briefly tells the issue
of this negotiation, which he justly describes as "an
important circumstance in his life, of a nature to
relieve him from the anxiety which he must other-

wise have felt as one upon the precarious tenure of
whose own life rested the principal prospects of his
family, and especially as one who had necessarily
some dependence on the proverbially capricious favour of the public." Whether Mr Pitt's hint to Mr
William Dundas, that he would willingly find an
opportunity to promote the interests of the author of
the Lay, or some conversation between the Duke of
Buccleuch and Lord Melville, first encouraged him
to this direction of his views, I am not able to state
distinctly; but I believe that the desire to see his
fortunes placed on some more substantial basis, was
at this time partaken pretty equally by the three
persons who had the principal influence in the distribution of the crown patronage in Scotland; and
as his object was rather to secure a future than an
immediate increase of official income, it was comparatively easy to make such an arrangement as
would satisfy his ambition.   George Home of Wed-
derburn, in Berwickshire, a gentleman of considerable
literary acquirements, and an old friend of Scott's
family, had now served as Clerk of Session for upwards of thirty years.   In those days there was no
system of retiring pensions for the worn-out func-
tionary of this class, and the usual method was, either
that he should resign in favour of a successor who
advanced a sum of money according to the circumstances of his age and health, or for a coadjutor to

be associated with him in his patent, who undertook
the duty on condition of a division of salary.   Scott
offered to relieve Mr Home of all the labours of his
office, and to allow him, nevertheless, to retain its
emoluments entire during his lifetime; and the aged
clerk of course joined his exertions to procure a
conjoint-patent on these very advantageous terms.
Mr Home resigned, and a new patent was drawn out
accordingly; but, by a clerical inadvertency, it was
drawn out solely in Scott's favour, no mention of
Mr Home being inserted in the instrument.   Although, therefore, the sign-manual had been affixed,
and there remained nothing but to pay the fees and
take out the commission, Scott, on discovering this
error, could not of course proceed in the business;
since, in the event of his dying before Mr Home,
that gentleman would have lost the vested interest
which he had stipulated to retain.   A pending charge
of pecuniary corruption had compelled Lord Melville
to retire from office some time before Mr Pitt's
death; and the cloud of popular obloquy under which
he now laboured, rendered it impossible that Scott
should expect assistance from the quarter to which,
under any other circumstances, he would naturally
have turned for extrication from this difficulty.   He
therefore, as soon as the Fox and Grenville Cabinet
had been nominated, proceeded to London, to make
in his own person such representations as might be

necessary to secure the issuing of the patent in the right shape.

It seems wonderful that he should ever have doubted for a single moment of the result; since, had the new Cabinet been purely Whig, and had he been the most violent and obnoxious of Tory partisans, neither of which was the case, the arrangement had been not only virtually, but, with the exception of an evident official blunder, formally completed; and no Secretary of State, as I must think, could have refused to rectify the paltry mistake in question, without a dereliction of every principle of honour. The seals of the Home Office had been placed in the hands of a nobleman of the highest character — moreover, an ardent lover of literature; — while the chief of the new Ministry was one of the most generous as well as tasteful of mankind; and accordingly, when the circumstances were explained, there occurred no hesitation whatever on their parts. "I had," says Scott, "the honour of an interview with Earl Spencer, and he in the most handsome manner gave directions that the commission should issue as originally intended; adding that, the matter having received the royal assent, he regarded only as a claim of justice what he would willingly have done as an act of favour." He adds — "I never saw Mr Fox on this or any other occasion, and never made any application to him, conceiving, that in doing so, I

might have been supposed to express political opinions
different from those which I had always professed.
In his private capacity, there is no man to whom I
would have been more proud to owe an obligation —
had I been so distinguished." *

In January, 1806, however, Scott had by no
means measured either the character, the feelings, or
the arrangements of great public functionaries, by
the standard with which observation and experience
subsequently furnished him.   He had breathed hitherto, as far as political questions of all sorts were
concerned, the hot atmosphere of a very narrow
scene — and seems to have pictured to himself White-
hall and Downing Street as only a wider stage for
the exhibition of the bitter and fanatical prejudices
that tormented the petty circles of the Parliament
House at Edinburgh ; the true bearing and scope of
which no man in after days more thoroughly understood, or more sincerely pitied.   The variation of
his feelings while his business still remained unde-
termined, will, however, be best collected from the
correspondence about to be quoted.   It was, moreover, when these letters were written, that he was
tasting for the first time, the full cup of fashionable
blandishment as a *London Lion;* nor will the reader
fail to observe how deeply, while he supposed his

----

* Introduction to Marmion, 1830.

own most important worldly interests to be in peril on the one hand, and was surrounded with so many captivating flatteries on the other, he continued to sympathize with the misfortunes of his early friend and patron, now hurled from power, and subjected to a series of degrading persecutions, from the consequences of which that lofty spirit was never entirely to recover.

" To George Ellis, Esq., Sunninghill.

" Edinburgh, January 25th, 1806.

" My Dear Ellis,

" I have been too long in letting you hear of me, and my present letter is going to be a very selfish one, since it will be chiefly occupied by an affair of my own, in which, probably, you may find very little entertainment. I rely, however, upon your cordial good wishes and good advice, though, perhaps, you may be unable to afford me any direct assistance without more trouble than I would wish you to take on my account. You must know, then, that with a view of withdrawing entirely from the Bar, I had entered into a transaction with an elderly and infirm gentleman, Mr George Home, to be associated with him in the office which he holds as one of the Principal Clerks to our Supreme Court of Session ; I being to discharge the duty gratuitously

during his life, and to succeed him at his decease.
This could only be carried into effect by a new commission from the crown to him and me jointly, which
has been issued in similar cases very lately, and is in
point of form quite correct.   By the interest of my
kind and noble friend and chief, the Duke of Buccleuch, the countenance of Government was obtained
to this arrangement, and the affair, as I have every
reason to believe, is now in the Treasury.   I have
written to my solicitor, Alexander Mundell, Fludyer
Street, to use every despatch in hurrying through
the commission; but the news of to-day giving us
every reason to apprehend Pitt's death, if that la-
mentable event has not already happened,* makes
me get nervous on a subject so interesting to my
little fortune.   My political sentiments have been
always constitutional and open, and although they
were never rancorous, yet I cannot expect that the
Scottish Opposition party, should circumstances bring
them into power, would consider me as an object of
favour: nor would I ask it at their hands.   Their
leaders cannot regard me with malevolence, for I am
intimate with many of them; but they must provide
for the Whiggish children before they throw their
bread to the Tory dogs; and I shall not fawn on

---

* Mr Pitt died January 23d, two days before this letter was
written.

them because they have in their turn the superintendence of the larder. At the same time, if Fox's friends come into power, it must be with Windham's party, to whom my politics can be no exception,—if the politics of a private individual ought at any time to be made the excuse for intercepting the bounty of his Sovereign, when it is in the very course of being bestowed.

" The situation is most desirable, being £800 a-year, besides being consistent with holding my sheriffdom; and I could afford very well to wait till it opened to me by the death of my colleague, without wishing a most worthy and respectable man to die a moment sooner than ripe nature demanded. The duty consists in a few hours' labour in the forenoons when the Court sits, leaving the evenings and whole vacation open for literary pursuits. I will not relinquish the hope of such an establishment without an effort, if it is possible without dereliction of my principles to attain the accomplishment of it. As I have suffered in my professional line by addicting myself to the profane and unprofitable art of poem-making, I am very desirous to indemnify myself by availing myself of any prepossession which my literary reputation may, however unmeritedly, have created in my favour. I have found it useful when I applied for others, and I see no reason why I should not try if it can do any thing for myself.

" Perhaps, after all, my commission may be got
out before a change of Ministry, if such an event
shall take place, as it seems not far distant. If it
is otherwise, will you be so good as to think and
devise some mode in which my case may be stated to
Windham or Lord Grenville, supposing them to
come in? If it is not deemed worthy of attention,
I am sure I shall be contented; but it is one thing
to have a right to ask a favour, and another to
hope that a transaction, already fully completed by
the private parties, and approved of by an existing
Administration, shall be permitted to take effect in
favour of an unoffending individual. I believe I shall
see you very shortly, unless I hear from Mundell
that the business can be done for certain without
my coming up. I will not, if I can help it, be flayed
like a sheep for the benefit of some pettifogging
lawyer or attorney. I have stated the matter to you
very bluntly; indeed, I am not asking a favour, but,
unless my self-partiality blinds me, merely fair play.
Yours ever,

WALTER SCOTT."

" *To Walter Scott, Esq., Edinburgh.*

" Bath, 6th February 1806.

" My Dear Scott,

" You must have seen by the lists of the new Ministry already published in all the papers, that, although the death of our excellent Minister has been certainly a most unfortunate event, in as far as it must tend to ·delay the object of your present wishes, there is no cause for your alarm on account of the change, excepting as far as that change is very extensive, and thus, perhaps much time may elapse before the business of every kind which was in arrears can be expedited by the new Administration. There is no change of principle (as far as we can yet judge) in the new Cabinet — or rather the new Cabinet has no general political creed. Lord Grenville, Fox, Lord Lansdowne, and Addington were the four nominal heads of four distinct parties, which must now by some chemical process be amalgamated; all must forget, if they can, their peculiar habits and opinions, and unite in the pursuit of a common object. How far this is possible, time will show; to what degree this motley Ministry can, by their joint influence, command a majority in the House of Commons; how far they will, *as a whole*, be assisted by the secret influence and power of the

Crown; whether, if not so seconded, they will be able to appeal some time hence to the people, and dissolve the Parliament—all these and many other questions, will receive very different answers from different speculators. But in the mean time it is self-evident, that every individual will be extremely jealous of the patronage of his individual department; that individually as well as conjointly, they will be cautious of provoking enmity; and that a measure patronized by the Duke of Buccleuch is not very likely to be opposed by any member of such a Cabinet.

"If, indeed, the object of your wishes were a sinecure, and at the disposal of the Chancellor (Erskine), or of the President of the Board of Control (Lord Minto), you might have strong cause, perhaps, for apprehension; but what you ask would suit few candidates, and there probably is not one whom the Cabinet, or any person in it, would feel any strong *interest* in obliging to your disadvantage. But farther, we know that Lord Sidmouth is in the Cabinet, so is Lord Ellenborough, and these two are notoriously the *King's* Ministers. Now we may be very sure that they, or some other of the King's friends, will possess one department, which has no name, but is not the less real; namely, the supervision of the King's influence both here and in Scotland. I therefore much doubt whether there is any man in the Cabinet who, as Minister, has it in his power to prevent your attainment of your object. Lord Melville, we know, *was* in a great measure the representative of the King's personal influence in Scotland, and I am by no means sure that he is no longer so; but be that as it may, it will, I am well persuaded, continue in the hands of some one who has not been forced upon his Majesty as one of his confidential servants.

"Upon the whole, then, the only consolation that I can confidently give you is, that what you represent as a *principal* difficulty is *quite imaginary*, and that your own political principles are exactly those which are most likely to be serviceable to you. I need not say how happy Anne and myself would be to see you (we shall spend the month of March in London), nor that, if you should be able to point out any means by which I can be of the slightest use in advancing your interests, you may employ me without reserve. I must go to the Pump-room for my glass of water—so God bless you. Ever truly yours,

G. ELLIS."

" To George Ellis, Esq., Bath.

" London, Feb. 20, 1806.

" My Dear Ellis,

" I have your kind letter, and am infinitely obliged to you for your solicitude in my behalf. I have indeed been rather fortunate, for the gale which has shattered so many goodly argosies, has blown my little bark into the creek for which she was bound, and left me only to lament the misfortunes of my friends. To vary the simile, while the huge frigates, the Moira and Lauderdale, were fiercely combating for the dominion of the Caledonian main, I was fortunate enough to get on board the good ship Spencer, and leave them to settle their disputes at leisure. It is said to be a violent ground of controversy in the new Ministry, which of those two noble lords is to be St Andrew for Scotland. I own I tremble for the consequences of so violent a temper as Lauderdale's, irritated by long-disappointed ambition and ancient feud with all his brother nobles. It is a certain truth that Lord Moira insists upon his claim, backed by all the friends of the late Administration in Scotland, to have a certain weight in that country; and it is equally certain that the Hamiltons and Lauderdales have struck out. So here are people who have stood in the rain without doors for so many years, quarrelling for the nearest place to the fire, as soon as they have set their feet on the floor. Lord Moira, as he always has been, was highly kind and courteous to me on this occasion.

" Heber is just come in, with your letter waving in his hand. I am ashamed of all the trouble I have given you, and at the same time flattered to find your friendship even equal to that greatest and most disagreeable of all trials, the task of solicitation. Mrs Scott is *not* with me, and I am truly concerned to think we should be so near, without the prospect of meeting. Truth is, I had half a mind to make a run up to Bath, merely to break the spell which has prevented our meeting for these two years. But Bindley,* the collector, has lent me a parcel of books, which he insists on my consulting within the liberties of Westminster, and which I cannot find elsewhere, so that the fortnight I propose to stay will be fully occupied by examination and extracting. How long I may be detained here is very uncertain, but I wish to leave London on Saturday se'ennight. Should I be so delayed as to bring my time of de-

* James Bindley, Esq., famed for his rich accumulation of books, prints, and medals, held the office of a commissioner of Stamps during the long period of 53 years. He died in 1818, in his 81st year. At the sale of his library a collection of penny ballads, &c. in 8 volumes, produced £337.

parture any thing near that of your arrival, I will
stretch my furlough to the utmost, that I may have
a chance of seeing you. Nothing is minded here
but domestic politics, and if we are not clean swept,
there is no want of new brooms to perform that
operation. I have heard very bad news of Leyden's
health since my arrival here — such, indeed, as to
give room to apprehend the very worst. I fear he
has neglected the precautions which the climate renders necessary, and which no man departs from with
impunity. Remember me kindly and respectfully
to Mrs Ellis; and believe me ever yours faithfully,

WALTER SCOTT.

" P. S.—Poor Lord Melville! how does he look?
We have had miserable accounts of his health in
London. He was the architect of my little fortune,
from circumstances of personal regard merely; for
any of my trifling literary acquisitions were out of
his way. My heart bleeds when I think on his
situation —

    ' Even when the rage of battle ceased,
     The victor's soul was not appeased.' " *

---

   * These lines are from Smollett's *Tears of Scotland.*

" *To the Earl of Dalkeith.*

" London, 11th Feb. 1806.

" My Dear Lord,

" I cannot help flattering myself — for perhaps
it is flattering myself — that the noble architect of
the Border Minstrel's little fortune has been sometimes anxious for the security of that lowly edifice,
during the tempest which has overturned so many
palaces and towers. If I am right in my supposition, it will give you pleasure to learn that, notwithstanding some little rubs, I have been able to
carry through the transaction which your Lordship
sanctioned by your influence and approbation, and
that in a way very pleasing to my own feelings.
Lord Spencer, upon the nature of the transaction
being explained in an audience with which he favoured me, was pleased to direct the commission to
be issued, as an act of justice, regretting, he said, it
had not been from the beginning his own deed. This
was doing the thing handsomely, and like an English
nobleman. I have been very much fêted and caressed
here, almost indeed to suffocation, but have been
made amends by meeting some old friends. One
of the kindest was Lord Somerville, who volunteered
introducing me to Lord Spencer, as much, I am convinced, from respect to your Lordship's protection

and wishes, as from a desire to serve me personally.
He seemed very anxious to do any thing in his
power which might evince a wish to be of use to
your protégé.   Lord Minto was also infinitely kind
and active, and his influence with Lord Spencer
would, I am convinced, have been stretched to the
utmost in my favour, had not Lord Spencer's own
view of the subject been perfectly sufficient.

" After all, a little literary reputation is of some
use here.   I suppose Solomon, when he compared a
good name to a pot of ointment, meant that it oiled
the hinges of the hall-doors into which the posses-
sors of that inestimable treasure wished to penetrate.
What a *good* name was in Jerusalem, a *known* name
seems to be in London.   If you are celebrated for
writing verses or for slicing cucumbers, for being
two feet taller or two feet less than any other biped,
for acting plays when you should be whipped at
school, or for attending schools and institutions when
you should be preparing for your grave, your notoriety becomes a talisman — an ' Open Sesame '
before which every thing gives way — till you are
voted a bore, and discarded for a new plaything.
As this is a consummation of notoriety which I am
by no means ambitious of experiencing, I hope I
shall be very soon able to shape my course northward, to enjoy my good fortune at my leisure, and
snap my fingers at the Bar and all its works.

" There is, it is believed, a rude scuffle betwixt our late commander-in-chief and Lord Lauderdale, for the patronage of Scotland. If there is to be an exclusive administration, I hope it will not be in the hands of the latter. Indeed, when one considers, that by means of Lords Sidmouth and Ellenborough, the King possesses the actual power of casting the balance betwixt the five Grenvillites and four Foxites who compose the Cabinet, I cannot think they will find it an easy matter to force upon his Majesty any one to whom he has a personal dislike. I should therefore suppose that the disposal of St Andrew's Cross will be delayed till the new Ministry is a little consolidated, *if that time shall ever come.* There is much loose gunpowder amongst them, and one spark would make a fine explosion. Pardon these political effusions; I am infected by the atmosphere which I breathe, and cannot restrain my pen from discussing state affairs. I hope the young ladies and my dear little chief are now recovering from the hooping-cough, if it has so turned out to be. If I can do any thing for any of the family here, you know your right to command, and the pleasure it will afford me to obey. Will your Lordship be so kind as to acquaint the Duke, with every grateful and respectful acknowledgment on my part, that I have this day got my commission from the Secretary's office? I dine to-day at Holland-house; I

refused to go before, lest it should be thought I was
soliciting interest in that quarter, as I abhor even
the shadow of changing or turning with the tide.

" I am ever, with grateful acknowledgment, your
Lordship's much indebted, faithful humble servant,

WALTER SCOTT."

" *To George Ellis, Esq.*

" London, Saturday, March 3, 1806.

" My Dear Ellis,

" I have waited in vain for the happy dissolu-
tion of the spell which has kept us asunder at a
distance less by one quarter than in general divides
us ; and since I am finally obliged to depart for the
north to-morrow, I have only to comfort myself
with the hope that Bladud will infuse a double influence into his tepid springs, and that you will feel
emboldened, by the quantity of reinforcement which
the radical heat shall have received, to undertake
your expedition to the *tramontane* region of Reged
this season. My time has been spent very gaily
here, and I should have liked very well to have remained till you came up to town, had it not been for
the wife and bairns at home, whom I confess I am
now anxious to see. Accordingly I set off early to-

morrow morning — indeed I expected to have done
so to-day, but my companion, Ballantyne, our Scottish Bodoni, was afflicted with a violent diarrhœa,
which, though his physician assured him it would
serve his health in general, would certainly have contributed little to his accomplishments as an agreeable
companion in a post-chaise, which are otherwise very
respectable. I own Lord Melville's misfortunes affect me deeply. He, at least his nephew, was my
early patron, and gave me countenance and assistance
when I had but few friends. I have seen when the
streets of Edinburgh were thought by the inhabitants
almost too vulgar for Lord Melville to walk upon;
and now I fear that, with his power and influence
gone, his presence would be accounted by many,
from whom he has deserved other thoughts, an embarrassment, if not something worse. All this is
very vile — it is one of the occasions when Providence, as it were, industriously turns the tapestry,
to let us see the ragged ends of the worsted which
compose its most beautiful figures. God grant your
prophecies may be true, which I fear are rather dictated by your kind heart than your experience of
political enmities and the fate of fallen statesmen.
Kindest compliments to Mrs Ellis. Your next will
find me in Edinburgh.   WALTER SCOTT."

" To George Ellis, Esq.

" Ashestiel, April 7, 1806.

" My Dear Ellis,

" Were I to begin by telling you all the regret
I had at not finding you in London, and at being
obliged to leave it before your return, this very
handsome sheet of paper, which I intend to cover
with more important and interesting matters, would
be entirely occupied by such a Jeremiade as could
only be equalled by Jeremiah himself. I will therefore waive that subject, only assuring you that I
hope to be in London next spring, but have much
warmer hopes of seeing you here in summer. I
hope Bath has been of service; if not so much as
you expected, try easy exercise in a northward
direction, and make proof of the virtues of the
Tweed and Yarrow. We have been here these two
days, and I have been quite rejoiced to find all my
dogs, and horses, and sheep, and cows, and two
cottages full of peasants and their children, and all
my other stock, human and animal, in great good
health—we want nothing but Mrs Ellis and you to
be the strangers within our gates, and our establishment would be complete on the patriarchal plan. I
took possession of my new office on my return. The
duty is very simple, consisting chiefly in signing my

name; and as I have five colleagues, I am not obliged to do duty except in turn, so my task is a very easy one, as my name is very short.

" My principal companion in this solitude is John Dryden. After all, there are some passages in his translations from Ovid and Juvenal that will hardly bear reprinting, unless I would have the Bishop of London * and the whole corps of Methodists about my ears.. I wish you would look at the passages I mean. One is from the fourth book of Lucretius ; the other from Ovid's Instructions to his Mistress. They are not only double-entendres, but good plain single-entendres—not only broad, but long, and as coarse as the mainsail of a first-rate. What to make of them I know not; but I fear that, without absolutely gelding the bard, it will be indispensable to circumcise him a little by leaving out some of the most obnoxious lines. Do, pray, look at the poems and decide for me. Have you seen my friend Tom Thomson, who is just now in London ? He has, I believe, the advantage of knowing you, and I hope you will meet, as he understands more of old books, old laws, and old history, than any man in Scotland. He has lately received an appointment under the Lord Register of Scotland, which puts all our records under his immediate inspection and control,

* Dr Porteous.

and I expect many valuable discoveries to be the consequence of his investigation, if he escapes being smothered in the cloud of dust which his researches will certainly raise about his ears. I sent your card instantly to Jeffrey, from whom you had doubtless a suitable answer." I saw the venerable economist and antiquary, Macpherson, when in London, and was quite delighted with the simplicity and kindness of his manners. He is exactly like one of the old Scotchmen whom I remember twenty years ago, before so close a union had taken place between Edinburgh and London. The mail-coach and the Berwick smacks have done more than the Union in altering our national character, sometimes for the better and sometimes for the worse.

" I met with your friend, Mr Canning, in town, and claimed his acquaintance as a friend of yours, and had my claim allowed; also Mr Frere, — both delightful companions, far too good for politics, and for winning and losing places. When I say I was more pleased with their society than I thought had been possible on so short an acquaintance, I pay them a very trifling compliment and myself a very great one. I had also the honour of dining with a

* Mr Ellis had written to Mr Jeffrey, through Scott, proposing to draw up an article for the Edinburgh Review on the Annals of Commerce, then recently published by Mr David Macpherson.

fair friend of yours at Blackheath, an honour which
I shall very long remember. She is an enchanting
princess, who dwells in an enchanted palace, and I
cannot help thinking that her prince must labour
under some malignant spell when he denies himself
her society. The very Prince of the Black Isles,
whose bottom was marble, would have made an
effort to transport himself to Montague House.
From all this you will understand I was at Montague House.

"I am quite delighted at the interest you take in
poor Lord Melville. I suppose they are determined
to hunt him down. Indeed, the result of his trial
must be ruin from the expense, even supposing him
to be honourably acquitted. Will you, when you
have time to write, let me know how that matter is
likely to turn? I am deeply interested in it; and
the reports here are so various, that one knows not
what to trust to. Even the common rumour of
London is generally more authentic than the ' from
good authority' of Edinburgh. Besides, I am now in
the wilds (alas! I cannot say *woods* and wilds), and
hear little of what passes. Charlotte joins me in a
thousand kind remembrances to Mrs Ellis; and I am
ever yours most truly,   WALTER SCOTT."

I shall not dwell at present upon Scott's method
of conduct in the circumstances of an eminently

popular author beleaguered by the importunities of fashionable admirers: his bearing when first exposed to such influences was exactly what it was to the end, and I shall have occasion in the sequel to produce the evidence of more than one deliberate observer.

Caroline, Princess of Wales, was in those days considered among the Tories, whose politics her husband had uniformly opposed, as the victim of unmerited misfortune, cast aside, from the mere wantonness of caprice, by a gay and dissolute voluptuary; while the Prince's Whig associates had espoused his quarrel, and were already, as the event showed, prepared to act, publicly as well as privately, as if they believed her to be among the most abandoned of her sex. I know not by whom Scott was first introduced to her little Court at Blackheath; but I think it was probably through Mrs Hayman, a lady of her bedchamber, several of whose notes and letters occur about this time in the collection of his correspondence. The careless levity of the Princess's manner was observed by him, as I have heard him say, with much regret, as likely to bring the purity of heart and mind, for which he gave her credit, into suspicion. For example, when, in the course of the evening, she conducted him by himself to admire some flowers in a conservatory, and, the place being rather dark, his lameness occasioned him

to hesitate for a moment in following her down some
steps which she had taken at a skip, she turned
round, and said, with mock indignation—" Ah ! false
and faint-hearted troubadour ! you will not trust
yourself with me for fear of your neck !"

I find from one of Mrs Hayman's letters, that on
being asked, at Montague House, to recite some
verses of his own, he replied that he had none
unpublished which he thought worthy of her Royal
Highness's attention, but introduced a short account
of the Ettrick Shepherd, and repeated one of the
ballads of the *Mountain Bard*, for which he was
then endeavouring to procure subscribers.   The
Princess appears to have been interested by the
story, and she affected, at all events, to be pleased
with the lines ; she desired that her name might be
placed on the Shepherd's list, and thus he had at
least one gleam of royal patronage.

It was during the same visit to London that Scott
first saw Joanna Baillie, of whose Plays on the
Passions he had been, from their first appearance,
an enthusiastic admirer.   The late Mr Sotheby, the
translator of Oberon, &c. &c. was the friend who
introduced him to the poetess of Hampstead.   Being
asked very lately what impression he made upon her
at this interview—" I was at first," she answered,
" a little disappointed, for I was fresh from the Lay,
and had pictured to myself an ideal elegance and

refinement of feature; but I said to myself, If I had
been in a crowd, and at a loss what to do, I should
have fixed upon that face among a thousand, as the
sure index of the benevolence and the shrewdness
that would and could help me in my strait.　We
had not talked long, however, before I saw in the
expressive play of his countenance far more even
of elegance and refinement than I had missed in
its mere lines."　The acquaintance thus begun, soon
ripened into a most affectionate intimacy between
him and this remarkable woman; and thenceforth
she and her distinguished brother, Dr Matthew
Baillie, were among the friends to whose intercourse
he looked forward with the greatest pleasure when
about to visit the metropolis.

I ought to have mentioned before, that he had
known Mr Sotheby at a very early period of life,
that amiable and excellent man having been sta-
tioned for some time at Edinburgh while serving his
Majesty as a captain of dragoons.　Scott ever retained for him a sincere regard; he was always,
when in London, a frequent guest at his hospitable
board, and owed to him the personal acquaintance of
not a few of their most eminent contemporaries in
various departments of literature and art.

When the Court opened after the spring recess,
Scott entered upon his new duties as one of the
Principal Clerks of Session; and as he continued to

discharge them with exemplary regularity, and to the entire satisfaction both of the Judges and the Bar, during the long period of twenty-five years, I think it proper to tell precisely in what they consisted, the more so because, in his letter to Ellis of the 25th January, he has himself (characteristically enough) understated them.

The Court of Session sits at Edinburgh from the 12th of May to the 12th of July, and again from the 12th of November, with a short interval at Christmas, to the 12th of March. The Judges of the Inner Court took their places on the Bench, in his time, every morning not later than ten o'clock, and remained according to the amount of business ready for despatch, but seldom for less than four or more than six hours daily; during which space the Principal Clerks continued seated at a table below the Bench to watch the progress of the suits, and record the decisions — the cases, of all classes, being equally apportioned among their number. The Court of Session, however, does not sit on Monday, that day being reserved for the criminal business of the High Court of Justiciary; and there is also another blank day every other week, — the *Teind Wednesday*, as it is called, when the Judges are assembled for the hearing of tithe questions, which belong to a separate jurisdiction, of comparatively modern creation, and having its own separate establishment of officers.

On the whole, then, Scott's attendance in Court may
be taken to have amounted, on the average, to from
four to six hours daily during rather less than six
months out of the twelve.

Not a little of the Clerk's business in Court is
merely formal, and indeed mechanical; but there are
few days in which he is not called upon for the
exertion of his higher faculties, in reducing the
decisions of the Bench, orally pronounced, to tech-
nical shape; which, in a new, complex, or difficult
case, cannot be satisfactorily done without close attention to all the previous proceedings and written
documents, an accurate understanding of the principles or precedents on which it has been determined,
and a thorough command of the whole vocabulary
of legal forms. Dull or indolent men, promoted
through the mere wantonness of political patronage,
might, no doubt, contrive to devolve the harder part
of their duty upon humbler assistants: but, in general, the office had been held by gentlemen of high
character and attainments; and more than one
among Scott's own colleagues enjoyed the reputation of legal science that would have done honour
to the Bench. Such men, of course, prided themselves on doing well whatever it was their proper
function to do; and it was by their example, not
that of the drones who condescended to lean upon
unseen and irresponsible inferiors, that Scott uni-

formly modelled his own conduct as a Clerk of
Session. To do this, required, of necessity, constant
study of law-papers and authorities at home. There
was also a great deal of really base drudgery, such
as the authenticating of registered deeds, by signa-
ture, which he had to go through out of Court; he
had, too, a Shrievalty, though not a heavy one, all
the while upon his hands; — and, on the whole, it
forms one of the most remarkable features in his
history, that, throughout the most active period of
his literary career, he must have devoted a large
proportion of his hours, during half at least of every
year, to the conscientious discharge of professional
duties.

Henceforth, then, when in Edinburgh, his literary
work was performed chiefly before breakfast; with
the assistance of such evening hours as he could
contrive to rescue from the consideration of Court
papers, and from those social engagements in which,
year after year, as his celebrity advanced, he was of
necessity more and more largely involved; and of
those entire days during which the Court of Session
did not sit — days which, by most of those holding
the same official station, were given to relaxation
and amusement. So long as he continued quarter-
master of the Volunteer Cavalry, of course he had,
even while in Edinburgh, some occasional horse
exercise; but, in general, his town life henceforth

was in that respect as inactive as his country life ever was the reverse. He scorned for a long while to attach any consequence to this complete alternation of habits; but we shall find him confessing in the sequel, that it proved highly injurious to his bodily health.

I may here observe, that the duties of his clerkship brought him into close daily connexion with a set of gentlemen, most of whom were soon regarded by him with the most cordial affection and confidence. One of his new colleagues was David Hume (the nephew of the historian) whose lectures on the Law of Scotland are characterised with just eulogy in the Ashestiel Memoir, and who subsequently became a Baron of the Exchequer; a man as virtuous and amiable, as conspicuous for masculine vigour of intellect and variety of knowledge.* Another was Hector Macdonald Buchanan of Drummakiln, a frank-hearted and generous gentleman, not the less acceptable to Scott for the Highland prejudices which he inherited with the high blood of Clanranald; at whose beautiful seat of Ross Priory, on the shores of Lochlomond, he was henceforth almost annually a visitor — a circumstance which has left many traces in the

* Mr Baron Hume died at Edinburgh, 27th July 1838, in his 82d year. I had great gratification in receiving a message from the venerable man shortly before his death, conveying his warm approbation of these Memoirs of his friend.—[1839.]

Waverley Novels. A third (though I believe of later appointment) with whom his intimacy was not less strict, was the late excellent Sir Robert Dundas of Beechwood, Bart.; and a fourth was the friend of his boyhood, one of the dearest he ever had, Colin Mackenzie of Portmore. With these gentlemen's families, he and his lived in such constant familiarity of kindness, that the children all called their fathers' colleagues *uncles*, and the mothers of their little friends *aunts;* and in truth, the establishment was a brotherhood.

Scott's nomination as Clerk of Session appeared in the same Gazette (March 8, 1806) which announced the instalment of the Hon. Henry Erskine and John Clerk of Eldin as Lord Advocate and Solicitor General for Scotland. The promotion at such a moment, of a distinguished Tory, might well excite the wonder of the Parliament House, and even when the circumstances were explained, the inferior local adherents of the triumphant cause were far from considering the conduct of their superiors in this matter with feelings of satisfaction. The indication of such humours was deeply resented by his haughty spirit; and he in his turn showed his irritation in a manner well calculated to extend to higher quarters the spleen with which his advancement had been regarded by persons wholly unworthy of his attention. In short, it was almost immediately

after a Whig Ministry had gazetted his appointment
to an office which had for twelve months formed
a principal object of his ambition, that, rebelling
against the implied suspicion of his having accepted
something like a personal obligation at the hands of
adverse politicians, he for the first time put himself
forward as a decided Tory partisan.

The impeachment of Lord Melville was among
the first measures of the new Government; and
personal affection and gratitude graced as well as
heightened the zeal with which Scott watched the
issue of this, in his eyes, vindictive proceeding; but,
though the ex-minister's ultimate acquittal was, as to
all the charges involving his personal honour, complete, it must now be allowed that the investigation
brought out many circumstances by no means cre-
ditable to his discretion; and the rejoicings of his
friends ought not, therefore, to have been scornfully
jubilant. Such they were, however — at least in
Edinburgh; and Scott took his share in them by
inditing a song, which was sung by James Ballantyne, and received with clamorous applauses, at a
public dinner given in honour of the event on the
27th of June 1806. I regret that this piece was
inadvertently omitted in the late collective edition
of his poetical works; but since such is the case, I
consider myself bound to insert it here. However
he may have regretted it afterwards, he authorized

its publication in the newspapers of the time, and my narrative would fail to convey a complete view of the man, if I should draw a veil over the expression, thus deliberate, of some of the strongest personal feelings that ever animated his verse.

" HEALTH TO LORD MELVILLE.

A IR — *Carrickfergus.*

" Since here we are set in array round the table,
    Five hundred good fellows well met in a hall,
Come listen, brave boys, and I'll sing as I'm able
    How innocence triumphed and pride got a fall.
        But push round the claret —
        Come, stewards, don't spare it —
With rapture you'll drink to the toast that I give :
        Here, boys,
        Off with it merrily —
MELVILLE for ever, and long may he live !

" What were the Whigs doing, when boldly pursuing,
    Pitt banished Rebellion, gave Treason a string ?
Why, they swore on their honour, for ARTHUR O'CONNOR,
    And fought hard for DESPARD against country and king.
        Well, then, we knew, boys,
        PITT and MELVILLE were true boys,
And the tempest was raised by the friends of Reform.
        Ah, wo !
        Weep to his memory ;
Low lies the pilot that weathered the storm !

" And pray, don't you mind when the Blues first were raising,
  And we scarcely could think the house safe o'er our heads?
When villains and coxcombs, French politics praising,
  Drove peace from our tables and sleep from our beds?
          Our hearts they grew bolder
          When musket on shoulder,
Stepp'd forth our old Statesmen example to give.
          Come, boys, never fear,
          Drink the Blue grenadier —
Here's to old HARRY, and long may he live!

" They would turn us adrift; though rely, sir, upon it —
  Our own faithful chronicles warrant us that
The free mountaineer and his bonny blue bonnet
  Have oft gone as far as the regular's hat.
          We laugh at their taunting,
          For all we are wanting
Is licence our life for our country to give.
          Off with it merrily,
          Horse, foot, and artillery,
Each loyal Volunteer, long may he live!

" 'Tis not us alone, boys — the Army and Navy
  Have each got a slap 'mid their politic pranks;
CORNWALLIS cashier'd, that watched winters to save ye,
  And the Cape called a bauble, unworthy of thanks.
          But vain is their taunt,
          No soldier shall want
The thanks that his country to valour can give:
          Come, boys,
          Drink it off merrily, —
SIR DAVID and POPHAM, and long may they live!

" And then our revenue — Lord knows how they viewed it
   While each petty statesman talked lofty and big;
But the beer-tax was weak, as if Whitbread had brewed it,
   And the pig-iron duty a shame to a pig.
         In vain is their vaunting,
         Too surely there's wanting
   What judgment, experience, and steadiness give;
         Come, boys,
         Drink about merrily, —
Health to sage MELVILLE, and long may he live!

" Our King, too — our Princess — I dare not say more, sir, —
   May providence watch them with mercy and might!
While there's one Scottish hand that can wag a claymore, sir,
   They shall ne'er want a friend to stand up for their right.
         Be damn'd he that dare not, —
         For my part, I'll spare not
   To beauty afflicted a tribute to give:
         Fill it up steadily,
         Drink it off readily —
Here's to the Princess, and long may she live!

" And since we must not set Auld Reikie in glory,
   And make her brown visage as light as her heart;*
Till each man illumine his own upper story,
   Nor law-book nor lawyer shall force us to part.
         In GRENVILLE and SPENCER,
         And some few good men, sir,

---

* The Magistrates of Edinburgh had rejected an application
for illumination of the town, on the arrival of the news of Lord
Melville's acquittal.

High talents we honour, slight difference forgive ;
        But the Brewer we'll hoax,
        Tallyho to the Fox,
And drink Melville for ever, as long as we live !"

This song gave great offence to the many sincere
personal friends whom Scott numbered among the
upper ranks of the Whigs ; and, in particular, it
created a marked coldness towards him on the part
of the accomplished and amiable Countess of Rosslyn
(a very intimate friend of his favourite patroness,
Lady Dalkeith), which, as his letters show, wounded his feelings severely,—the more so, I have no
doubt, because a little reflection must have made
him repent not a few of its allusions. He was consoled, however, by abundant testimonies of Tory
approbation ; and, among others, by the following
note from Mr Canning :—

            " *To Walter Scott, Esq., Edinburgh.*

                                " London, July 14, 1806.
" Dear Sir,
        " I should not think it necessary to trouble you
with a direct acknowledgment of the very acceptable
present which you were so good as to send me
through Mr William Rose, if I had not happened to
hear that some of those persons who could not indeed
be expected to be pleased with your composition,

have thought proper to be very loud and petulant
in the expression of their disapprobation. Those,
therefore, who approve and are thankful for your
exertions in a cause which they have much at heart,
owe it to themselves, as well as to you, that the expressions of their gratitude and pleasure should reach
you in as direct a manner as possible. I hope that,
in the course of next year, you are likely to afford
your friends in this part of the world an opportunity
of repeating these expressions to you in person; and
I have the honour to be, Dear Sir, with great truth,
your very sincere and obedient servant,

GEORGE CANNING."

Scott's Tory feelings appear to have been kept in a
very excited state during the whole of this short reign
of the Whigs. He then, for the first time, mingled
keenly in the details of county politics,—canvassed
electors — harangued meetings; and, in a word,
made himself conspicuous as a leading instrument of
his party—more especially as an indefatigable local
manager, wherever the parliamentary interest of the
Buccleuch family was in peril. But he was, in truth
earnest and serious in his belief that the new rulers
of the country were disposed to abolish many of its
most valuable institutions; and he regarded with
special jealousy certain schemes of innovation with
respect to the courts of law and the administration of

justice, which were set on foot by the Crown Officers for Scotland.   At a debate of the Faculty of Advocates on some of these propositions, he made a speech much longer than any he had ever before delivered in that assembly; and several who heard it have assured me, that it had a flow and energy of eloquence for which those who knew him best had been quite unprepared. When the meeting broke up, he walked across *the Mound*, on his way to Castle Street, between Mr Jeffrey and another of his reforming friends, who complimented him on the rhetorical powers he had been displaying, and would willingly have treated the subject-matter of the discussion playfully.   But his feelings had been moved to an extent far beyond their apprehension: he exclaimed, " No, no—'tis no laughing matter; little by little, whatever your wishes may be, you will destroy and undermine, until nothing of what makes Scotland Scotland shall remain."   And so saying, he turned round to conceal his agitation — but not until Mr Jeffrey saw tears gushing down his cheek — resting his head until he recovered himself on the wall of the Mound.   Seldom, if ever, in his more advanced age, did any feelings obtain such mastery.

STEVENSON AND CO. PRINTERS,
THISTLE STREET.

www.ingramcontent.com/pod-product-compliance
Lightning Source LLC
Chambersburg PA
CBHW020933030726
47496CB00005B/1163